THE TIGHTENING STRING

Books by Ann Bridge

PEKING PICNIC

THE GINGER GRIFFIN

ILLYRIAN SPRING

THE SONG IN THE HOUSE

ENCHANTER'S NIGHTSHADE

FOUR-PART SETTING

FRONTIER PASSAGE

SINGING WATERS

THE HOUSE AT KILMARTIN

AND THEN YOU CAME

THE DARK MOMENT

A PLACE TO STAND

A FAMILY OF TWO WORLDS

THE LIGHT-HEARTED QUEST

THE PORTUGUESE ESCAPE

THE NUMBERED ACCOUNT

THE TIGHTENING STRING

with Susan Lowndes:

THE SELECTIVE TRAVELLER IN PORTUGAL

A NOVEL BY

The dates on each country indicate
exactly when that country came
under the control of the Nazis

New York / Toronto / London

ANN BRIDGE

THE TIGHTENING STRING

1939 • WARSAW

POLAND

• KIEV

• LWOW

RUSSIA

SLOVAKIA 1939

• BUDAPEST

UNGARY

February 1941

RUMANIA

• BUCHAREST

1941

arch

• BELGRADE

UGOSLAVIA

ALBANIA

TIRANA

BULGARIA

• SOFIA

MOSCOW •

ISTANBUL •

McGraw-Hill Book Company, Inc.

THE TIGHTENING STRING

First Edition

07734

AUTHOR'S NOTE

Apart from historical figures like the Regent and the Prime Minister of Hungary, the characters in this book, with three exceptions, are fictitious. There was a real British Legation in Budapest in 1940–41, full of real people, of whom I was one—the Minister's wife; in the novel they have been exchanged for purely invented characters. But the facts given—the long delay in parcels from England reaching the prisoners-of-war in Germany, and the extraordinary generosity of the Hungarians in helping to meet their needs—are purely a piece of modern history. "Prince Willie Tereny" is dead—I am happy to have given him this small memorial. "Mr. Smith"—whose name is not Smith—is alive; so is Mrs. Starnberg, who also bears another name—I should like them both to accept this tribute of gratitude for all they did for British officers and men in their need.

Ann Bridge

1

The big Legation Humber bowled smoothly along the wide blue road leading out from Budapest to the air-port at Buda-Örs. Mrs Eynsham, the Counsellor's wife, seated in the back, was grateful to the Minister for the loan of it—David, her husband, was using their own car, and she had felt a desperate need that afternoon to get out of the city and among trees and fields and growing things, if only for an hour. So she had telephoned to Sir Hugh, and of course he had said Yes. This was the very end of May 1940, and Rosina Eynsham, like thousands of other English mothers, was in desperation about her son. Dick was in a county regiment, the Gloucestershires; the Belgians had just surrendered, leaving the British left flank in the air; Panzer divisions were fanning out all over northern France, and pressing the English troops back onto the coast; the French were apparently in flight, and the Americans still on a "cash-and-carry" basis.

Mrs Eynsham always heard whatever news was going, because her daughter Lucilla regularly monitored the huge official wireless, to suck out information for the *Bulletin* which the Legation daily put out to give the Hungarians accurate news; good or bad, it had to be accurate—and just now it was appalling.

The car pulled up well short of the air-port, at one end of a small rocky ridge clothed with immature pines—the Minister's chauffeur had often driven Mrs Eynsham here before. She got out, and walked along a small track between the slope of dark trees and the flat land below it, at the further side of which the

1

airfield lay; a tiny yellow lily starred the grass beside the path —absent-mindedly she picked some, thinking all the time of the Stukas dive-bombing those Flemish roads blocked with refugees, and the German artillery pounding the retreating British troops from the rear. Here all was peace; out to her left civilian planes rose from the airfield, or hummed gently down onto it; between, in the soft sunshine, slender high-bred horses, yoked to the plough, turned up the rich brown earth in clean shining furrows, or harrowed the sown ground. Mrs Eynsham, born a country-woman, had been astonished when she first came to Hungary not long before to see such horses doing field-work; some of them looked, she told her husband, almost like race-horses. David Eynsham had laughed.

"You're not so far out, Rosie. Most of them have some Arab blood—they rather fancy that here, even for heavy work, and keep Arab stallions at stud for the peasants' mares, if they care to use them." And he had driven her out to one of the State-owned stud farms, where in long sheds hundreds of slender nervous Arab mares, their big veins standing out under their delicate skins, suckled their graceful leggy foals. Rosina remembered now, distraught as she was with her personal anxiety, the words the director of the stud had used to describe the qualities which Arab blood gave to horses: "Härte, Adel, Dauer" —firmness, nobility, endurance. Tears sprang to her eyes. Just what Dick and his men needed at this moment—oh, God preserve them all!

At its further end the little ridge sloped down into broken ground, with oak-scrub and hazel-thickets in the hollows. These were ringing with the song of nightingales; Mrs Eynsham sat down on a bank to listen to the glorious jug-jug-jugging, and "the fervour of the four long notes"—but she could only hear guns. Restlessly she got up, and strolled about; then looked at her watch. Yes, she had better go back; it was the Min's ghastly *jour* today, and she must change.

Sir Hugh Billingshurst, the Minister, was a bachelor, who took his duties seriously; when the Eynshams arrived in Budapest, he as Counsellor, he sized up Mrs Eynsham at once as a person who could help him with his official entertaining, and forthwith instituted a weekly At Home day, at which she acted as hostess. It would make a sort of rallying-point for the few British left in Budapest, he explained, in his cool, half-amused manner— and to the Hungarians and the diplomatic corps it was a way, unobtrusively, of showing the flag—"quite a small flag," he had added, with his sidelong smile. "But it will only come off if you will play. I can't do it alone." And of course Mrs Eynsham, in duty bound, had had to agree to play—only stipulating that this performance should take place in the middle of the week.

"Oh, why? I understand that in old days the Legation *jour* was always on Monday."

"Yes, and wreck all our week-ends! *No*, dear Sir Hugh—of course I'll do whatever you want, but do let it be on a Wednesday or a Thursday." And on Wednesdays, accordingly, the *jour* took place.

During the latter part of the Phoney War these occasions were not too bad. Sir Hugh provided strong and excellent drinks, and was rather lavish with his nibbles. But even then the *jours* served as a sort of barometer for the view taken in Central Europe of England's chances of success—any reverse, such as the sinking of a battleship or the torpedoing of a convoy always reduced the Hungarian attendance considerably. This used to irritate Mrs Eynsham; she liked the Hungarians for their wit and warmth and gaiety, but was impatient of their ambivalent attitude in a conflict where—to her it seemed so simple—human freedom was at stake. But her husband scolded her when she criticised them. "Don't be a fool, Rosina. These people are in an impossible situation—the frontier is only three and a half hours drive away! If we were not to win they would be utterly at the Germans' mercy. You can't blame them for watching their step."

The Eynshams had rented a house in Buda in the same street as the Legation, and barely 100 yards from it; the car dropped her at her door, and when she had changed she stepped along

3

between the pretty old yellow plastered houses and turned in at the big *porte-cochère* leading through into the large court-yard round which the Legation was built. It was really an old palace dating from the Turkish occupation in the 17th century; a reminder of those days remained in the wrought-iron gates of another archway at the further end of the courtyard, giving onto the garden; the rooms opening off this arched passage, and the garden itself, had once constituted the *harem-lik,* or women's quarters. Mrs Eynsham however went through a door within the *porte-cochère* itself and up the broad balustraded stone staircase to a long, wide upper hall off which the main rooms opened—footmen were lurking at the foot of the stairs; Anton, the Viennese butler, waited at the top and showed her into the still-empty drawing-room. "I will inform His Excellency," he said.

Mrs Eynsham moved over to the windows and looked across the street at the small greengrocer's shop exactly opposite. Yes, there they were, as usual, sitting by the thrown-up windows on the first floor—a small man with a pair of field-glasses, another with a notebook open on the sill; both ready to check on who-ever entered the Legation. "Schmutz!" Rosina muttered—she was both emotional and a good linguist.

"My dear, how good and punctual you are," Sir Hugh said, coming in. "Was it nice out at Buda-Örs?"

"Yes lovely—thank you so much." She gestured towards the window. "Are those unworthy little *spotteurs* across the road Gestapo, or just *Deuxième Bureau?*"

"I simply don't know—and I think it more prudent not to find out" he said, with his rather sidelong smile. "Is David coming?"

"*I* don't know that either" Rosina replied. Her husband's al-lergy to any form of social occasion was one of the many dif-ficulties of her married life—in fact she had become allergic herself to telling white lies in his excuse, merely because he didn't want to attend some function to which, strictly, he ought to have gone. The *jour* was not one of these, fortunately.

"Oh well, where should we be without him, whether he

4

comes to parties or not?" the Minister said. "I can't tell you what it means to me to have someone with his command of this impossible language, and his knowledge of the people. How is his aunt, by the way?"

An aunt of David Eynsham's had, rather late in life, married a certain Count Pongracz and gone to live in Hungary; from his preparatory schooldays onwards the boy had stayed with her for long holidays, and thus acquired a mastery of Hungarian very uncommon in western Europe—to say nothing of that peculiar intimacy with a foreign way of life which children find it so easy, and adults so difficult, to achieve.

"She's getting old—" Mrs Eynsham was beginning, when Anton announced the first guests.

The *jour* was ill-attended, as was only to be expected since things were going so badly for the Allies. There were a few Poles, who had managed to escape to Hungary; some rather pitiful and worried members of the small British colony; a sprinkling of faithful Hungarians who clung to the association with England, come Hell and high water, like the old Marquess Pálfalvy, his son Jenkö, and a Count and Countess Táray—also a few of the Allied diplomats. Mrs Eynsham, who was still a good-looking woman, had put on a really good frock, and moved about, talking cheerfully in English, French and German, trying to bring a still-born party to life. In this effort she was energetically supported by Martha Beckley, whose official job was to edit the Legation Bulletin, but who also acted to some extent as the Minister's private secretary—a big gaunt black-haired girl in her middle thirties, with an ugly clever face, a lively tongue, and an inexhaustible fund of commonsense. She too—in a quite hideous dress—not only mixed with and shifted the rather dreary company about, but occasionally slipped out to tell Anton to put more gin in the cocktails; she really ran Sir Hugh's household for him. Sir Hugh himself preserved a rather monolithic attitude on such occasions. He stood opposite the door by which people entered, sipping sparingly at a glass of whisky, and shook hands with such of his guests as had the courage to come across to him—but he seldom left his stance except to greet the elderly and important, like the old Markgraf Pálfalvy and the American Minister. These stayed for some time beside him, also drinking whisky—a thing then practically unobtainable in Central Europe except by diplomats; but Sir Hugh went out of his way to go forward and speak courteously to several of the drabber and more discouraged English residents, halted in mid-room.

Halfway through this wretched entertainment two individuals walked in, a few minutes apart; the appearance of each created an appreciable stir of interest and pleasure. There are people who have this quality, though they are rare; Frances Cornford has described most exquisitely the effect of Sir Philip Sidney's entrance into a room—the alteration in the whole atmosphere. However neither of these two were men, nor in any sense famous. The first was a very tall girl, beautifully though rather carelessly dressed, with masses of pale gold hair wound closely and unfashionably round her small head, and a classically beautiful face—"The Princess Oria Tereny" Anton announced. She went straight across to Sir Hugh.

"Oh my dear Oria, I had no idea you were up. How delightful to see you. How is your Father?"

"Daddy meant to come, but the Old Boy has kept him. He's so sorry" the girl replied, in perfect English. Sir Hugh smiled; he recognised the reference—Prince Willie Tereny, Oria's Father, always referred to the Regent of Hungary as "the Old Boy."

"Are you up for long? Could you both come to luncheon tomorrow?" he asked.

"Dear Sir Hugh no, though thank you so much. Daddy has to rush back first thing tomorrow morning. But I popped in; I hoped I might see Lucilla—as well as *you*. Is she here?"

"Not so far, I don't think" the Minister said. "I expect she's glued to that horrible wireless."

"Oh, what a pity." The girl turned and greeted the American Minister and the old Marquess, who kissed her hand—an unusual gesture in Hungary to an unmarried girl; but Oria's

6

Father was a *Durchlaucht,* a Prince, though not of royal blood, and an important figure. "I will go and see Martha," Oria said, and moved away. Even as she did so, Lucilla Eynsham slid into the long drawing-room through a door from the small morning-room at one end. Lucilla presented the greatest possible contrast to Oria Tereny. She was very small indeed, exceedingly slender, with immense grey eyes in an almost colourless face under curly hair of a warm brown, and heavy brown eyebrows—but she was extraordinarily pretty, with a delicate grace of figure and movement that arrested the attention. Sir Hugh always said that Lucilla had "a thread of silver"; this perfectly described her curious cool and aloof charm. At her entrance also heads turned, smiles appeared involuntarily on people's faces—and she too went fearlessly up to Sir Hugh.

"Sorry I'm so late, Min dear—that wretched Betty wasn't up to time, and I couldn't leave the machine. Oh, how do you do, Mr Milward? And you, dear Mar*quess?*" She made a mocking inflection on the last syllable—the old Hungarian laughed and tapped her pale cheek. "You are saucy!" he said, in English as good as her own.

"Yes I know—but you don't really mind, do you? Dear Min, is Oria here? She rang up to say she might come. Oh yes—there she is; how good." And Lucilla flitted away.

"Such a pretty child!" the old Markgraf said benignly. "And even her impertinences are well-bred."

But the advent of Oria and Lucilla could not really save the party. Mrs Eynsham, in this prolonged act of failure, wondered privately which was worse?—open commiseration on the disastrous news from France, or the polite ignoring of some diplomats. As she took a cocktail from one of the footmen—goodness, how these awful affairs made one want to drink!—an Englishwoman married to a Hungarian came up to her, with the disturbed expression which seemed to be common form today.

"Oh good evening, Mrs Eynsham. I hope you don't mind my asking, but do you think there's anything in these rumours in the Hungarian Press about a Scottish regiment having been practically wiped out on the Flemish coast? You see I have a nephew in the Argylls."

"I'm so sorry, Mrs Starnberg, but I've no idea. I'm not being diplomatic!—only I can't read Hungarian." As she spoke Rosina was conscious of an acute sense of guilt—Lucilla's fiancé, Hamish MacNeil, was in the Argylls, but in her anxiety about Dick she had quite forgotten him, out at Buda-Örs that afternoon.

"Oh, there's Mr Milton! Let's go and ask him—he's sure to know" Mrs Starnberg said eagerly.

"Yes, do" Rosina said. But she let Mrs Starnberg go alone to accost the Press Attaché, who had just come in. She had what she considered good reasons for disliking and distrusting Geoffrey Milton. He was married, but his wife was in England, and no one knew what, exactly, their relations were; meanwhile Budapest gossip, usually as well-informed as it was free, credited him with latterly living with Sonia Marston, an English journalist representing the Anglo-Global News Agency. But just recently he had shown marked signs of pursuing Lucilla, greatly to her Mother's vexation—married men were the worst of all! And Milton was an obvious womaniser, and "lefty" to boot. Lucilla's Mother glanced across, with marked distaste, at the tall, dark, handsome but rather fleshy man who now bent his immense melting eyes—like giant gooseberries, she thought irritably— on Mrs Starnberg. He was being polite, she could see—which was something; but the gooseberry eyes strayed down the long narrow room to where Lucilla was laughing with Oria Tereny in a corner.

It was an understood thing, considerately laid down by the Minister, that except for Martha and Mrs Eynsham the members of the staff were under no obligation to attend the *jours* —so if the Press Attaché had come, he had come for his own purposes. However these were thwarted, for even as he shook off Mrs Starnberg and began to move down the room, Oria and Lucilla came up it and joined Rosina.

"Daddy is *so* glad that you will come down on Sunday— Siraly is looking lovely just now" Oria said.

"Yes—I'm looking forward to it very much. You realise that

8

David can't come?" Mrs Eynsham said—her husband would never stay in Hungarian, or indeed any other country-houses if he could avoid it.

"Oh yes; Daddy knows how busy he is" Oria said with calm politeness.

"Mummy darling, I must flash home and get a bite, and then go on the job" Lucilla said, giving her Mother a kiss. " 'Bye. Oh, good evening" she said in a light chilly voice to Milton as he came up. "I'm just off."

"Can I see you home? Good evening, Mrs Eynsham."

"See me a hundred yards?—what rubbish!" Lucilla said laughing, and slipped out.

The party ended at last. It had become a habit for the Minister, Mrs Eynsham, and Martha to repair to the boudoir to conduct a sort of post-mortem on the afternoon over a last whisky, while the men-servants cleared up the drawing-room; they did so now.

"No, no drink for me, Min," Martha said. "I must do a little editing for tomorrow's issue"—and in spite of his hospitable protests she took herself off.

"Well, it wasn't much of a success, was it?" Sir Hugh said, sitting down after bringing Mrs Eynsham a whisky. "It would have been disastrous but for you. You *are* good."

Rosina had long realised, with a certain embarrassment, that the Minister had a slight *tendre* for her.

"You look tired" he added solicitously. "Have you got a headache?"

"No, thank you—yes, I am a little tired. Oh well, it might have been worse"—to her own surprise and exasperation she burst into tears.

He let her cry for a moment or two before he went over and patted her shoulder.

"I expect you're in torture about Dick" he said quietly. "It is a torturing situation."

She looked up at him, relieved to have her trouble brought into the open, and wiped her eyes.

"*Yes.* And what is so frightful is that I'd quite forgotten about

9

Hamish, Lucilla's young man. He's in the Argylls, and that Mrs Starnberg says that the Press here is full of a story that a Scottish regiment has been practically wiped out somewhere along the Flemish coast. She has a nephew in the Argylls."

"Have you any reason to believe that the Argylls were near the Flemish coast?"

"Well Lucilla has always known—till quite recently, anyhow—where Hamish was; I didn't have a chance to ask her this evening."

"How did she know? They aren't allowed to say."

"Oh, she and Hamish each bought a copy of the *Guide Gastronomique* for France before he went out, and all he had to do was to write "I dined last night at the *Chapon Fin* off ..." and then mention some special regional dish and some wine referred to in the book; and all Lucilla had to do was to look through northern France at all the *Chapon Fins* till she found the one with the right dish and the right wine—then she knew what town Hamish was near."

He laughed. "How ingenious. There's really no controlling these young creatures—they're far too clever for us!" He went back to his chair. "I'll ring up the M.A. and see if he's heard anything," he said, lifting the receiver of a telephone beside him as he spoke. All the main rooms in the Legation had telephones.

"Colonel Morven, please." A pause—then a conversation—during which Mrs Eynsham waited quietly; she was ashamed of having cried, but felt more relaxed after having spoken to someone about Dick. With her husband she dared not discuss her anxiety; it upset him too much. Oh dear, she and David were so far apart nowadays—one might as well not be married! He was nearly always so cross and repressive; he shut her up if she tried to consult him even about Lucilla and the various young men who were running after her, like Hugo Weissberger—who was certainly in earnest—and Endre Erdöszy, who still more certainly wasn't!

At last Sir Hugh put down the receiver.

"Yes, he's had two telegrams today. He gathers, I'm afraid,

10

that the 7th and 8th battalions of the Argylls have been pretty well chewed up—his expression—on the Somme, somewhere between Abbeville and the sea; the fighting seems to have been quite desperate; Rommel already held two bridgeheads, and they were stretched out far too thin to do much; the Panzers simply flooded through and surrounded them. The few who weren't killed or wounded have been taken prisoner, he thinks."

"Oh how awful! Oh dear! Poor Lucilla!"

"Her Hamish may have been one of the lucky ones—*and* Mrs Starnberg's nephew. Let's hope so. As for the main Expeditionary Force" he went on, "the news is rather better. They have reached the coast near Dunkirk, and a most extraordinary effort is being mounted to get them out—every private yacht or small launch along the whole of the South Coast is being mobilised and sent across to collect them; and the Navy is there too, of course. They seem to be getting away in considerable numbers, in spite of the bombing."

"Bombing? There on the coast?"

"Oh yes, the Stukas are at it—but so is the R.A.F. Seriously, I do think there's a fair chance that most of them will get out —although we have to rescue the French as well, poor creatures."

"Bother the French! And bother the Belgians too!" Mrs Eynsham exclaimed vigorously. "*Miserable* wretches, running out on us!" She got up. "Thank you so very much. I must go home now."

"You wouldn't stay and dine?"

"Really no, thank you. I must give David his supper. But I'm immensely grateful to have this news. The awful thing out here is the endless rumours, and never *knowing* anything for certain."

"Oh come—with the Bulletin we know a good deal more than most people" Sir Hugh protested.

"Yes—we do of course. Only somehow not enough! Goodnight."

As she walked home Mrs Eynsham regretted her hasty remark. The Bulletin, she knew, was the Minister's pride and joy; later in the war these productions became common to most Embassies and Legations, but Budapest was the first British Mission to have one. In theory it came under the authority of the Press Attaché; in practice it was edited by Martha Beckley, while Lucilla did most of the monitoring of the broadcasts, since she, like Martha, knew shorthand; and as the demand for it grew two more girls had been got out from England to help with the mechanical tasks of roneoing and folding the pages. Martha had worked in a newspaper office, and knew her business; the news was well and clearly presented, and though people had to come and collect it, either from the Legation or from the Consulate down in Pest, the Bulletin already had a daily circulation of over 1200 copies. To accommodate it Sir Hugh had sacrificed most of his spare-rooms, over in the old harem quarters on the ground floor at the far side of the courtyard; beds and dressing-tables had been taken out of one set of rooms and stuffed into the opposite suite—rendering this practically unusable—and replaced by large tables, kitchen chairs, typewriters, and the roneo machine; the huge and enormously powerful radio receiver lived in the bathroom—where whoever was doing the monitoring perched uncomfortably on a cork-topped stool. It was all rather improvised, but it was the first of its kind, it was doing a valuable job well, and the Minister was justifiably proud of it. Hence Rosina's repentance.

As she walked in to her house Lucilla came out of it.

"Oh good, there you are. Daddy's just come in—he's pretty sour! But Margit has made a smashing goulasch—that may cheer him up. 'Bye—I must relieve Betty." And she darted away along the street.

So there was still no opportunity to tell her about the disaster to the Argylls. Well, the young were very resilient; if she did hear about it from the B.B.C. Overseas Service she would probably prefer it that way, Mrs Eynsham thought as she ran a comb through her hair, washed her hands, and powdered her face, before joining her husband.

"Party a flop, I suppose?" David Eynsham said as she came in. "Bound to be, with the news the way it is."

"Yes it was, rather. Very few Hunks, at least of the sit-on-the-

12

fencers." (Mrs Eynsham, like most English diplomats in Hungary, habitually used the deplorable abbreviation "Hunks" when speaking of their hosts; in English speech it has no injurious overtones, it is just a piece of diplomatic slang.) "But the M.A. says there seems quite a good chance of our people getting out."

"Oh, Morven showed up, did he?"

"No—the Minister telephoned to him and asked."

"Oh. Well let's have some dinner, shall we?" He rang the bell, and walked fretfully about the room till the meal was announced. David Eynsham was tall, thin, and so fragile-looking that one half expected a piece of him to break off at any moment; his narrow face with the high forehead, beaky nose, and the same immense grey eyes as Lucilla's was enormously intelligent, but almost shockingly sensitive; he had a slight tic in his right eyelid, which became more marked when—as so often—he was irritated or anxious. He ate his dinner in gloomy silence, which his wife was too wise to interrupt; quite at the end he asked —"What exactly did Morven say about our troops getting away from France?"

"That every single yacht and launch on the South Coast had been mobilised, and were being sent across to bring them home."

"Where from?"

"A place called Dunkirk. That seems to be where they've got to." She wondered if she dared to mention the disaster to the Argylls, but decided against it—David's eyelid was ticking furiously. Through the open windows came the song of the golden orioles in the trees on the slope below the Bastion, the fortification surrounding the old city of Buda; the Eynshams' house was perched on the very lip of this slope, and the loud, sweet, repeated note, "Oriole, Oriole," filled the room—as it was to fill every room for the next few days. For years afterwards Mrs Eynsham couldn't bear to listen to golden orioles; they reminded her too much of those prolonged hours of sickening anxiety about her son.

13

2

A few days later—it was a Sunday, the first in June—Lucilla came dancing into her Mother's bedroom at seven in the morning, waving a telegram.

"He's out! Dick's out! He's back in England—he wired to Grannie. Look"—she held out the paper. Mrs Eynsham took it and read: "Richard wires from Dover safely returned asked me to cable you thank God Mabel Eynsham."

Rosina leant back against her pillows, feeling almost faint with the sudden relief. "Why should he wire to Grannie?" she asked, dazedly.

"Oh don't be silly, Mummy darling! A foreign telegram! —what a botheration, when thousands are sending them. The M.A. told me last night that each man was being allowed to send just one when they landed. But isn't it *lovely?*" She gave her Mother a kiss.

"Yes, wonderful. Does your Father know?"

"No—you come first! I'll put it under his door. He was working till all hours last night; I saw his light on when I came in at two—I went dancing with Erszi; after I finished work." She looked at her Mother's face, still bemused with relief. "Hurry up and drink your tea, darling; you've got to be dressed in half an hour. Belinda's train goes soon after eight."

Mrs Eynsham obediently drank her tea. She was having it thus early because she had undertaken to see off one of the Legation typists, whose mother was dying, by the Nice Express from the West-Bahnhof. (So early in the war it was still possible to cross France from Nice to one of the Channel ports, and so on

14

to England.) But she did everything as if in a dream; Lucilla had to remind her to take the box of Gerbeaud chocolates and the Penguin which she had bought to lighten the girl's journey. And when the long train had drawn out, and she and Lucilla were back in the car, Rosina told the chauffeur to drop her at the Kronungskirche before taking the gnädige Fräulein home. Lucilla asked no questions about this move; she merely said—

"I'll tell Bertha to bring you your breakfast in bed when you come in. I think you'd better rest this morning. I daresay we shall get a wire from Hamish presently, though the M.A. seems to have an idea that the Argylls were a bit further north."

Mrs Eynsham did not feel that she could comment on this. "Bless you, my darling" she said to her considerate child as she got out of the car.

The Kronungskirche is the old Coronation Church, standing in a large open space at the edge of the Bastion; it was barely a hundred yards from the Legation. Mrs Eynsham had got into the habit of going there on Sundays after the Anglican parson had been evacuated, with many other British subjects, in the previous September on the outbreak of war; the only alternative was a service conducted in a bare school hall by the Presbyterian Minister, who thanks to his close links with the local Calvinists—30 per cent of the inhabitants of Hungary were Calvinists—had felt it safe to remain. Mrs Eynsham however found that she preferred Mass in the Kronungskirche; puzzling as the Roman Liturgy seemed to her, there was a sort of *reality* about the Mass which she found supporting. So often, even before the Phoney War ended, she had slipped in there to pray for Dick's safety; this morning she wanted to go and give thanks.

Mass was going on at the High Altar; she dropped on her knees in a pew. But when she tried to find words of thanksgiving, none came, only floods of tears; helplessly, she simply cried and cried while the service took its splendid course—so lofty, so related to Heaven, so far above all earthly concerns, and yet so closely linked to them. Now the congregation stood for the *Credo;* Rosina, still on her knees, knew the meaning of the Latin words. "Who for us men, and for our salvation, came down from Heaven... *et Homo factus est.*" And making a final effort she prayed that her tears might be accepted as the thanksgiving she could not put in words, and for safety for Hamish. Then she slipped out, and walked back along the yellow street to her house.

Yes, Lucilla's idea was a good one—she threw off her clothes, got back into her freshly-made bed, and took her rolls and coffee. Bertha had put the latest issue of the Legation Bulletin on the tray, and she read it while she ate. Oh, awful—town after town in France bombed and burning; she read the familiar names with dismay.

She was half asleep when Martha Beckley looked in to congratulate about Dick. "And here's a note from H.E.—he's got to see Czaki this morning, or he'd have come himself. It is wonderful, isn't it?—so many out, when it seemed quite hopeless. Everyone is ringing up to congratulate." Mrs Eynsham had never seen Martha so enthusiastic; her harsh face was almost radiant. "Oh, and Prince Willie—yes, he rang too—says Pista Táray is coming down to Balaton-Siraly by the late train as well, so he will look after you. There's a diner on that train. He doesn't mind your coming a day late a bit—I reminded him about Belinda, and that being the reason you couldn't go yesterday."

That was Martha all over. She was always tying up loose ends and smoothing things over for everyone in the Legation, not only for the Minister, to whom alone she had any obligations of the sort; but it was all done so casually and off-handedly that it seemed almost accidental. "Why on earth do you waste your time clearing up my wife's muddles? She's quite old enough to know better than to make them" David Eynsham said to her one day, in his most *cassant* manner.

"Oh, the show must go on!" Martha had replied coolly. "Anyhow, David, why do you have to be such a toad about Rosina? She's much nicer than you are; and can't a poetess ever be absent-minded?" (Mrs Eynsham had had a very minor poet's reputation before she married.) He laughed when Martha called

16

him a toad, and scowled at the reference to his wife's poetry. "Hardly anything of hers was the slightest good" he had said coldly—"and anyhow she's stopped it now, thank goodness."

"Very *un*thank goodness! But she can't help having a poet's mentality. You pipe down, David, and count your blessings, you silly man!" Martha had finished, making him laugh again—she blew him a kiss as she went away. Everyone came to her for advice; this she never volunteered, but appeared to give with reluctance. "Oh well, in your place I *rather* think I should do so-and-so" she would say, almost vaguely—and add that she must hurry off! There was always plenty of work for Martha Beckley to hurry off to; she had a lot on her plate. But before hurrying off on that Sunday morning the reserved creature did something almost unprecedented: she leaned over the bed and gave Mrs Eynsham a kiss. "I *am* so glad" she said. "Bless you, Rosina."

The railway from Budapest to the Yugo-slav frontier, leading on to Trieste and Italy, runs close beside the southern shore of Lake Balaton for almost the whole of its length of fifty miles; it is Hungary's largest lake, slanting very slightly from north-east to south-west. Sitting in the dining-car opposite Count Pista Táray, who had carefully ordered a table on the lake side of the train, Mrs Eynsham looked out at the trees bordering the quiet waters, faintly coloured in the sunset light; and then, as twilight fell, watched lights springing out in the villages along the farther shore. Her morning rest had calmed her to some extent, but she was still in a rather wrought-up mood, after her days of anxiety and the sudden relief. This tranquil scene, and above all the lights so fearlessly shown—the black-out had begun before she left England—plucked at her emotions.

"Pista" she said as they drank their coffee, "I feel a poem coming on. Can we go back to our carriage for me to write it?"

"How splendid! Yes of course. A poem about Hungary?"

"Well about the Balaton."

But when they got back to their coach they found it in darkness; the lights had failed. Count Táray flicked on his briquet and located the bell, which he pressed; presently the little train-conductor appeared, a sort of policeman's lantern stuck in his belt.

"We require light" Pista said.

"Excellency, the lights do not function. I apologise."

"Nevertheless, light we must have. This lady from the British Legation desires to write a poem." Whereupon the conductor drew out the little lantern from his belt and set it on the table by the window. "I hope this will serve" he said, bowing, and withdrew. And by that faint light Rosina Eynsham, on sheets of airmail paper from her despatch-case, wrote her poem.

> "*The poplars stand by Balaton*
> *And over them the stars—*
> *With lights across the water*
> *And the low planet Mars—*
> *His red alone reminding*
> *Of aeroplanes and wars.*
>
> *The chestnuts stand by Balaton—*
> *Their flowers fall on the grass*
> *From white and coral candles*
> *Like candles at the Mass;*
> *And Amiens lies in ashes,*
> *And Bapaume, and Arras.*
>
> *The acacias stand by Balaton—*
> *Their sweetness fills the night;*
> *They droop above the water*
> *Like lovely ghosts in white.*
> *But in the whole of England*
> *Shows not a single light.*
>
> *The reed-beds stand round Balaton,*
> *Whispering, grey, and tall—*
> *The water talks along the shore*
> *Where flowers in silence fall.*

18

And there's barbed wire in Downing Street
And sentries in Whitehall.

When day breaks, over Balaton,
Will rise the cattle grey
To browse through dew-grey pastures
By waters grey as they—
While from the aerodromes at home
The pilots roar away.

So deep the peace round Balaton,
But no peace there for me
While England stands in peril
By land, and air, and sea—
And her most beautiful and brave
Fight, now, to keep her free.

I must get out by Balaton
The train goes on to Nice.
Perhaps if I were going home
My heart might find some ease—
To be in England at war
Might bring my spirit peace."

She screwed the cap onto her pen when she had finished, and began to fold the sheets of paper together.

"Might one see? Only if you wish" Count Táray said.

"Oh yes, of course. I expect it's silly" Mrs Eynsham said, handing the poem over. Pista Táray drew the lamp towards him, and read it, slowly.

"This is not silly" he said when he had finished. "First, it is beautiful; one *sees* our Balaton. But I wish all our people felt so—and with such conviction. Few Hungarians, I think, would *wish* to be in Hungary at war. Would you really be happier now in England?"

"Oh yes, so *much* happier! Look, Pista, it's lovely being here, and everyone is so kind; but one isn't *doing* anything, don't you

19

see? One's just comfortable and safe—or fairly safe. At home one could be an air-raid warden, or work in a canteen, or something."

"I wish more of our people felt so," he repeated.

It was nearly eleven by the time they were driven up to the great house, where six men-servants, all in elaborate Hungarian livery, met them in the hall; old Bentö, the major-domo, led them up to where the Prince awaited them at the head of the broad staircase. "I am so *thankful* about your boy" he said, as he kissed Mrs Eynsham's hand. "Now I will take you to your room—you will not want to meet people tonight. Pista, Bentö will see to you; come along to my study presently for a night-cap." The Prince's mother had been the daughter of a Scottish Duke, and his English was indistinguishable from that spoken in good society in England.

Balaton-Siraly, to give it its full name, was nearly half the size of Versailles; Mrs Eynsham, who had often stayed there, always carefully timed the distance from the stair-head to her bedroom, in order not to be late for the formal assembly in the drawing-room before meals—the Prince had a thoroughly Scottish sense of punctuality. Tonight the walk took a full three minutes. "I have put you in the Hapsburg suite," Prince Tereny said as they walked along broad corridors—"I think you have not been in that before. The portraits are quite interesting." Then he turned to a more immediate subject. "Countess Dolinsky is staying here" he said. "She telephoned and asked to come, and her husband is such an old friend of mine that on this occasion I did not like to refuse her." Mrs Eynsham smiled to herself, though she was embarrassed at the idea of Countess Dolinsky's presence in the house; the lady was notoriously and rabidly pro-Axis and anti-Ally. And Willie Tereny seldom had any inhibitions about telling unwanted guests that it was "inconvenient" to receive them. Something must be up.

"I hear she's so charming" she said carefully, wishing that she needn't be careful at this time of night. "The French Minister

20

once told me that any man who sat next to Countess Dolinsky at dinner was sure to be well looked after!"

He laughed, pleased.

"Well, you shall not sit next to her! You will sit by me, and I hope be well looked after too. But—a little caution would be wise."

"I'll try. You know I'm not very good at caution. Thank you. Goodnight"—for they had at last reached her quarters. The Prince kissed her hand again as he said—"Sleep well."

Her cases had come up, and two pretty Hungarian maids were unpacking them—the nightdress already lay on the huge bed, with its cobweb-fine linen sheets and lacy quilt, her brushes and toilet-effects were being ranged on a vast antique toilet-table in front of a big mirror framed in silver. The bedroom was the size of an ordinary billiard-room; portraits of Hapsburgs, with their gloomy expressions and long chins, hung on all the walls; through an open door Mrs Eynsham caught a glimpse of an even larger sitting-room full of French furniture, where the soft glow of rose-shaded lamps revealed yet more Hapsburg emperors and their wives in massive frames. She found the "suite" rather depressing, but was touched by old Willie's gesture in giving her the most famous set of rooms in the house precisely at this moment. She realised exactly what it meant, for all the Prince's moves were most carefully calculated—it was a salute, not to her, but to her country. Good for him, bless him.

A sound of running water disturbed her reflections. She had been taking off her coat, hat, dress and so on all this time, and as fast as she did so one of the maids hung them over a delicate walnut clothes-rack, to be carried away and pressed. Through another open door she saw that a bath was being run for her in a large bath-room—Prince Tereny had made Siraly completely up-to-date in those respects. In her rather halting Hungarian she told the maid that she would take her bath in the morning, that she wanted tea at 8, her breakfast at 9, and a glass of cold milk *now*. Rosina did not pretend to speak the language socially,

21

but she had prudently mastered such words and phrases as would get her what she wanted in Hungarian country-houses, where she often stayed, and where few of the servants ever spoke even German. It always amused her that at Siraly there were no bells in the rooms—from 6.30 a.m. onwards a man-servant or maid-servant, according to the sex of the visitor, stood outside the bedroom doors, to be summoned by a call from the inmate! At first she had found all this service and formality, and indeed the sheer *size* of the house, rather oppressive; but this feeling gradually disappeared as she came to recognise how good the relations were between the Prince and his people; a tireless and devoted care for their interests on his side, a contented and affectionate response on theirs. It was just a different order of things, no longer familiar in western Europe—though probably mediaeval England had been like that, when England was still merry.

The normal hour for visitors at Siraly to make an appearance in one of the smaller drawing-rooms was at 11 a.m.—by which time Prince Tereny, who rose early, had already interviewed his bailiff on estate matters, seen the chef about the meals, the head-gardener concerning what flowers should be cut and sent in to the florists in Budapest for sale, and after going through his mail had dictated several letters to his secretary, besides scribbling notes for replies on those which the secretary could handle. After this he was ready to devote himself to his guests. Not all this methodical activity was typically Hungarian: most of the *Magnaten,* the big landed aristocracy, took pains to run their estates well, but they didn't start so early in the morning, and few would have dreamed of making a profit out of their gardens and green-houses by selling flowers commercially—that was Willie's Scottish practicality coming out.

Rosina Eynsham was familiar with this time-table, but she often found it rather a bore to assemble with the other guests, march downstairs, be handed fly-whisks in summer or be put into snow-shoes in winter by the men-servants in the lower hall, and then walk slowly about out of doors. On that Monday morn-

ing in June, 1940, after a good night's sleep—the best for days—
she took a bath between her morning tea and breakfast, and
was down and out, alone, well before ten.

She loved the gardens at Siraly. They were rather informal—
great stretches of lawn surrounded by shrubs and flower-beds,
and long cool avenues shaded by that loveliest of trees, the silver
lime, *Tilea argentea,* whose leaves are almost white on the
underside. Barefooted girls in bright dresses, with kerchiefs on
their heads, were mowing the lawns with scythes—their rhythmic movements and gay colours were as pretty as a ballet. An
ignorant stranger would have condemned the Prince for not
installing motor-mowers, but Mrs Eynsham already knew the
reason for this occupation. The Hungarian government, in some
ways much wiser than the English or the Russians—or indeed
the Americans—had realised the importance to the vitality, the
morale of a nation of keeping a large proportion of the popula-
tion on the land; hence restrictions had been placed on the use
of agricultural machinery, including lawn-mowers. That was
why half-Arab horses pulled the plough in the rich fields all over
Hungary, and girls gave the Prince's lawns a close-cut shave
with the scythe—and, incidentally, why Hungary had no dust-
bowl, since its soil was held firm by organic manure, not crum-
bled by powdery fertilisers out of sacks. Country-bred Rosina
applauded this wisdom, and smiled on the pretty mowers.

On her way back to the house to appear at the appropriate
time she encountered the Prince, returning from the kitchen
garden, at a crossing of two of the lime avenues.

"You are out early! Did you sleep well?"

"Very well, thank you. The Hapsburgs must have blessed my
slumbers!"

"I am glad. Now, I have had an idea—it is excellent that I
should meet you now, so that we can arrange it quietly. I must
drive over to Devis to see my new developments there—would
you care to come with me this morning? The lake is pretty. My
sister and Oria can look after the others."

"Yes, I should love to." Crafty old Willie, Rosina thought

gratefully—keep me and the Dolinsky apart for the morning, anyhow!

"Then go in by that door, and get your hat; it is the shortest way to your room. In ten minutes, here?" They were approaching the immense yellow-grey façade of the house, which had several entrances besides the one normally used, at the foot of the main staircase.

"How beautiful it is" Mrs Eynsham said, pausing to look at the great sub-baroque building. "Your great-great-grandfather, or whatever he was, knew what he was about."

The Prince was pleased; his small, sharp-featured, aristocratic face creased into a smile.

"Yes, he did indeed. But not only by building the house. Do you realise that he founded here, in the village, the first agricultural college in Europe?—which means in the world!—so that young men might come and learn the principles of agriculture and viticulture, and go out and teach their fellow-countrymen?"

"No, I'd no idea. How extraordinary! Does it still go on?"

"Oh yes—with State grants now, of course" Prince Willie said Scottishly. "And he began the library. Have I shown you the library?"

Rosina said he hadn't.

"Oh well, I shall show you that—perhaps after tea. I have added to it considerably myself, with the help of my excellent librarian, a most learned little Dominican. We do not keep the collection of Napoleon's letters there—they are in an *armoire* in the gold drawing-room."

"Goodness, have you got a collection of Napoleon's letters? *Why?*"

"Because an ancestress of mine was one of his step-daughters; she married the King of Bavaria, and Buonaparte was always writing to give her advice on how to behave to the Germans, and to enquire about her *grossesses*. He had an absolute obsession with children" the Prince said, looking amused.

"Oh, *could* I see those? I should love to."

24

"Of course. Tomorrow. I wish you would catalogue them—no one has."

"Dear Willie, you are really quite mad! Have a collection of Napoleon's letters and *not* catalogue them! I never heard of such a thing! Can't your Dominican do it?"

"He only works in the library" the Prince said, laughing a little at her emphasis, but quite unoffended. "Now go and get your hat, or I shall not have enough time at Devis."

Devis was a small watering-place, based on the hot radio-active springs which occur here and there in Hungary; at Devis many of them emerged into a small lake, so that swimmers could get the benefit of the waters while taking exercise. The place was on Prince Tereny's property, and he had decided to add a couple of modest but modern hotels to the collection of rather tumble-down boarding-houses which had hitherto accommodated the health-seekers. When they arrived he was at once fastened on by his architect and the clerk of the works. "Can you amuse yourself for an hour?" he asked Mrs Eynsham.

"Yes—I should like to swim. Only I didn't bring my bathing-dress. Oh what a pity!"

The architect, who spoke English, at once said that she could hire one at the bathing-establishment, a wooden building projecting out into the lake on stout pine-wood piles. Thither she went, and while the Prince discussed his new hotels Rosina Eynsham donned a rather lumpy bathing-gown, and walked down some wooden steps into the lake. It was the most entrancing bathe she had ever known. The water was blue-green and clear, its temperature that of a good hot bath; willows and chestnut trees in bloom overhung the little lake, and when she swam towards the shore floating blossoms brushed against her chin. Magical, she thought, turning over onto her back to float and look up at the pink and white flowers against the blue sky; if Willie really developed this place it would be famous throughout Europe. Where else could one bathe in such surroundings?

She spoke of this to him as they drove back.

"No," he said. "I shall only do it on a small scale, for connoisseurs—like you! For one thing I do not want a huge resort on my doorstep; and for another, a big fashionable place would corrupt the people. High wages and a bad example for three months of the year, and discontent for the rest of it! No" the Prince repeated. "There are higher values than money, useful though that is; any development, in any country, should be related to local values, local traditions. Have I ever shown you my cellars?"

"No."

"Well, I will. The peasants here have always grown their own wine, but in the past rather ignorantly, and from poor vines. I have built on this tradition: given them good stocks from Germany, and taught them better methods. They sell their grapes to me, and I arrange the bottling and marketing—Siraly-Riesling now commands a high price. It is profitable for them as well as for me; it gives more employment, and the land is not wasted by misuse. I hate waste!" the Prince said with energy, as the car crackled up over the gravel sweep to the front door.

Rosina only just reached the drawing-room in time, after a hurried change before luncheon; she fairly ran along those endless corridors, and arrived rather out of breath. She paid her respects to the old Princess, Willie's sister, who like her brother was small, with sandy hair slowly turning grey above a little peaky face—kissed the tall Oria, and then met the large company. Countess Dolinsky certainly was *very* pretty, with a face as animated as a squirrel, and hair of a squirrel's golden red; but in spite of her smile Mrs Eynsham thought that she looked wicked as well as clever, and was confirmed in this view when the young woman said—"I am so hurt that your charming Minister never asks me to his delightful *jours*. Why not?"

"Oh, because no one is ever *asked*—anyone who wants to just comes. We keep open house on Wednesdays" Rosina replied. This was an attack, she felt; glancing at the Prince she saw a lightning gleam of approval on his astute face, and was glad.

26

"Then may I come the day after tomorrow?"

"Of course—please do. You will meet lots of English people, and some charming Poles" Rosina said, passing to the attack in her turn. Again she glanced furtively at Prince Willie; he sketched a tiny nod just as old Bentö announced that the Princess was served, and they all moved into the dining-room.

Rosina Eynsham was by nature rather greedy; that is to say that she cared about good food, and was at pains to provide it for her family—today, after her swim, she was hungry as well. And the food at Siraly, she knew already, was something quite out of the world of even the best restaurants—something miraculous. If old Willie encountered some heavenly sauce in a princely house in Poland or Austria, or in some restaurant in Paris or Monaco, he would send his chef there for a fortnight to learn the secret. Mrs Eynsham saw no harm in this; again it belonged to an unfamiliar order of things, like the stately formalities of this sub-royal household—a vanishing world, but not a bad one, and with more moral values attached to it than to most industrialised societies. She ate heartily of the delicious food, judiciously praising items of it to the Prince—beside whom, as he had promised, she sat. On her other side was Count Endre Erdöszy, a very slim pale young man, with pale grey eyes and an amused expression which never left his long hatchet face, but was intensified when he found something particularly entertaining.

"And how is my little Biedermeier?" he asked Mrs Eynsham when her host turned to speak to the woman on his other side. Rosina stared at him coldly. She knew perfectly well that he was referring to Lucilla, and liked the aptness of the comparison between her child and the 18th century elegance of Biedermeier furniture; but Count Endre was running after her, as he ran after every pretty woman in sight, and was quite unscrupulous. "Plait-il?" she said warily.

"But of course I ask after your lovely daughter. She really is *pure* Biedermeier; the delicacy, the restraint—not in the least like most girls today."

"Oh, I see. I didn't understand you" Mrs Eynsham said rather repressively. "She is well, thank you. But she is very anxious and unhappy about her fiancé. He is with a Scottish regiment, in France, and the news we get of them is rather alarming."

"But I thought all the English troops were getting out from Dunkirk—so marvellous, all those little boats going across to fetch them! Who but the English could organise such a thing? The Prince told me that your son is safe—may I say how glad I am?"

Rosina made a polite response to this—any reference to Dick disarmed her. But she noticed that Count Endre made no further reference to Lucilla's fiancé. She was relieved to observe him, later in the day, flirting violently with, in turns, Anna Dolinsky and a beautiful young girl, Christina Fugger, who belonged to the famous German banking family.

Next day Princess Oria, who like so many Hungarian women was as active and athletic as she was long-limbed and slender, suggested that they should bathe in Lake Balaton before luncheon. "If one keeps fairly near the shore it is not *too* cold, though it is not very warm yet." Besides Mrs Eynsham only the younger ladies in the house-party acceded to this suggestion: Erszebet Erdöszy, Count Endre's sister, who had become a friend of Lucilla's; the Fugger girl, and, slightly to Rosina's embarrassment, Countess Dolinsky. The Terenys had a large bathing-hut on a quiet part of the shore, with plenty of cubicles for changing in; the party presently emerged onto the beach of flat water-worn stones in their various bathing-dresses. Rosina's was much lighter and prettier than the one she had hired at Devis the previous day, a brief flowered tunic-cum-shorts with a tiny discreet little skirt; Countess Dolinsky however appeared in the first Bikini any of the others had ever seen. Oria glanced at it with surprise, but made no remark except to praise Mrs Eynsham's rather pointedly.

The shallow water near the shore was warmed with the sun, but further out it was still fairly cold; most of the party turned back after about 100 metres, but Rosina, who was a strong swimmer, pushed on, as she thought alone; there were birds swimming about some distance off shore, and she wanted to get close enough to see what they were. Suddenly one of her feet was caught from below, and she was pulled right under; she was really frightened. But after a few seconds her foot was released by whatever held it, and she came up, spluttering and gasping—as she wiped the water from her eyes with one hand she saw Countess Dolinsky's laughing face a yard away.

"That gave you a surprise, didn't it?" the young woman said. "I'm rather good at swimming under water."

"I don't think it was very funny" Mrs Eynsham said, trying to exercise the caution the Prince had enjoined on her.

"Did you mind? Oh, then I am so sorry. I thought the English liked jokes."

"Yes—but this was what we call 'a practical joke', meaning a rather pointless trick" Rosina said, rightly guessing that to criticise Countess Anna's command of English was the surest way of snubbing her, and forgetting about caution.

"So. Then a joke is what?"

"Something verbal, and really witty. I am sure you are as good at that as at swimming under water." She looked towards the shore. "Aren't we rather a long way out?"

"Yes, perhaps. Shall we go back?"

"Do—I'll follow you in a few minutes."

"You want to get rid of me!" Anna Dolinsky said reproachfully.

"Well I don't want to be drowned again!" Rosina said laughing—really she was a beguiling creature.

"Then let us go back together—I promise I won't touch you!"

"Good. But I want to go on and look at those birds."

The Countess trod water, and gazed over the silky shining surface of the lake. "They are just ducks" she said—"and they are a *long* way away!"

"Yes—we frightened them with our talking, of course. But they're not ducks. I believe they may be Great Crested Grebes, and I want very much to see them. Countess Anna, do please be a dear, and go away."

"What is this, grebe?"

"Oh, a water-bird" Mrs Eynsham said impatiently. "The English like birds much more than they do practical jokes! You go on back—I'll follow you. You've come quite far enough; you look cold" she said, a little concerned at a bluish tinge on that pretty face.

"Yes, it is rather cold. I will go back"—and she turned and swam away.

Mrs Eynsham, with a slow powerful breast-stroke, swam on towards the birds; as she drew near them she stretched her arms out in front of her, quite still, to support her body, and swam only with her legs, very gently. Yes, they *were* Great Crested Grebes, with those enormous chestnut frills projecting on either side of their faces, and the funny horns of feathers from the back of their heads; but what delighted Mrs Eynsham was that they were surrounded by their striped offspring and were feeding them—as she trod water, only a few yards away, she watched the parent birds dive, come up with a beakful of small fish, and thrust them into the little gaping beaks. She had never seen this process going on at a distance of only a few yards—how many naturalists had, she wondered? Since she kept perfectly still the birds completely ignored her, and she could watch as she chose, out on the sunny water, with the low green shore opposite making a background to the beautiful creatures. But presently she remembered luncheon and Prince Willie's passion for punctuality, and struck out vigorously towards the shore.

There Princess Oria stood waiting for her, fully dressed.

"I sent the others home in the car. Countess Dolinsky had got chilled, and felt unwell" she said. "But it will be back in a few minutes."

"Right—I'll get dressed. I do hope I'm not late?" Rosina said, pulling off her rubber cap and shaking the water out of it. "Goodness, my hair's soaking!"

"Did Anna do something foolish?" Oria asked, with large serious eyes.

"To me, do you mean? Yes—she dived down and pulled me

30

under, silly little thing" Rosina said, shaking her head like a wet spaniel, and beginning to rub it with a towel from her cubicle.

"I thought she seemed upset—I think it was as much that as the chill that made her feel unwell. I am so sorry that this should have happened, here. She is impulsive, often, and unwise."

"Don't worry, Oria dear. It didn't matter. She was *really* cold, too—she was turning quite blue when I sent her back. I hope she'll be all right. But you'll have to lend me a bit of veiling to put over my hair for lunch—I shall never get it dry in time."

"Of course I will do this—and my maid shall set it for you afterwards. She has had a coiffeur's training."

"Oh, lovely."

"Leave your bathing-dress—one of the servants will come down to rinse and dry them" Oria called after her, as she went in to dress.

They were just in time for luncheon—at which Countess Dolinsky did not appear; she had gone to bed, she was unwell. As Mrs Eynsham expressed polite regrets about this to the old Princess she saw the Prince watching her, with an eye like a Red Indian's; but he said nothing till after the meal was over, when he took her aside in the big florid salon where coffee was served.

"You are kind, and clever" he said then. "Oria tells me there was a contretemps at the Balaton. What happened?"

She told him. "I had no idea she was following me—I was swimming out to see the grebes. But it didn't matter; it was just a prep-school boy's trick."

"I did not think even Anna, who is very foolish, would have ventured to treat one of my guests so" he said. "I do apologise most deeply."

"Oh as the Americans would say, 'Forget it', dear Willie. She's a foolish creature as you said—though mind you she's really rather sweet. She'd get round anyone—she quite got round me, when I ticked her off."

He laughed.

"You are gracious! And I should like to have heard you

31

'ticking her off' out in the middle of the Balaton!" Then he turned serious again.

"If you ever want help about anything here—quite quietly and discreetly—please let me know. I can always go and have a little talk with the Old Boy."

Mrs Eynsham smiled. "To have a little talk" was Prince Willie's invariable phrase for conducting a major intrigue. But she was grateful as well as amused.

"Thank you, dear Prince. I shall take you up on that if I ever do want help" she said—little guessing how soon she was going to apply to him.

In the afternoon several of the company went out to the stud-farm, where Prince Tereny bred his race-horses; he wanted to show his yearlings to Count Erdöszy, who only bred Arabs, but was a good judge of horse-flesh. They stood by the railings of a large green paddock while grooms led round, first, the solid sober-sided dams, "Those four in front are from the Aga Khan's stable" the Prince told Count Endre—"and the next three I got from Lord Derby. Those two following are French; the French breed well, now. The last five are my own." Then the beautiful rough-maned leggy colts were brought out—walking, to begin with; at the second and third rounds they were hustled into a gallop, to show their pace and movement. Endre Erdöszy watched them closely, and when eventually the lovely creatures were led up to the rails he climbed through, and passed a knowing hand down their slender, knobby legs. "This is quite exceptional, Willie—and this one, and this; and these three. Shall you be able to get them to Doncaster this year?"

"That is what I am considering. Last year, as you know, the Sale was cancelled—and though there was a second one later at Newmarket, with all the confusion after the outbreak of war I didn't attempt to send anything. But I believe that this year there will be a mixed Sale at Newmarket in October, in which they propose to include yearlings. I should like to send some of these, I must say—I feel sure Lord Derby would send them up from his stud, if I could get them to England."

"How should you send them?"

"They could go by train to Genoa, since Italy is neutral, and be shipped from there—though I do not care about a long sea-voyage for horses. I thought that possibly I might get them through France to Lisbon by train, and ship them from there."

"H'm. Wouldn't it be rather a risk to send them through France? I believe the French still mobilise horses! And I wonder how long one can count on Italy's remaining neutral. I hear—" he related some apparently inspired rumours from the Italian Legation about Mussolini being pressed by Hitler to become a more active partner in the Axis.

Mrs Eynsham listened to all this with mounting dismay. Only the day before yesterday she had seen that typist off, to travel through Italy and so home; not so long before the two new girls had come out by the same route to help with the Bulletin. If Italy were to come into the War—undoubtedly on the German side, if she did—the only way out, if the worst happened, would be south through the Balkans to Turkey, and so on to Palestine and Egypt. All routes to the north were through enemy territory—Austria, Germany, German-occupied Poland; to the north-east Czecho-Slovakia was what the Germans called a *Protektorat*, i.e. under German control, and recently they had been sending officers and troops into Rumania, to instruct and bolster up the Rumanian Army—so they said. In effect they now controlled that country too; the Hungarians, laughing, called it the *Instruktorat*. Rosina Eynsham had long had the uncomfortable feeling of living in a sack, whose mouth grew narrower and narrower as the string at the neck was drawn ever more tightly. If Italy came in, the mouth of the sack would be very narrow indeed.

3

The *jour* on the Wednesday when Mrs Eynsham returned from Balaton-Siraly was exceptionally well-attended. No one could call Dunkirk a victory, indeed it ought to have counted as a disaster; the fact that by an amazing feat of improvisation it wasn't somehow turned it into a triumph. It caught the Hungarian imagination, as it did that of much of the world, and people flocked up the wide stone staircase and into the long drawing-room to congratulate, to praise, to exclaim. If amateur yachtsmen and little launch-owners could bring 350,000 men across the Channel, at no notice, perhaps England was not sunk, not *foutu*—it seemed that she could do almost anything; she might win after all. But among all the throng there was no sign of Countess Dolinsky. Mrs Eynsham had seen the Minister in the morning, and reported her adventures—"Shall I ring up and remind her to come? Would that be a good move?" she asked.

"No. Let her come if she has the nerve, after that" Sir Hugh had replied. "Brazen little creature! Willie Tereny was very upset—he telephoned to apologise last night."

"Did he? I told him not to worry."

"Yes, you seem to have done admirably; he was full of your praises."

One of Mrs Eynsham's preoccupations in Budapest was to get exercise, both for herself and Lucilla, in their rather indoor life; and after her return from Siraly she started a new routine. Martha Beckley professed herself quite willing to do the monitoring from 7.30 till 9.30 a.m., so every morning the Eynshams, mother and daughter, drove down in bathing-gowns and bath-robes to the big swimming pool on the Margit-Insel, the lovely green island in the middle of the Danube, and swam—four lengths of the pool equalled half a kilometre, and they both did it every morning. Then Lucilla would go and do her ballet-exercises on the lawns set with young willows—looking like a solitary Sylphide, her Mother thought; she, being rheumatic, went and lay on a submerged marble couch in the hot radio-active spring beyond the big pool, and smoked a cigarette while she studied her Hungarian grammar—the submerged couches most conveniently had un-submerged marble armrests, with ashtrays. Afterwards they both put on their bath-robes again, and had coffee and rolls in the sun at the open-air restaurant by the water's edge—and then drove home, exercised and refreshed, to dress and tackle the day's work.

On the morning of June the 10th—they both remembered the date—Lucilla said to her Mother over their breakfast "Did you see Sonia?"

"Sonia Marston? No. Was she swimming? I didn't know she did."

"Well I suppose she can, up to a point; anyhow she was out in the middle of the pool nattering away to Egon von Schaffhausen—you know, that very good-looking man in the German Legation—for *ages,* while you were boiling and learning Hungarian. The privatest place in all B.P., at this hour in the morning" Lucilla said. "No walls to have ears, no hidden mikes, no cover for eaves-droppers! Erszi told me she'd rather taken up with him lately"—a faint blush, very comprehensible to her Mother, appeared in Lucilla's clear pale cheeks as she said this. "But she oughtn't to, ought she? I mean, he is a German, and she's English. And why at the pool, if it isn't secrets? Ought we to tell the Min?"

"I'll think—and ask your Father. Don't talk about it, darling."

"O.K." Lucilla said vulgarly, making her Mother smile. Everything about the "little Biedermeier" was so utterly *un*vulgar that common expressions, in her mouth, became actively funny.

Thanks to Budapest gossip, and to a letter from a friend at

home, Mrs Eynsham had quite recently learned something of the journalist's background. A Russian Mother, a hard-drinking mining engineer for a Father; the parents divorced when Sonia was in her early teens, and the Russian woman given the custody of the child. Rosina was familiar with the deplorable results of "broken homes" on the psychology of the children—only she, being Scottish, thought of these results more in terms of morals than of psychology. But her sense of compassion—rarely aroused, but strong when it was—had now extended itself to Sonia Marston, in so far as this was compatible with security. She realised too that the girl's position in Budapest was made more difficult by the fact that she had succeeded a delightful and brilliant creature, Yvette Yarnton, who had been universally liked, when the latter was sent down to the Balkans; comparisons are as inevitable as they are odious, and Mrs Eynsham had by now heard plenty of laments over Miss Yarnton's departure, and complaints about her rather *difficile* successor.

During the day the news that Italy had entered the war on the German side broke on the world—and on the Legation. When she heard it Mrs Eynsham remembered Endre Erdöszy's words out by the paddocks at Siraly, only a few days before. Too right, he had been!—the mouth of the sack was getting pretty narrow. But Lucilla remembered what she had seen at the bathing-pool that very morning.

"I bet von Schaffhausen knew then, and was telling Sonia" she said. "Mummy, I do think you ought to tell the Min."

"All journalists like to get scoops" Mrs Eynsham said temperately. "And I don't think most of them worry much about what sources they use."

"Well, I think you ought to let the Min know" Lucilla persisted. "She oughtn't to do it. She may tell *him* things."

"I don't think she gets much from the Legation nowadays" Mrs Eynsham said thoughtlessly, bringing that blush of Lucilla's out again.

"Oh don't be a *beast*, Mummy! I loathe Geoffrey. *I* didn't ask him to chuck Sonia."

"I know, poppet. I'm sorry I said that—it was just *une consta-*

36

tation" her Mother replied, causing Lucilla to smile rather unwillingly. *Une constatation* was a tiny joke between them.

Two days later Lucilla ran in and asked—"Mummy, what are you doing tonight?"

"Nothing—well only writing a speech I've got to make for Emmi's mother when I open her bazaar for The Save The Children Fund."

"Then *could* you monitor for me? I said I'd be on from 9.30 to 11.30, and now Emmi, as a matter of fact, has asked me to go with her and Hugo to the Arizona—they've made up a sudden party for some Austrian friends. I *would* like to."

"Yes, of course I will." Mrs Eynsham approved of the Weissberger brother and sister, Emmi and Hugo, and indeed of the whole family, far more than she did of many of her daughter's friends. All the Weissbergers were serious and immensely given to good works in the slums of Budapest. All the same she groaned mentally: two hours perched on that small cork-topped stool in the bath-room of the guest suite, her pad perched on the rim of the bath, was an unpleasing prospect. "What do I have to monitor?" she asked.

"Oh, only the B.B.C.—the English of course, and the German and French emissions. And then you might try Radio Toulouse; they sometimes have something. Don't worry with the German stations—they're mostly lies, and so are the Ities. Thank you— bless you! Leave your notes in the Chancery when you've finished." She kissed her Mother and hastened away.

Mrs Eynsham couldn't write shorthand, like Martha and Lucilla and the other regular monitors; but she had a good verbal memory, and knew French and German well; she had occasionally helped in this assignment before, and even her daughter, let alone Martha, always passed her notes as adequate. At dinner her husband asked where Lucilla was? She told him, and that she was taking the evening turn of duty. David Eynsham grumped. "That child ought to stick to her last."

"She doesn't often miss, David. And I think the Weissbergers are some of the more reputable of her friends."

"Well better than that creature Milton!—who's chasing her,

37

I hear. I don't trust him, *or* his girl-friend Sonia—if she still is his girl-friend. They say she's taken up with von Schaffhausen since Lucilla wiped her eye with Geoffrey. I mean to tell H.E. to be rather careful about briefing her."

"I wish you would—" and she told him what Lucilla had observed at the bathing-pool two days before.

"Why on earth didn't you tell me at once? Two days ago!—the very day the Ities came in. *Really*, Rosina!"

All conversations with David were like that nowadays, Rosina thought sadly, as she walked along the yellow street to the Legation through the warm night; the scent of flowers from hidden gardens made the air sweet. The night-porter let her in when she explained her errand—latterly the big wooden doors of the *porte-cochère* were kept locked after dark. He was a tall cheerful creature called Tom, a middle-weight boxer; after some assaults on the Kings Messengers who were taking the diplomatic bags down to the train, escorted by rather frail and elderly porters, Sir Hugh had applied to London for two new ones, and specified that they must be high-class boxers. They were—Tom in particular.

The moon was high as she crossed the courtyard; some lights were still on in the Chancery to her right, and in the glass-windowed passages which the Office of Works had added all round the first floor of the old building when they built on a third storey to house the kitchens and pantries, and the servants' quarters. She passed through the iron gates into the second archway, and turned right along a passage to the bath-room where the wireless set was housed; the door was open, and as she appeared at it Ginny Coombe, the girl she was to relieve, rose from the cork-topped stool—but perched on the rim of the bath sat Sonia Marston, smoking a cigarette.

"All right, Ginny—I'll take over now" Mrs Eynsham said. "Good evening, Miss Marston." She sidled past that young woman's long legs, seated herself on the stool, and took her block and pencil out of her bag.

"Good night, Ginny. Good night, Miss Marston" she said very

firmly—the two young women went away, and Rosina Eynsham applied herself carefully to the knobs on the huge aluminum receiver—their one real contact with the outside world, there in the enclosing sack.

It always gave Mrs Eynsham a sense of mystery and amazement to hear news crackling along the air all over the Continent, in endless different languages. She could only understand four —English, French, Italian and German; though she could recognise Hungarian, Rumanian and Czech she always cut these out, since she couldn't follow them. Dutifully she tuned in to the B.B.C., and picked up the news in French and German—nothing much there. She made some notes on her pad. Then, as Lucilla had bidden her, she began twiddling the knobs to try to get Radio Toulouse. Mrs Eynsham wasn't really very good at dealing with a wireless set; in her vague searching of the air she was suddenly arrested by the words "The Highland Division" in English, in that curious sub-American accent which was later to become so notorious. She held the knob still, and listened carefully.

"Most of the Division" the voice went on, "surrendered to the German Commander at 10.30 this morning at St-Valéry-en-Caux. The surrender was made by General Fortune, commanding the Division. The English prisoners amount to something over 30,-000; this is not counting those who were surrounded and captured some days ago on the Somme, near the coast, among whom were the 7th and 8th Battalions of the Argyll and Sutherland Highlanders. The Black Watch was among the regiments which surrendered this morning, and. . . ." The horrible voice went on, intoning the name of regiment after regiment.

Mrs Eynsham listened appalled. She was half-incredulous, but the facts were so detailed that it sounded as if they must be true. She knew General Fortune personally, and that he was commanding the Highland Division; knew too that many of the regiments mentioned formed part of it. But where was this news coming from? While the curiously monotonous voice went on about the "disaster to one of Britain's crack divisions" she scribbled down the time, and the place of surrender, the names of regiments and so on, listening all the while; at last the voice said—"This news comes to you from Deutschland-Sender Hamburg," and ceased.

So it came from Germany! But who would be broadcasting in English from Hamburg? In June 1940 "Lord Haw-Haw" was not as familiar to English listeners as he became later on; it was only in August that he was identified by the B.B.C. as William Joyce, the Irish-American. To Mrs Eynsham, hearing him for the first time, the whole thing was as puzzling as it was alarming. Thoroughly disturbed, she bethought her that she hadn't yet got Radio Toulouse; she did so eventually, but too late for the news bulletin. She tried the B.B.C. again—still nothing there. At 11.30, cramped, stiff, and anxious, she switched off, clipped her notes together, locked the outer door of the Bulletin office and re-crossed the courtyard, wondering as she went if she ought to contact the Minister and report this to him. By now the Chancery windows were all dark; at the entrance she rang the night-porter's bell to be let out; when Tom appeared she held out the keys and her notes—"Put these on Miss Beckley's desk, Tom, please."

But at that moment there was a second ring, and Tom, instead of taking the keys and notes, hurried over to unbolt the big doors and admitted the Minister's car. The little pavements in the *porte-cochère* were barely two feet wide; Rosina squashed herself against the wall to let the car pass, but of course she was clearly visible in the headlights; and as Sir Hugh got out—"What on earth are you doing here at this hour?" he asked.

"I've been monitoring."

"Oh, I see. Spoiling your child! Any news?"

"Well I'm not really sure." He was struck by the hesitant phrase, and a certain distress in her voice. "I suppose I couldn't see you for two minutes? It's rather late, I know."

He opened the glass door and ushered her into the hall. "Are those for Tom?" he asked, glancing at the keys and papers still in her hand, while the porter hung in the doorway.

40

"Oh yes—for Miss Beckley, Tom" she said for the second time; the man closed the door and went away.

"Rosina, you can always see me, as you very well know, for as many minutes as you like" Sir Hugh said then. "And for Hungary 11.45 is *early*, not late! Come up to my study and have a drink, and tell me what's been upsetting you."

The Minister's study was a large comfortable room next to the drawing-room; besides his desk and some steel filing-cabinets ranged along the walls it contained several comfortable arm-chairs and a long table on which, together with some red diplomatic boxes, stood a tray of drinks.

"Whisky?"

"Oh yes, please."

"I know you like soda, and ice" Sir Hugh said, unscrewing a Thermos ice-bowl and squirting from a syphon into her glass. "What a comfortable woman you are, with these wholesome appetites!" He filled his own glass and sat down, pushing a small table with ash-trays and a cigarette box in between their two chairs. "Now, what is it?"

Rosina told him what she had just heard. "And you see it was so detailed—mentioning the Black Watch and the Camerons and all the rest, and General Fortune having made the surrender. Do you think it *can* be true? The B.B.C. never said a word about it."

"I'd better have a word with the M.A." the Minister said, getting up and going over to his desk. This was of course furnished with a telephone; but because microphone installations were suspected the instrument was housed in a wooden box lined with thick baize, to prevent ordinary conversations in the room being overheard. He lifted the lid of the box and asked for Colonel Morven.

Colonel Morven was out, the Legation operator said after a brief pause.

"We must just wait till tomorrow, then" Sir Hugh said, replacing the lid over the telephone. "It does sound rather disturbing."

"So many things are disturbing" Rosina said. "When I went

into the wireless room tonight Miss Marston was sitting on the edge of the bath; obviously she'd either been listening in with Ginny, or pumping her. She oughtn't to, ought she?"

"Certainly not. Wonder how she got in? I'll speak to Tom about that—and to Martha too. Those new children are so silly; they're sent out to us knowing absolutely nothing. Journalists have no business in the Bulletin office."

"Least of all Sonia, I feel—though perhaps Geoffrey Milton got her into the habit." Sir Hugh laughed, rather shortly, at that. "No, but listen—I'm not gossiping for gossip's sake, but two days ago when we were down swimming before breakfast Lucilla saw her out in the middle of the pool, having a heart-to-heart with von Schaffhausen. The very day that Italy came in!"

"Did she indeed? That's quite interesting—though I wonder why he didn't give her a curtain lecture about it" Sir Hugh said coarsely, making Mrs Eynsham laugh. "Why the pool?"

"Oh, no mikes! I must go home" she said, getting up. "Thank you."

"Thank *you*." He took her downstairs, Tom let her out, and she walked home along the quiet street under the moon, hoping confidently that the Minister was letting Tom have it for admitting Miss Marston.

The following day Sir Hugh rang her up. "Would it be very inconvenient for you to come round? There *has* been something on the B.B.C.—Martha picked it up—and we should like to check it with what you heard. Fairly soon?—I've got the M.A. here now."

"I'll come now" Rosina said, after a glance at her watch. 5.40 —she would just have time to get back and change for the cocktail at the American Legation.

"Good—thank you."

In the Minister's study Mrs Eynsham found a small group assembled: Martha, Sir Hugh, and Colonel Morven, the Military Attaché, a big, gaunt, gruff Highlander, singularly without the normal charm of his race, with a rough tongue.

"Now, Mrs Eynsham, what's this you think you heard last night about the Highland Division having surrendered?" he began.

"I didn't *think* I heard—I heard, and wrote it down at the time" Rosina replied stoutly. "Martha, you've got my notes? But first I should like to hear what the B.B.C. has vouchsafed" she said, turning to Sir Hugh.

"Of course. Precious little!" the Minister replied. "Martha, would you read it?"

Martha Beckley, who unlike most women who profess to write shorthand could read her own notes back without hesitation, read out rapidly:

"The following announcement was made this morning by the War Office.

" 'One of our divisions, which was operating on the North Coast of Normandy, had its communications cut by German forces which had penetrated further to the South. A part of this division, together with other Allied troops, was eventually surrounded by superior forces. Attempts to evacuate these troops by sea were only partially successful and it is feared that a number of them have been made prisoners. The remainder of this division has been embarked and landed again in France.'

"A later statement says it is believed that the number taken prisoner is about six thousand."

There was a short silence. "Sounds like playing something down, to me" Martha Beckley said.

"Now can we have again what Mrs Eynsham got last night" the Minister said. "Just to refresh her memory." And Martha read out Rosina's notes, including the names of the various regiments.

"Were these all in the 51st Division, Morven?" Sir Hugh asked.

"Yes—as far as the make-up of the Division goes it's perfectly accurate, except for the Argylls; and we know that Rommel mopped up most of them a week ago, on the 5th. But Rommel certainly didn't take six thousand prisoners up on the Somme." He turned to Mrs Eynsham.

"You say you heard all this in English. In an English voice?"

"Well not *very* English—rather odd and affected, I thought. It wasn't like an ordinary Englishman speaking."

"And it came from Hamburg?"

"Yes—Deutschland-Sender Hamburg."

"H'm. All very odd." Colonel Morven raised his long knobbly body out of his chair.

"If you'll excuse me, H.E., I think I'll go and make a signal. I should like to get to the bottom of this."

"Do" Sir Hugh said.

But by the following day all the Hungarian and Austrian newspapers, which suffered from none of the inhibitions imposed on the B.B.C. by the Ministry of Information, were full of the fact that most of the Highland Division had been surrounded and forced to surrender—they gave the figure for the prisoners at nearer 40,000 than 30,000, and some of the correspondents explained quite openly the circumstances which had brought this disaster about. The English could not leave the French in the lurch—but while the Highland Division had ample transport, the French had none; this limited the rate of withdrawal to 20 kilometres, or 12 miles, a day. (Winston Churchill was to write gloomily later, in his History of the War:—"I was vexed that the French had not allowed our Division to retire on Rouen in good time, but had kept it waiting till it could neither reach Havre or retreat southward, and thus forced it to surrender with their own troops.") There was more commiseration to be faced at parties—"These wonderful Highlanders! I suppose they were all wearing kilts? Oh, how tragic." The next *jour* was dimmer than ever. In spite of Dunkirk, Central Europe was again convinced that England was sunk; the Americans clearly weren't going to come in, and what could she do alone? The Russians were of course allied to the Germans, after the signing of the Ribbentrop-Molotoff pact the previous August.

The very young find this kind of situation easier to bear then the middle-aged; they can always dance, and dancing is a peculiarly good form of narcotic. Lucilla, nervy with the absence of news about her Hamish, was cross to her Mother and pert to her Father—but she was always ready to dance, and one day came and told Rosina that she was invited to one at the Stefan

44

Tárays three days hence. "They've got the *best* gypsies coming to play; it ought to be smashing. I can go, can't I?"

"Yes of course, darling." But for once Mrs Eynsham displayed a certain, and rather unusual, maternal firmness. Count Stefan Táray had married a sister of Endre Erdöszy's, and she had a very fair idea of what their parties were like; when Lucilla had gone back to the Bulletin office she rang up Countess Táray, thanked her for her kindness in inviting Lucilla, and expressed the hope that she, Mrs Eynsham, might have the great pleasure of coming too? The Countess could of course only say Yes— "*Too* delightful to have you; how good of you to spare the time. I did not venture to ask you. And your husband also?"

"Alas, no—he has so much work at night."

"Oh, what a pity! Alors, on Thursday, about eleven-thirty. Enchantée, Madame Eynsham."

Lucilla was not particularly enchanted.

"Did she *ask* you, Mummy?"

"No—I asked myself. I would rather be with you when you go to the Tárays. As a matter of fact I think she was rather flattered," Mrs Eynsham said astutely.

"I shouldn't wonder." Lucilla was also quite astute. "But I think it's rather silly—you'll only get tired, and I should be quite all right alone." Her Mother wisely made no reply.

The Tárays had a big apartment on the Buda side of the Danube overlooking the river; as usual in flats in Budapest the large openings between the living-rooms had no doors, only looped-up curtains. Dancing took place in the big drawing-room, where a few chairs stood round the walls; the other rooms were agreeably arranged for sitting-out with easy-chairs in pairs. At first a small but very good band played rumbas, fox-trots, and waltzes; later, about 1 a.m., the gypsies arrived in their bright clothes; they played the czardas. With their advent the tempo of everything hotted up—of music, of dancing, of emotion. At one point Mrs Eynsham noticed that her daughter had not been visible on the dance-floor for sometime, and decided to make a cast round. She rose and strolled through into the next room;

there the lights were on, but in the three others leading off it they had been extinguished—just the sort of thing one would expect at Countess Táray's parties! And from one of the darkened doorways a voice, unmistakeably Endre Erdöszy's voice, suddenly and irritably pronounced in English—"You are like a hot-water-bottle with cold water in it!"

Mrs Eynsham almost laughed. Endre making a pass at Lucilla, of course—and fortunately, bless the child, getting no change. She moved slowly forward and stood for a few moments, knowing herself clearly profiled in the lights, opposite the doorway whence the voice had come; then she returned to the drawing-room. As she had expected Lucilla shortly reappeared, followed after a discreet interval by Count Endre, who proceeded to gather up another young woman to dance the czardas, at which he excelled. Lucilla didn't; one must be born Hungarian to dance the czardas properly.

It was not long after the Táray's dance that an edict went out in the British Legation that all members of the staff, with their wives and other belongings, must both be vaccinated, and get a T.A.B. inoculation—T.A.B. standing for Typhoid Fever plus Para-Typhoid A. and B. "You see my dear," the Minister explained to Rosina, "we might have to quit at short notice, and get down through Palestine to Egypt—and the *only* way to get into Palestine is a certificate of recent vaccination and a T.A.B. inoculation." (Palestine in 1940 was still a British mandated territory, under the old League of Nations.)

"Oh very well—of course we'll get done" Mrs Eynsham replied, feeling again that unpleasant in-drawing of the string round the neck of the sack. "What a bore, though. How do we get to Palestine? Walk?"

"It might come to that" Sir Hugh replied, laughing.

Rosina was a regular Boy Scout about "being prepared," and she took the Minister's remark about walking quite seriously; indeed other members of the staff, she found, were all discussing that possibility, among others—though laughing about it as he had done. She made her dispositions. She had a large pigskin bag with a zip top and strong handles, and in this she proceeded to accumulate what she thought would be most useful on a journey of several hundred miles, on foot or otherwise. A set of spare underclothes, a thin blouse, a sweater; three pairs of ankle-socks and two of light string-soled shoes, which she preferred for walking in; handkerchiefs, a First-Aid Case. First Aid made her think of health needs, in a large party, and in went a bottle each of Chlorodine, aspirin and quinine; a bottle of gin in case anyone's kidneys went wrong, of whisky against chills, of brandy as a restorative, and of rum as an all-purposes cheer-bringer. Cigarettes of course—500, in those handy little sealed tins of 50, as supplied to Legations; matches, and a bottle of lighter-fuel. What else? Some plain chocolate, and two or three aspirin-phials full of salt; finally, a last notion, she made a corner for a small aluminium saucepan.

When the bag was full, zipped, and locked Mrs Eynsham lifted it, consideringly. It was far too heavy for anyone to carry, if it should come to walking. Sling it on a stick, and let two people carry it so? Possible. Then she had an idea. David's aunt, old Countess Pongracz, had been mad on gardening, and used to possess one of those baskets on wheels with a walking-stick handle to cart her weeds about in—to the astonished mirth of her Hungarian gardeners. If it still existed it would be the very thing—and she drove out to the old lady's house on the Rosza-Dom and called on her. The poor old Countess was by now rather gaga, but she remembered the wheeled basket, and said that of course dear David's wife could borrow it. She sent for the gardener—she seldom left the house any more—and gave her orders; the man led Rosina to a tool-shed where, dusty and rusty, but still mobile if pushed, stood the weed-basket, which she took home in the car. Her chauffeur cleaned it, and oiled it till it ran smooth and free; it held the pigskin bag nicely, and was stowed in the back of the garage. With her supplies locked in the bag under her bed-table, and its transport secured, Mrs Eynsham, in spite of her husband's mockery, felt ready for any emergency.

47

But she was rather busy for several days—opening Baroness Weissberger's bazaar, entertaining for the Minister, social doings of one sort or another; it was nearly a fortnight before she got round to the far more essential job of getting herself and Lucilla vaccinated and inoculated—Rosina was poor on priorities. When she eventually rang up the doctor who attended the Legation he was much distressed.

"The small-pox is easy—I can do that. But there has been such a demand for the typhoid inoculations that I have no cultures left; so many people have asked for them: the French, the Dutch, the Belgians, even some of the Americans. None is left in Budapest."

"Oh how awful! How soon can you get more? Can't you give us *anything* now?" Rosina asked desperately, rightly feeling guilty at her negligence.

"Gnädige Frau, what I *could* get is some of what we give to our troops when they are going on manoeuvres; but this is very severe—it has the anti-cholera in it also."

"Oh, never mind the cholera! Can you have that today? Right —we'll be down about 5.30, my daughter and myself."

In fact the Hungarian Army inoculations were very severe indeed. The doctor wanted to put them into the trunk, but Mrs Eynsham unwisely insisted on having hers in her thigh; the result was that her whole leg swelled up to an enormous thickness, and was extremely painful—for some days she could only walk with difficulty. Lucilla had much less discomfort—the doctor had been quite right, as doctors so often are. But it passed off in time—in fact just in time, for a few days after Rosina was mobile enough to swim again, about the third week in July, when she and Lucilla were already having raspberries with their coffee and rolls down by the bathing-pool on the Margit-Insel, the cards began to arrive.

4

The first postcard with the printed heading "OFLAG VII C" to reach the Legation was addressed to the Minister; it came from a second Lieutenant in the Highland Light Infantry whose sister had once acted as secretary to Sir Hugh; the writer asked for food, cigarettes, socks, a shirt, and above all a pair of pyjamas. Next day Colonel Morven had three from officers in the Cameron Highlanders, his own regiment; these, rather more literate, made the same requests, and explained the reason for the straits the prisoners were in. The Division had been sent to Germany practically in what they stood up in: three weeks march to the Dutch coast, just west of Antwerp, had finished their socks (besides leaving them almost starving) and though some enterprising officers had tried trailing their single shirt overboard on their voyage up the Rhine by barge, to wash the sweat out of it, this had been frowned upon by their captors. In fact they were hungry, filthy, and in need of almost everything —and very concerned about their men, from whom they had been separated. "We gather they are being sent to another type of camp, called STALAGS" one officer wrote. "I wish we could have stayed together." The day after that Lucilla, at last, got a card from Hamish, also from OFLAG VII C and also asking for food, clothing, and cigarettes.

"Well anyhow he's alive" Lucilla said. "But we simply *must* send him some clothes and eats, Mummy."

Everyone in the Legation felt the same; and within a few days the trickle of cards became a flood. But sending parcels to British prisoners in Germany was easier said than done. En-

quiries from the Hungarian Post Office were discouraging—
"Unless, of course, parcels are sent through the Red Cross. These
go *Fracht-frei* (free of charge) and have a priority." But the
Hungarian Red Cross, when approached, was cagey and not very
co-operative—and the British Red Cross was in London, hundreds of enemy-held miles away.

At this point Mrs Eynsham remembered Prince Tereny's
promise to help her if ever she needed it, and she rang him up.
He was coming to Budapest next day, and called on her; she
explained the difficulty.

"I will have a little talk with the Old Boy" Prince Willie said.
He did. British prisoners-of-war in Germany from 1940 to 1945
owe more than they know to that old half-Scottish aristocrat.
The result of his intervention with Admiral Horthy, the Regent,
was that the Hungarian Red Cross received instructions to supply
their own labels for parcels to British P.O.W.s in Germany, and
to send a man up to the Legation as required to affix their own
leaden seals. The first parcels ever to reach the P.O.W. camps
in Germany were so sent off.

But as the cards continued to pour in it became obvious that
an effort on a much larger scale would be needed. Hungary was
herself suffering from severe shortages of many essentials, mainly
as a result of the British blockade of Central Europe; tea was
almost unobtainable, coffee cost approximately 45 shillings (or
six dollars fifty) per pound. The export of all woollen goods was
forbidden, since Hungary, which breeds cattle rather than sheep,
had run out of wool—so how to get shirts, or wool to knit socks?
The only permitted exports were luxury products like paté de
foie gras, very high-class chocolates, and smoked goose-breast
—a delicious edible; these the Legation staff sent off under the
cover of the Hungarian Red Cross label, adding tins of their own
ration of cigarettes—but clearly this would not suffice. And the
men in the STALAGS—something must be done about them, too.

Martha Beckley and Colonel Morven decided to form a little
Committee to deal with supplies for the P.O.W.s—it met, that
first time, in his room in the Chancery. Besides the Military

Attaché and Martha there was Mrs Chalgrove, the Consul's wife, Wheatley, the First Secretary, with his wife, Mrs Eynsham, and Mrs Morven. Horace Wheatley was tall and thin, and stooped; he had a curious habit of waving his long hands about like fins or flippers, and usually spoke in a rather low soft voice—these characteristics frequently misled people into underestimating him. In fact he was highly intelligent, a tiger for work, and capable of ruthless determination. His wife, Eleanor, was equally misleading: small and pretty, with a sort of fair elfin charm, her manner usually displayed an easy affectionate friendliness; but she was as stupid as sin, as obstinate as a mule, and rather spiteful—in fact she constituted Number One problem in the small Legation community. Mrs Eynsham, that first morning, noted her presence with dismay; she guessed, rightly, that Eleanor Wheatley had insisted on taking part in anything that was going on.

Gina Morven, on the contrary, was a delight—in every way the greatest possible contrast to Mrs Wheatley. She was Italian; the Colonel had married her when he was Assistant Military Attaché in Rome. Short, dark, crisp of hair and crisp of manner, well-read and well-dressed, she was an asset, not a liability; she always had a contribution to make to any conversation, generally a highly original one, and the more entertaining for being expressed in the most execrable English, practically the music-hall version of Italian speech. She had now been living with a British husband for ten years, much of the time in Great Britain; but she was still incapable of pronouncing the letter H, and added that redundant A to most words which ended in consonants. Everyone wondered why she had not troubled to learn her husband's native tongue—but they wondered still more how the vivid creature contrived to remain so devoted to her rather heavy Hugo. In fact, everyone loved her.

By now all those present at that first momentous Committee, except Gina, had received cards from OFLAG VII C; Mrs Eynsham had even had one from STALAG XX, one of the camps containing "other ranks"—from a corporal who had been underkeeper on her Father's estate in Scotland before he joined up.

"The nights are cold here, for all it's summer" Corporal Fraser wrote—"and we have but the one blanket, a poor thin thing; and we sleeping in our shorts." When she read this out it added to the general sense of urgency and desperation. The prisoners had *got* to be helped, but in Hungary the wherewithal to satisfy their needs simply did not exist. After a good deal of rather fruitless discussion Martha said, in her cool firm voice—"Mrs Eynsham, couldn't you go down to the Balkans, and see what you can scrape up from the Jugs and the Bulgars?—or even the Turks? You'd do it very well, and you *could* get away. Lucilla can look after her Father."

"Yes, I suppose she could" Rosina said, rather hesitantly, startled by the idea. To everyone's surprise Gina put in her oar.

"Meessis Eynsham, you must do zis! Unless someone goes to ozzer countries, and get food-a, it is absolutely 'op'less."

"Oh bless you, Gina" Horace Wheatley said, with a warmth rather unusual to him. "You're quite right. Mrs E., will you go?"

"Just one moment, Horace" Colonel Morven put in. "I agree that Mrs Eynsham would form an admirable buying commission of one—but how is it all to be financed? I suppose most of us could shell out something, but not on the scale that's going to be necessary—nothing like it."

The Consul's wife, a quiet unassuming woman, here observed that her husband had told her to say that several of the English business-men still in Budapest would be willing to contribute to any fund set up for prisoners' relief.

"That's excellent, Mrs Chalgrove" Martha said.

"And a lot of the wives will be glad to knit—socks, or whatever is needed" Mrs Chalgrove pursued, encouraged.

"But what earthly use is it their being willing to knit, when there's no wool to knit with?" Eleanor Wheatley asked scornfully.

"Don't be bloody-minded, Eleanor" her husband said, in his low slow tones, as calmly as if he were offering her some toast. "It may be a great deal of use when Mrs Eynsham sends us back hundred-weights of wool. You keep them ready for action, Mrs Chalgrove." Mrs Chalgrove, who had appeared rather dashed, looked relieved; Rosina looked startled; Colonel Morven looked positively appalled.

"But my good fellow, Mrs Eynsham can't go off buying wool by the hundred-weight without knowing how it's to be paid for. I've already telegraphed to find out if we can get anything from regimental funds. Mrs Chalgrove, did your husband give any figure for these local contributions?"

Mrs Chalgrove, dashed again, said No.

"Well ask him to find out, will you? That would be a great help" the Colonel said politely. "But we ought to have a budget, and settle how much Mrs Eynsham can spend before she starts" he told the Committee firmly. "Agreed?"

During these interchanges Rosina had had time to recover from her initial surprise and hesitation—she had begun to *see* the thing as a whole: the need of those men in the camps, and the possibility of meeting the need; her imagination was alight. Now she spoke.

"*No*, Hugo—not agreed. I'll go, but I'll go without any budget. I shall get whatever I can, on tick; we can think about raising the money afterwards."

"But how?" the Colonel asked.

"By begging, for one thing. I'm a good beggar!"

Gina Morven jumped up and hugged her.

"You are good everysing! I know you get-a ze money!"

On the whole the little Committee approved of this rather optimistic approach, though Eleanor Wheatley muttered to Mrs Chalgrove that she didn't see why an Italian had to be so keen on helping British prisoners. "Shut up, Eleanor" Martha Beckley said coldly—she had overheard. "Learn to knit!"

Few husbands are enthusiastic at the prospect of their housekeeper leaving her job for an indefinite time. David Enysham was not, but he raised no serious objections, and three days later his wife set off. The Minister was much more positively co-operative; he sent word to the Legations in Belgrade and Sofia, and to the Consulate-General in Istanbul, that she was coming, and the nature of her errand, and asked them to help her in every way. In fact Mrs Eynsham knew the Ministers in both the Balkan posts slightly; they invited her to stay, and promised all assistance. By the time she left the financial situation was already brighter; most members of the staff had begun to receive cheques from prisoners' relations, begging them to send what they could from neighbouring Hungary to poor Tom, or Dick, or Harry. Unwisely, as it proved, most of the staff instructed their banks in London to place these cheques in a special "prisoners relief" account—later the War Office froze them all.

"Well, we shall miss you, but this is a job well worth doing" Sir Hugh said to Rosina before she left. "I've telegraphed to the Red Cross asking if they can help with funds."

"Oh good. Anyhow the American Minister has given me a thousand dollars already—in notes!"

"No! Well bless you—take care of yourself."

The Minister in Belgrade was a shrewd little bachelor, with a rather unusual capacity for assessing situations.

"I've got all the local ladies coming at eleven for coffee" he told his guest at breakfast—the night train from Budapest got in early in the morning. "If one is going to drive a coach-and-four through an Act of Parliament, women are the ones to do it!—and knowing you, Mrs Eynsham, I feel fairly confident that you will be up to some illicit activities."

"Oh, I hope not! What I *should* like, Sir Monty, is a list of your prohibited exports, here. Then I shall know how to go on. In Hungary it covers practically everything!"

"I'll get the Commercial Attaché to produce that" Sir Montague said. "And I've arranged for the M.A. to come in and see you at 10.30—he may have some ideas. You'll come tonight to the concert? Prince Paul will be there. How's David?"

Belgrade proved to be a rather fruitful source of supplies. Yugo-slavia had an infant canning industry which produced a quite tolerable tinned goulasch—Mrs Eynsham sampled it; and the export of this was not only permitted but encouraged. In

54

the recent process of industrialisation mills had also been set up to spin Macedonian cotton into flannellette; but owing to wartime difficulties of transport the manufacturers had stocks on their hands which they were not only willing but anxious to dispose of, and Mrs Eynsham at once thought of pyjamas. But here the Military Attaché had something to say.

"Whatever you buy, Mrs Eynsham, you must get it dyed khaki, or the prisoners won't be allowed to have it. I know this from"—he hemmed. "Well my German opposite number here is a splendid chap; we used to be great friends, and he knows how upset I am about the 51st Division being mopped up. He tipped me the wink."

"How good of him!" Rosina considered. "Are there dye-works here who can do khaki?"

"I *think* so; but ask Mrs Henderson—she knows everything. And by the way, when you're shopping here don't speak German, or you'll get nowhere. These people absolutely loathe the Huns!"

Mrs Eynsham spent a strenuous week in Belgrade. With the help of the local ladies, who also formed themselves into a small Committee, she placed orders for tinned goulasch, and arranged with Mrs Henderson's help for the dyeing khaki of several hundred metres of flannellette. But all these things had got to be conveyed to Budapest somehow.

"Look, Sir Monty dear, can't the K.M.s bring some of this stuff along when they come up from you to us? Fatted creatures, always travelling about in single first-class sleepers!—they might do a hands' turn for the prisoners."

The Minister laughed.

"What did I say about your attempting illicit activities? King's Messengers are only supposed to convey diplomatic bags. However, we'll see. Anyhow, I and my staff have coughed up a very small contribution to your funds"—and he handed her a cheque for three hundred pounds. "Nearly all from the staff."

Rosina took his hand. "Darling Sir Monty, bless you all. Tell them, will you?"

Sofia was rather different. The Minister there was married, but his wife was in England coping with children's school holidays—however he too showed a desire to help the prisoners. Bulgaria had more wool, since sheep are bred in the mountains; and being nearer to the Mediterranean coast somehow seemed to feel the blockade less—Mrs Eynsham ordered a lot of wool, after fingering samples carefully. Rather coarse, but it would make socks all right.

"I thought they might be glad of some chocolate" the Minister said, "so I have arranged for you to meet one of the principal manufacturers here. I expect you know that Bulgaria makes something like one-third of Europe's chocolate."

Mrs Eynsham didn't know this, but gladly went to interview the chocolate-maker. After fixing a price—a little less than cost price was all he would charge—she told him exactly what she wanted: a half hundred-weight (56 pounds), in half-pound slabs, every week.

"I can do this" the Bulgarian said—"but I shall not pack it in slabs. I shall have each quarter kilo put up in fourteen fingers, separately wrapped in silver foil."

"Oh, but that isn't in the least necessary" Mrs Eynsham protested. "And it will make it more expensive, surely?"

"No—the cost will be what we have agreed. This is something I do for your prisoners." He leaned back in his chair, not smiling, but with a very benevolent expression.

"In the last war I was myself a prisoner for nearly two years, in British hands; and I learned then that one of the few things one could do for one's fellow-prisoners was to make them little presents: a few cigarettes, or a piece of chocolate—naturally my family sent me chocolate from the firm. But a stick broken off a slab of chocolate—what an inelegant present this is! So in time I got them to send my chocolate wrapped in fingers—and your men now shall have it so. The English treated us well."

Mrs Eynsham was greatly touched by this—it was really the brightest spot among her efforts in Sofia, where in fact she experienced a certain sense of frustration. Once again the question of transport to Budapest arose; the Minister was adamant against using King's Messengers for the purpose. Another little committee of women was formed, who undertook to buy wool and Macedonian cigarettes at intervals, and seek means of getting them up to Hungary; one or two of the wives on the Legation staff volunteered to come up themselves and bring all they could —with their *laissez-passers* they would have no trouble at the Customs. "Anyhow Budapest is such heaven, compared to this dump!" one lively young woman said. "I'd adore to come, as often as ever I can."

The Minister, like Colonel Morven, was concerned about finance. "I've passed the hat round, naturally" he said, "but the thing ought to be put on a proper basis. The Red Cross are the people who should pay—they have endless funds. Have they been approached?"

"Sir Hugh was going to, when I left."

"Well I hope he will. If your parcels really reach the camps, and they know this, there ought to be no difficulty." (In this he was wrong, as it turned out.)

"Meanwhile" he went on, "for your immediate purposes I think it might be useful if you met the American Minister here. He is intensely pro-British; he served with our Navy in the last war, before America came in. He is having a birthday party tomorrow night at the Brown House—shall I ask him if I may bring you?"

"Oh do by all means. What is the Brown House?"

"The principal hotel here, the Bulgaria. It has a restaurant with a good dance-floor and band, but it's cram full of Nazis; they're trying to take over this wretched little country, and the place is alive with them—naturally they have all congregated in the best hotel, so it's known as the Brown House, after the original Nazi head-quarters in Munich."

The American Minister's birthday party at the Brown House in Sofia was a very lively affair—unexpectedly so. The restaurant was circular in all respects: the band played on a circular platform, surrounded by an open space for dancing, which in turn

57

was surrounded by a triple ring of tables; upstairs there was a balcony, like a dress-circle at the theatre, also full of tables for those who wished to eat rather than dance. The Minister had a large table adjoining the dance-floor; the balcony, as he pointed out to Mrs Eynsham, was filled with German officers in uniform. The food was good; Rosina, hungry after a hard day of going round to shops and factories in search of supplies, ate heartily. At a pause in the music the American diplomat clicked his finger and thumb at the band-master; when the man came over to the table he handed him a folded wad of leva notes, with the single word "Tipperary." The band-master bowed; when he returned to his round platform the band struck up that tune—so value-less in itself, so symbolic to two whole generations, not only in England, but throughout Europe.

"Shall we dance?" the Minister said.

"Yes, rather." Rosina was kindled by the meretricious music; it was nice to dance to "Tipperary" in the depths of the Balkans; her heart warmed to the American. They rose and began to jig round the floor; so did several other couples. In the case of Bul-garians to do this was brave; it amounted to a political demon-stration, with all those Germans sitting up on the balcony—but a few risked it, as well as some other Americans, and various Allied diplomats—soon the small floor was crowded. All this annoyed the Germans, and one officer, who had drunk a good deal, presently flung an empty champagne-bottle from the bal-cony down onto the round orchestra dais. It only hit a music-stand before smashing harmlessly on the parquet floor, but the trombonist, a huge Bulgarian, was annoyed in his turn. He put down his instrument, ran up the stairs, seized the German officer and threw him bodily over the balcony rail onto the floor below; he landed with the astonishingly loud sound that a human body makes when it falls on something hard.

No one was hit. The band went on playing, louder than ever, while waiters hurried to pick up the fallen man, and answer the protests of the other Germans, who came pouring down the stairs; the trombonist returned to his trombone and emitted a loud blare. Oddly, to Rosina, the dancers went calmly on dancing, still to the strains of "It's a long way to Tipperary."

"D'you mind?" the American Minister asked, continuing to twirl Mrs Eynsham round.

"Well, he asked for it" Mrs Eynsham said, though in fact she was rather shaken by this display of crude violence. Perhaps it was just the Balkan idea of clean fun, but the sight of the German officers, so ill-behaved, added force to her words when later she told the American, who raised the subject, of the reason for her mission.

"Yes, your nice Minister told me about that. It's too bad, losing all those prisoners. I and my staff would like to help—in fact I made a little collection this morning, after I heard I would have the pleasure of meeting you tonight." He drew out his wallet. "How would you like it?—in dollars or leva?"

"Oh, in dollars, I think. They take dollars here, don't they?"

"Mrs Eynsham, they take dollars everywhere! And I hear you're going on to Turkey, where they like dollars particularly. There!" He handed her a roll of notes so large that she had some difficulty in stuffing it into her bag—when she counted them over before going to bed she found that she had been given 3000 dollars, at the then rate £750. Before she slept she scribbled a note to Martha, reporting her purchases, present and future, and the encouraging fact that between the two British Legations, and the U.S. Minister, she had already netted £1150. She set out for Turkey in high heart.

Istanbul, however, at first proved discouraging. The ladies of the large—and rich—English colony there were already hard at work knitting—but for the crews of mine-sweepers! Mrs Eynsham tried to divert their activities to socks for the prisoners, without much success. They met to knit in the huge and mainly deserted British Embassy, that stately building copied from the Farnese Palace in Rome; the Ambassador was at the new Embassy up in Ankara—if he had to come down he lived on the official yacht, *Makook*. The abandoned kitchens and pantries of the great house were full of chests and crates containing the silver of most of the Ministers in South-East Europe, which they had prudently sent down to the Mediterranean sea-board to be shipped home when opportunity offered—in those days Ministers and Ambassadors were still expected to furnish their official dinner-tables with their own family possessions, as they had to supply their own table-and-bed-linen, their glass and china. (Mrs Eynsham had already noticed in her scour through the Balkans that one now used, at Ministerial tables, nickel-plated forks and spoons to eat with.)

However in spite of the local obsession with mine-sweepers she persevered with her task. She arranged sources for wool—in Turkey abundant and quite good; for sultanas and dried figs, which would help to replace sugar in the prisoners' diet; she placed orders for considerable quantities of all these. But by now it was August; winter cold would be upon those men in Germany in three months' time, and Rosina was obsessed by the picture which Corporal Fraser's card had conjured up of the one thin blanket. If they were chilly by night in July, what would it be like in November? Escorted by one of the English ladies she made an expedition to the *Bazar*, that extraordinary roofed-in market, covering acres, on the European side of the Galata Bridge, to try to buy blankets. The kind woman who took her spoke some Turkish, but not very well, nor had she fully mastered the art of bargaining, so essential in Turkey—it usually involves leaving a given stall at least three times before a price is fixed. The Turkish blankets were very coarse, and heaver than they were warm; the price asked was exorbitant. Mrs Eynsham, profoundly discouraged, decided not to buy any.

Most fortunately some Turkish diplomats, friends of hers, were at home on leave, and she went out to spend a couple of nights with them at Büyük Ada, the resort in the Marmara; when she explained her problem her hostess at once said "But quilts!" And when she returned to Istanbul the Turkish lady came with her, and led her to the arcade devoted to the wadded cotton quilts under which poorer Turks sleep. Mrs Eynsham was thrilled by these. They are normally covered in thin cotton in bright Paisley patterns, but she insisted that she only wanted them in the plain strong unbleached calico in which the cotton-wool itself is quilted, and of specified dimensions: 6 feet 10 inches long by 4 feet 10 inches wide. She reckoned that these, folded over and sewn or pinned down one side and along the bottom would make fine warm sleeping-bags for even big men. The price finally agreed on for these articles, after some hard bargaining in Turkish, was, if bought by the thousand, 16/- shillings each, then a little over three dollars—cheaper, and far warmer, than any blanket.

Much encouraged, Mrs Eynsham went as usual to the Embassy to cash a cheque and pick up her letters. Among these was a note from the Ambassador's wife at Ankara, asking if she could possibly go up there for a few days to discuss supplies for the prisoners?—Ankara too, it seemed, had been getting cards from the camps. By this time Rosina would have gone to the North Pole to discuss supplies, let alone secure them; she asked if she could telephone from the Embassy, and did so, suggesting coming at once—she set off the following evening.

Ankara of course is in Asia, or at least in Asia Minor; hence Turkey's two capitals, the old and the new, are separated by the waters of the Bosphorus, so that the journey from Istanbul begins with a crossing by ferry to Haidar Pasha, the Anatolian terminus of the railway to the South. Most fortunately a junior attaché was also travelling up, and brought a dragoman—an Embassy servant—along to deal with the swarming so-called porters who fasten on travellers' luggage and race away with it, no one knows where—unless they can speak Turkish, which Rosina couldn't. So presently she found herself installed in a comfortable sleeper, and later eating an excellent dinner in the restaurant-car opposite the young attaché, as the train, leaving the shores of the Marmara, turned inland. Here too lights showed across water; Turkey, in spite of all the astute von Papen's efforts, was still neutral, and remained so to the end. Turkey had come in on Germany's side in World War I, only to lose all her European possessions as a result; as far as the Turkish people were concerned they had had it, in regard to Germany. But they have not received sufficient credit for the risks they took in not succumbing to the intense pressure put on them by the Reich. Within weeks of Mrs Eynsham's visit German squadrons were installed on the Bulgarian airfield at Chataldja, only a few minutes flying-time from Istanbul, then still a city built mainly of wood—it was within their power to reduce the place to ashes in a matter of hours. There were threats, but the Turks stalled —they are very good at stalling—and in the event they did as they intended, and preserved their neutrality.

The atmosphere in Ankara was quite different from that prevailing in Istanbul, and to Rosina much more satisfactory. There was a lot of knitting—the Ambassadress even knitted during her parties; but it was pull-overs for the prisoners, not leg-stockings for mine-sweeper crews. She and Mrs Eynsham went through the cards together; there seemed to be a lot of duplicates. "Lady P. writes from Athens that she has had a lot too" the Ambassadress said, when Rosina recognised several names. "Do you think they can be writing to *all* of us?"

"I shouldn't wonder a bit. I think we'd all better make lists: you give me yours, and ask Lady P. to send me hers—and when I get back I'll send both of you the names we've sent to from B.P. We don't want to send too much to some, and leave the rest without."

"That's a good idea. I think you had better be the clearing-house, since you can really get your parcels in through the Hungarian Red Cross—that's so wonderful. Lady P. says that a Greek merchant has offered 100,000 cigarettes a week, but she doesn't know how to despatch them safely."

"Tell her to send them to us, and we'll get them off" Rosina said confidently. "And so we will anything that you send up." Then she raised the question of the quilts. The Ambassadress was enthusiastic—"*What* a splendid idea!"

"I think we ought to send one to every single prisoner," Rosina said. "But that will cost quite a lot—far more than we can manage unless the Red Cross helps."

62

"Let's talk to my husband about it" her hostess said.

The Ambassador was equally pleased with the idea of the quilts. "But my Military Attaché says that there are nearer forty thousand than thirty thousand prisoners, he hears. At sixteen shillings per man"—he did a rapid sum on the telephone pad—"that comes to thirty-two thousand pounds. No, the British Red Cross will have to help with this. And I wonder if we can get so many. Who's your merchant?"

Mrs Eynsham delved in her handbag and brought out the note-book in which all her sources of supply were written down.

"Oh, old Panoukian. Yes, he's perfectly reliable, and in a very big way of business indeed. Funny how these really important merchants still work from a potty little stall in the bazaar —but that's the local tradition. He could certainly produce forty thousands quilts within a few weeks, at the outside." He reflected. "I think I'll telegraph to the Red Cross via the Foreign Office. The sooner we start on this, the better."

"Won't it cost a lot to send all that mass of quilts up?" his wife asked.

"Not if we send them through the Red Crescent, consigned to the Hungarian Red Cross—all Red Cross goods are supposed to go free of charge. But I will check on that." He pressed one of several flat bells on a table; Rosina's travelling companion appeared almost immediately.

"Oh Ralph, I want someone to get onto the Red Crescent and confirm that they can consign goods *in bulk* to the Hungarian Red Cross in Budapest, for our P.O.W.s, with no charge for freight. I'd like the answer *quickly,* even if they are all sun-bathing at Büyük-Ada!"

The young man grinned.

"Right. I'll see to that at once. That all?"

"Yes, for the moment. I shall be sending a cable to the Red Cross later."

"Who are the Red Cross to answer to?—you or us?" Mrs Eynsham asked, not very grammatically. "I mean, we shall want to know too, if we are going to despatch the things." She was

63

thinking of *where* 40,000 quilts were to be packed, and *who* would pack them, in the already over-crowded Legation.

"Yes, that's a point. I'll tell them to reply to Hugh, with a copy to us" the Ambassador said. "Is lunch ready?" he asked his wife. "I've promised to ride with the Foreign Minister this afternoon."

5

The Turkish Red Crescent did ultimately agree that goods for prisoners-of-war could be sent free of charge, but this was not before Mrs Eynsham's departure, so she left Istanbul on the Simplon Orient Express with her sleeper crammed with sacks of figs and sultanas and wool. By the time she had picked up half a hundred-weight of that specially-wrapped chocolate in Sofia, and several bales of khaki-dyed flannellette in Belgrade, there was no room for her in the sleeper at all; even the berth was piled high with stuff, and she couldn't get near the basin to wash. Perfectly content, she put her despatch case under her head and slept all night on the floor of the corridor.

Greatly to her surprise, David was at the Keleti-Station to meet her, though the train got in soon after 6 a.m.

"You look fit enough" he said, after a rather perfunctory kiss. "But what have you done to your dress? It's all crumpled, and dusty."

"Oh is it? Yes, I daresay—I slept in it. David, I think we shall want a taxi as well as the car—I've brought rather a lot of stuff."

"What on earth is all this?" David Eynsham asked, as bales, sacks, wooden cases, and cartons were bundled down out of the *Wagons Lits* coach.

"Prisoners' stuff. Haven't I got a splendid lot?" She studied his face. "You look tired, David. How are you? And how's Lucilla?"

"I'm all right. Lucilla seems perfectly fit, in spite of working all day, and dancing all night with her various admirers" he said with a wry grin. "But you'll find the house upside-down."

This is the sort of phrase which most appals a woman on returning after an absence—Rosina had visions of the cook having left, or the always uncertain kitchen range having finally conked out.

"Goodness, what's wrong?" she asked anxiously.

"That woman Martha would get round the devil himself" her husband replied obliquely, as they walked towards the station entrance. "She said they absolutely must have a room to pack the prisoners' parcels in, as close to the Legation as possible, and that our dining-room would be just the thing, it's so big and so near —in fact she practically requisitioned it!"

"Oh." Rosina laughed, relieved. "So where do we eat?"

"In your little morning-room. Where you'll keep all your trash and write your letters I can't imagine." He told the chauffeur to get a taxi, and they stood in the cool morning air while the miscellaneous collection of bundles was stowed.

"It had all better come to our house, so" Rosina said, checking her acquisitions carefully from a list.

"*Everything* comes to our house—and everybody! People tramp in and out all day long. Thank goodness that infernal little man from the Hunk Red Cross has stopped coming up with his wretched labels and seals" Eynsham said as they drove off.

"Oh dear! Why? And now what happens?"

"*Why*, I imagine because he found it too much trouble! But he left the seal in the Legation, with endless strips of lead, and Morven or Horace seal the parcels themselves. And Chalgrove arranged for us to use their block, and have the labels printed ourselves."

"But with the Hungarian Red Cross name on it?" Rosina was thinking of those quilts, and the cigarettes from Athens, for which this cover was so essential.

"Certainly. I *said* we used their block—you don't listen. Oh, a lot has gone on while you were away" David said, looking slightly amused. "That woman Martha! She's had writing-paper printed with a quite *brazen* letter-head:

66

Not a word about the Legation!—and how are the Boches to know that it lives at No. 1 Verböczy utca? There are no flies on Martha."

Rosina did certainly find her entrance-hall rather dusty, and bits of straw and paper blowing here and there; but she didn't mind—in fact she was delighted. After an early breakfast, while she was taking up again the reins of her easily-running household, checking the cook's account-book, and hearing Bertha's eager recital of what the Fräulein had worn to what parties, the front-door bell rang.

"That will be Herr Schmidt" Bertha said. "Will the lady see him?"

Herr Schmidt proved to be Mr Smith, an English business-man from the town; while work was slack, owing to the war, he had taken on the formidable task of doing most of the actual packing of parcels for the prison-camps. With him Mrs Eynsham now entered what had been her dining-room; she stared in astonishment. The carpet had gone; a trestle-table stood down the middle of the long room, with two smaller ones at each end, one covered with flaring red-and-black Red Cross labels, balls of string, a huge set of kitchen scales, and the sealing-machine with its attendant strips of lead; the other piled with heaps of chocolate, cigarettes, and various tinned edibles. The things she had brought had been dumped down under the windows; against the opposite wall strong cardboard boxes in various sizes were neatly ranged.

Mr Smith explained all the arrangements enthusiastically. The Hungarians were being absolutely splendid; they made special cartons for the Relief Organisation at cost price or below, and a lot of the food-merchants sold their goods at the same rate. As for him, he loved doing the packing—"And the staff are so

67

busy, it's more than enough for them to go and buy things." His
eye lit on the pile of bundles under the windows—"Oh, is this
what you've brought? How grand! May I undo them?" Mrs
Eynsham said by all means, and left him muttering and chuck-
ling joyfully over the chocolate, the cigarettes, the khaki flannellette, the figs and sultanas.

> "Let us now praise famous men,
> Men of little showing"

—men like Mr Smith, to whose labours in the Eynsham's dining-room thousands of prisoners, who never heard his name or
knew that he existed, owed the well-packed parcels which did
so much to lighten their lot during those first terrible six months
when practically nothing reached them from England. Others
packed too: Gina Morven, with her small strong hands, and
Horace Wheatley, whose fins were more efficient than they
looked; the Colonel tugged at knots on parcels for the Camerons. But Mr Smith carried the main burden. Over 100 5-kilo-
gram parcels, the maximum permitted weight, were already
being sent off every week—not only to those whose wives or
parents sent cheques, but to all camps whose initials and numbers were known—so Mrs Eynsham learned from Martha later
that morning; some had already been acknowledged. "They seem
to get there in about four weeks; some in less."

"Oh, excellent."

"But someone will have to keep the lists" Martha pursued.
"We must know what has been sent to whom, or to which camp.
So far we've just scribbled it all down in a copy-book, but that's
very muddly and unmethodical." Mrs Eynsham realised that
she would have to keep the lists, and volunteered to do so.

"Good, I was sure you would."

"I'm not very methodical."

"Oh, Horace will keep you up to the mark—he's a mammoth
for method!" Martha said, with her brief laugh. "But Mrs E.,
we must find out somehow how *many* of our people there are
in each camp. Look at this." She took from her desk—they were

68

talking in Martha's office—a letter in German from an indignant Camp-Commandant; Rosina could not help laughing as she read it. The Hauptmann X's complaint was that *eight* parcels of food had been sent to his camp by the Prisoners' Relief Organisation in Budapest, for British prisoners—"whereas here I have of these only six, all diabetics or with stomach ulcers, who are receiving special foods from the International Red Cross in Geneva. Such cannot eat smoked goose-breast and chocolate!" He ended by saying that he had sent on the parcels to the nearest Stalag, where there were over 1000 British prisoners.

"Well, that's splendid of him," Rosina said, still laughing.

"Yes—but will you answer it? He ought to be thanked, but I simply haven't the time. And this nonsense has got to stop. We *must* know how many of our people are in which camps; we can't waste our parcels. Could you find out?"

"I'll try. Is H.E. free? If so I'll go up and see him. Oh and Martha, when you have a moment I wish you'd come over and see my wool; the Turkish stuff is lovely."

"*More* wool? Pounds and pounds have come up from Sofia already."

"Really? Good. But this is better quality. Anyhow now we can start Mrs Chalgrove's ladies knitting."

"That's something *you* will have to do" Martha Beckley said firmly. She and Rosina were on such good terms that they could afford to be firm with one another. "You might talk to the Min about it. I think it ought to be done here—doling out the wool, and checking the products; all that part. In the mornings—we could give them coffee; they'd like that. I'm sure the Min will give the drawing-room once or twice a week."

"Of course the Legation is the proper place" Rosina said. "Right. Can you find out if H.E. is free now?"

The Minister was free, and Mrs Eynsham went up to his study, taking with her the letter from the indignant German Hauptmann. Sir Hugh studied her face rather more carefully than her husband had done, but reached much the same conclusion.

"Well apparently you haven't killed yourself, as I fully expected you to" he said. "In fact you look remarkably well." (By now Rosina had changed out of the crumpled dress in which she had slept on the corridor floor.) "Now sit down and tell me everything."

Rosina told him enough to amuse him; the episode in the Brown House she reserved for a later occasion, since she had business on hand. When she had made him laugh about his Belgrade colleague's remarks about women's illegal activities, she raised the question of the knitting-parties. As Martha had foretold, Sir Hugh at once promised to give the use of his drawing-room once a week, and to provide coffee for the knitting ladies. Rosina suggested Thursday mornings—"The day after the *jour,* and well before the week-end." He agreed. "But I suggest that you rope in that Mrs Starnberg to help you over this" he said. "She's far the most competent of the Englishwomen here."

"How *do* you know that?"

"Knowing is my business. Do you agree?"

"Yes, entirely—only I can't think how *you* find these things out." Then she produced the German Camp-Commandant's letter. When he too had finished laughing over it she explained that she had told Martha that she, Rosina, would keep the lists of parcels. "But look, H.E. dear, how are we to find out how many of our men are where? Obviously we must do that."

"I always like your calling me 'dear,' but from you, especially, I dislike the expression H.E.," the Minister said. "Wouldn't it be much simpler if you called me Hugh?"

"Nothing would induce me to, while we're in the same post." Rosina spoke as firmly as Martha. "Terribly bad for discipline, and—and morale, and so on" she said, blushing a little. "You *are* a dear" she added; "so now be your name, and tell me how to find out how many prisoners of ours are in each camp."

He laughed a little ruefully.

"Oh, you dedicated women! Well if you are going to do all the office-work for the P.O.W.s you must have a room in this house, with the use of the Legation telephone, and of a typist. I know

70

your scrawl—it wouldn't be much use for official records!" She laughed. "There's a little room across the landing—come and look" he said, and led her out of the study. The room was certainly small, and rather dark, but it contained a desk with a lamp, a telephone, two tables, and some bookshelves.

"Perfect" Mrs Eynsham said. "I'll tell Martha to send her papers up here. Oh, but I shall want something to keep files in—shan't we have to have files? What about one of those spare-room chests of drawers that were cleared out to make room for the Bulletin?"

"I'll send something up. Come and have a drink—it's after twelve."

Back in his study, over sherry, the Minister proceeded to answer Mrs Eynsham's question about how to ascertain in which camps the British prisoners were.

"The International Red Cross in Geneva will know that" he said, "and by now they should have the figures for all the camps."

"But how do I get hold of the Red Cross in Geneva?"

"Ring them up, of course. When you've finished your sherry go across to your little new office, and ask Hanna or Bertha to put you through."

Rosina was so startled by this idea that she abandoned her sherry and went straight across to her room to try it out; Sir Hugh looked gloomily after her.

"I want the International Red Cross in Geneva" she told the girl operator.

"Any particular section? This may save time" the girl said.

"Yes—whoever deals with British prisoners-of-war."

"I will ring you back." And within ten minutes Rosina was having the first of many conversations with a Mademoiselle O. in Geneva about the prisoners and their needs. Mrs Eynsham put her question—how many, in which camps, and their correct addresses?

"We have the total figure, about forty-four thousand" the lady replied. "But I cannot give you the numbers in each camp off-hand. Can I ring you up this evening? Say at 6.30?" Rosina said Yes. And in under seven hours she took down, over the telephone, the exact numbers of prisoners in each Oflag and Stalag in Germany—this at a time when letters from the British Red Cross in London were taking six weeks to reach Geneva, telephone communication between the two places was impossible, and all telegrams subject to censorship and delays.

On her return to lunch David said, to her surprise—"I've told Ernest Erdöszy that we'll all go down to Terenczer this weekend. Martha says she can spare Lucilla, and I think the child could do with a breather. So could I, come to that—and it's one of the few houses where they *will* let one go to bed if one wants to. You're free, aren't you?"

Rosina was free—but she would have broken almost any engagement to get David away into the country for two or three days. And she loved Terenczer, with its lake where one swam, and the quiet country life on the edge of the Bakony—the great forest, the second oldest in Europe to have been felled and replanted continuously for six centuries; it stretched for miles, and was still full of wild life: deer, roe, wild boar, wolves. Ernest Erdöszy was a cousin of Count Endre's, but of a very different stamp. He hated Budapest and lived on his estate, which he farmed with knowledge and enthusiasm; he bred Arab horses, was a fine shot, and—curiously—was also an eager student of modern philosophy; learned men came gladly to stay in his rambling comfortable house. He had surprised everyone by his choice of a wife, a girl from Vienna with no country roots at all; but Margit had taken to the life at Terenczer like a duck to water; she rode and drove splendidly, and had become as good a shot as her husband, or better. She filled her house with guests as often as possible—and even philosophers like a gay pretty hostess, who sees to their every comfort. Budapest, that hot-bed of gossip, speculated as to how Margit Erdöszy passed the winter evenings, when the children were in bed and her Ernest in his library with the philosophy books; in fact she spent them doing exquisite smocking, copying patterns from an old English book, on frocks for her little girls, and listening to Mozart records on her huge radiogram. She only left her husband about once every three months, to see her dentist in Budapest about her teeth, of which she was rather vain.

The Eynshams drove down to Terenczer on the Friday; so did the Morvens, who were invited too. Like so many other things petrol was in very short supply in Hungary in 1940, and diplomats, who could get all they wanted, were frequently asked to give lifts to fellow-guests. So the Morvens took down Count Endre and his sister Erszi, and the Eynshams (David grumbling) went to the Duna-Palota, the Budapest Ritz, and collected a rather fat and dreary man of learning from Dresden. (One of the things Margit Erdöszy had not learned was that one shouldn't ask diplomats to carry enemies in their cars.)

Before she left Rosina had telephoned to Mrs Chalgrove, the Consul's wife, and told her to muster all the English knitting ladies she could at the Legation at 10.30 on the following Thursday morning, to be given wool and to drink coffee; then, as the Minister had advised, she called on Mrs Starnberg. She soon realised how right Sir Hugh had been. Like most Scotswomen Rosina had been accustomed to knitting shooting-stockings and socks for her men-folk all her life, and imagined that all women could do likewise. Mrs Starnberg knew better.

"Most of them won't have the faintest idea" she said. "But I have an old knitting-book which has all the directions for socks and gloves and so on in it." She produced a rather tattered paper-covered pamphlet. "I thought it might be a good idea to have the recipes, if that's what one calls them, for socks and gloves typed out, so that you could hand one to each person who is given wool."

Rosina had never thought of any idea so practical as this; but she seized on it, and on the shabby book.

"I'll get that done. Thank you."

"And needles" Mrs Starnberg had pursued. "Most of them won't have any; and of course the size depends on the thickness of the wool."

Rosina hadn't thought of that either.

"Could you buy sets of needles, if you saw the wool?" she asked.

"Oh yes, I'd gladly do that."

And there and then Rosina had swept the sensible creature off to her house, where she furnished her with samples of Bulgarian and Turkish wool, and an ample supply of *pengoes* with which to buy needles. Then she went along to her little office in the Legation, and rather nervously rang up Horace Wheatley, who was Head of Chancery and controlled all the staff.

"Oh, Horace, the Min said I could have a typist—for the prisoners, you know—if I needed one. Do you think I could have someone?"

"*Now?*"

"Well not to *type* now—only to be given a job to do in the next few days."

"Right. Where are you? At home?"

"No—in that funny little room opposite the study. That's my new office."

"Very handy. Right" he said again. And a typist had come up and been told to make 60 copies each of recipes for gloves and socks from the tattered book, to be ready by the following Wednesday. After which Rosina went off to the country with a quiet mind.

She never forgot the drive down, it was so beautiful. Also it was the last time for many a long day that she was driven by David. Lucilla sat with her Father in front; Rosina and the learned German behind—fortunately he was rather silent. The road-side banks, in the open undulating country, were covered with a mauve salvia, on which white butterflies were settling in thousands; as the car passed they rose in silvery clouds—Rosina could see them settling again through the back window. Her frequent movements to do this presently aroused her companion from his philosophical absorption—"Something happens behind us?" he asked.

"No—only butterflies."

74

"So." He relapsed into silence.

Terenczer was a long, low, white building, elegantly plain without, combining elegance with countryfied comfort within— none of the splendours of Siraly, but a benevolent homeliness. The beds, for instance, had fine modern hair mattresses coated with lambswool; but instead of an under-blanket a soft-cured deerskin, gentle as chamois-leather and nearly half an inch thick was tucked in by the legs under the bottom sheet, a thing which always delighted Rosina.

After tea Margit asked the Eynshams if they would care to drive to one of the villages on the estate? "I must take some medicine to an old woman who is sick—the Morvens so kindly brought it down." David thought he would rest and look at some papers; Rosina went. A light waggonette was drawn up at the front door, with four white Arab horses—so much nicer than a car, Rosina thought. The village, only a few miles away, was typically Hungarian: all the houses set end on to the street, not facing it, and surrounded by gardens bright with flowers; under the deep eaves red peppers hung like crimson fingers against the white walls; huge yellow gourds were ripening on the roofs. The interior of the house where the old woman lived with her daughter and son-in-law fascinated Mrs Eynsham, who had never before penetrated into a Hungarian peasant's home. The floor was of earth, but trodden dark and smooth and as hard, almost, as parquet, and covered with arabesques scrawled in white chalk—these, Margit told her, were renewed every day, after the floor had been wiped over with a damp cloth. "And you see" her hostess added practically, "here there is no home for bugs. Bugs live between the cracks in wooden floors; but if no wood, no bugs! Americans think it so *low* to have floors made of earth; but in Harlem and in the Bronx there are often bugs, no?"

"I daresay; there certainly are in Whitechapel and Bethnal Green." But Rosina was comparing the *riches*, here, with the interiors of crofters' cottages in the Highlands, or the dreary little houses in the older parts of Oxford; let alone the bungalows in which so many of the English working-classes lived—the cheap "suite" of an undersized sofa and two armchairs, the fumed oak table, the general mass-produced hideousness. Here hand-made walnut chairs stood round a big solid table; beautiful earthenware, patterned in local designs, hung from hooks on the walls; at the further end of the room a bed was piled with *seven* goose-down quilts, its sheets of hand-woven linen heavily embroidered in red. Everything was the direct product of honest local craftsmanship; nothing had been produced in bulk for profit, but made on the spot for daily use—hence, inescapeably, it was beautiful.

Some time after the medicines had been handed over to the daughter—while the old lady sat, dignified and talking politely in an upright chair—they took their leave. Two village boys had been holding the Arabs' restless heads; the lovely creatures bounded forward when released, up the long dusty village street —Rosina commented on the well-kept gardens on either side.

"Yes, they love their gardens; and they keep their plots so well, too."

"Plots?"

"Oh yes, each house has a plot, half-a-hectare about, to grow their own vegetables in, and sun-flowers for oil, and poppies for their bread." (This did not puzzle Rosina, who already knew how good bread sprinkled with poppy-seed tasted; she also knew that all peasants who worked for a "*Magnat*" got their supply of bread-grains from their employers as part of their wages.)

Up by the whitewashed church they turned and started to drive back, but half-way down the street Margit checked the horses with an exclamation of dismay. "Oh dear, we are too late! Here come the animals." She pulled in to the side of the road and called to another couple of boys to hold the horses' heads. In the distance a cloud of dust appeared, golden in the evening light, from which as it drew nearer came a loud noise of squealing and lowing. Scores and scores of the leggy Hungarian pigs came galloping along, small parties peeling off and turning in smartly at the gateway of the house where they be-

76

longed; after them, more soberly, cows and calves, who did likewise; bringing up the rear, white under the golden cloud of
dust, a flock of geese stepped sedately, pausing to bite at the
roadside grass, and being chivvied on by a girl with fair plaits
who tapped them with a long willow wand to direct their
progress.

"Where are they all coming from?" Rosina asked, amused.

"Oh, they have been out grazing all day. Ernest gives them
the grazing free, of course, and pays the wages of the cowherd
and swineherd."

"Good gracious!" Again Rosina was thinking of small Highland crofts, and of the conditions under which English agricultural labourers worked. "How many animals does Ernest feed
free, for goodness sake?"

"Each house may graze five cows and their calves; but for pigs,
not more than forty. The geese no one counts, of course; they
do not eat much."

"My dear Margit, they *do!* And foul the land frightfully into
the bargain."

"So? Well anyhow, Ernest doesn't pay the goose-girl" Margit
said laughing, as they drove off again through the cloud of dust
which still hung over the road.

Dressing for dinner that evening, Rosina noticed a curious
thing. Rather than ring for a housemaid—there were bells at
Terenczer—she asked David if he would fasten her dress, and
stood before the tall cheval-glass while he tugged at the zip,
grumbling that she had been putting on weight; once or twice
he let go, and shook his hands impatiently. When he did this,
in the glass she saw the palms of his hands more clearly than
one usually does see the palms of anyone's hands, and was struck
by the fact that the outer bottom corner of each, opposite the ball
of the thumb, was bright pink. She considered asking him about
this odd phenomenon, but decided not to—David hated being
questioned; she soon forgot about it.

Margit Erdöszy was fond of David, and he of her; next day
she took him for a drive in the Bakony, again in a waggonette

77

with white Arabs. Rosina stayed behind to write to prisoners' relations acknowledging their cheques and promising to send parcels; outside the window Lucilla, Endre, Erszi and a young cousin of Margit's played desultory tennis, and then sat in the shade—looking up from her writing now and again Rosina observed that Lucilla, however elegantly, was flirting with the pale young man in a way which troubled her. She decided to speak to her daughter. But then before lunch David came in, happy and enthusiastic as he seldom was except about natural objects —Margit had known exactly where to go along the grassy rides; more than once they had caught glimpses of stags, and had visited two of the muddy wallows in which the wild boar cooled and cleansed themselves—one old brute, snorting and grunting, had heaved his great bulk up out of the slough and lumbered off dripping under their very eyes. In the afternoon everyone but David and the German went off to ride, and in the evening the young people danced to the gramophone, when the flirtation was more marked than ever—there was no convenient opportunity to speak to Lucilla. Oh well, tomorrow.

Tomorrow was Sunday, and Mrs Eynsham, who had a thoroughly Scottish feeling about keeping up some form of religious observance on the Sabbath, accompanied her host and hostess to Mass at ten, as did Gina Morven and Erszi Erdöszy; Count Endre said he had been at eight, which nobody believed. The village church was only a short distance from the house; Count Ernest and his party installed themselves in the large family pew, at one side of the chancel and raised a foot or so above it, so that the occupants had a good view of the whole congregation. This completely filled the church: many of the men, in dark sober Sunday cloth, stood at the back, while all the children were congregated in the chancel itself—the little kneeling figures in their bright costumes made it as gay as a flower-bed. The prettiest sight imaginable, Rosina thought, watching the little sun-browned hands fingering their rosaries, their small dark or tow-blonde heads devoutly bent.

The service ended unusually soon; the priest, Count Ernest

78

told his guests as they walked back to the house, had explained that he must hurry away to take Extreme Unction to a dying man—"They have to work hard, our priests" he said. As he spoke he opened a small door leading into the garden, and stood aside to usher Mrs Eynsham through it—there, in an arbour, she saw Count Endre holding Lucilla's hands and kissing them in turns; Lucilla was making faces at him.

Both were too well-bred to do anything so awkward as to spring apart. Lucilla stood perfectly still; Count Endre dropped her left hand and raised the other to his lips, rather formally; then he walked over with casual ease towards the party coming in by the garden door. How much the others had seen Mrs Eynsham couldn't know, but when Lucilla also joined them she said, equally casually—"Darling, come and help me to stamp my letters; there are such masses."

Up in the big bedroom Rosina threw off her hat, and began to run a comb through her hair in front of the looking glass—she wanted to gain time.

"Whatever you want to say, do please say it" Lucilla said, in a curious uneven voice—looking round her Mother saw that the child was almost shaking with nerves.

"I really don't know what to say" Rosina said frankly, putting down the comb, "I should *like* to say something that you would find sensible, and a help, if I could. What would *you* say, in my place?"

At that the nervous tension broke. Lucilla first laughed, then began to cry; and went on laughing and crying.

"Oh Mummy, you are a devil! No, in a way you're rather angelic. Only—I wonder if you can possibly understand? It's just because I'm so frantic about Hamish, shut up and lousy and half-starved, that I simply must have some distraction—man-distraction, don't you see? I mean, what other is there?" She paused. "Anyhow Endre's simply a clown; I like Hugo *much* better" she added inconsequently.

While Mrs Eynsham was wondering if she *did* understand, and what, if anything, to say next, there came a tap on the door

—Lucilla hurriedly escaped into the bathroom. It was Margit Erdöszy, come to suggest that they should all drive to the pool and have a swim before luncheon. "Your husband says he will come."

"Yes, we'd love to."

"In about ten minutes, then." She closed the door again.

Even that brief interruption had enabled Mrs Eynsham to know what she wanted to say to her daughter, and when that young woman emerged from the bathroom she said it at once.

"*I* trust you, Lucilla—and if you are sure you can trust yourself, that's all right, at least where Endre is concerned. I'm not so sure about Hugo, though."

Lucilla had seated herself at the dressing-table, and was using her Mother's cream and powder to restore her face. She surprised her parent by saying—"D'you remember what you said when you were giving me a pep-talk about sex, before my Confirmation?"

"No—I've no idea."

"Well I remember, because I thought it made sense. You said people had come to have such a bogus idea of female "virtue," as a wretched sort of wilting flower that had to be protected at all costs; whereas really the word came from the Latin *virtus*, strength, and that one should be ready to take almost any risks, provided one had a sense of responsibility for the other person— that was the one important thing."

"Good gracious!" Parents are always astonished when their children recall, let alone quote, heavy advice given in the past. "Fancy your remembering! Well, I daresay I did—it's what I believe, anyhow." The thought of Sir Hugh flicked, unbidden, into her mind as she spoke.

"Well I haven't ever forgotten, and I shan't forget—about Hamish, or about Hugo either." She got up and gave her Mother a quick kiss. "You funny pretty Mummy! You still have *your* problems, don't you? I must go and get my swim-suit." She ran off, leaving Mrs Eynsham aghast at the perspicacity of youth.

80

6

As the party was assembling in the hall the telephone rang. Margit Erdöszy went into her little morning-room to take the call; she came out looking pleased.

"It was Anna Dolinsky. She asked if they could bring their house-party over to swim, and come back for drinks before lunch."

"What did you say?" her husband asked, with a rather disturbed glance in Mrs Eynsham's direction.

"Oh, but of course Yes! Isn't it nice?" Margit said innocently. "She is so gay" she added, turning to her principal guest. "Don't you think so?"

"She has her own sense of humour" Rosina replied equably. But when she was seated beside her host on the box of the first waggonette he said in a low voice—"I am sorry about this. Margit is rather *une tête folle;* she cannot remember to be discreet socially."

"Oh don't worry, Ernest. Anna *is* rather fun, really. So long as you don't let her try to drown any of us today!" She had already realised that the Balaton episode must have become public property, probably through Anna's own lively tongue.

"Nothing untoward shall happen, I assure you" the Count said, as earnest as his name.

The pool where one bathed at Terenczer was not in the least like a swimming-pool in the commonly accepted sense of the word—a thing all cement, with paved walks surrounding it. Here was a small lake on the edge of the forest, with huge oak trees overhanging its further end; where the carriages drew up on a gravelled space with the usual bathing-hut it was open and sunny, the grassy banks covered with wild-flowers. Rosina Eynsham had had a dress made of the same material as her bathing-suit, and—partly with the rather futile idea of creating an impression, especially on Anna Dolinsky—stood smoking and chatting till that lady and her party drove up; then, after greetings and introductions, she simply unbuttoned her frock and threw it over a bush, before taking a header into the lake.

In fact she did create an impression on Countess Anna.

"*Aber!* This I never saw before" she said to Margit. "How clever." David Eynsham grinned—however contemptuous he might be *to* his wife, like all husbands he liked to see her scoring off another woman.

Soon the lake was full of swimming figures—men's heads, sleek and dripping, and the variously-coloured bathing-caps of the women; there was laughter and splashing. All this rather bored David Eynsham; he swam off a little way up the lake, and amused himself by climbing out and doing running dives from the shore, over and over again. It was Count Endre who first noticed what happened. He had left the pool and was standing on the bank, sunning himself and smoking, and chatting with Countess Dolinsky, who lay floating in the water at his feet. "*You* can't dive as well as Mr Eynsham" he mocked her. "Come up and watch." The pretty woman took his outstretched hand, sprang up, and stood beside him.

"Yes, that was a beautiful dive" she said, as the Englishman's lean fragile body took the water so cleanly and smoothly that there was hardly a splash. But when David Eynsham surfaced, instead of swimming back to the shore he put both hands to his chest, and then began rather feebly to struggle towards the bank, gasping; suddenly, as Count Endre watched, puzzled, he went under. Anna Dolinsky had turned away to speak to the German; she swung round sharply as the Count exclaimed—"Jesus Maria! He has a cramp!"

"Who? Eynsham?" Without another word she dived in and swam off up the lake. Count Endre called to his cousin that something was wrong— "Are there blankets? Get them out"—and then swam after her. Rosina, who had been keeping a wary eye on Countess Anna, overheard part of this, and scrambled hastily up the bank. "Where's David?" she asked her host, who had also climbed out by some wooden steps. "He was diving in up there a moment ago; but now I can't see him."

"I know nothing—excuse me, I send for blankets." He gave orders to a groom and one of the waggonettes went racing off along the forest road, the hooves of the four Arabs raising the dust in clouds. Rosina looked up the lake again—Countess Anna had reached the spot where David had been diving. Suddenly she submerged—a thing only experienced swimmers can do from the surface of the water; there was splashing, and then she appeared again, with David's head beside hers. By now Count Endre had come up with her; he took Eynsham's body in his arms, turned on his back, and swam swiftly, towing his inert burden, the short distance back to the steps. "Give a hand" he called to Count Dolinsky; between them they lifted Eynsham up onto the bank, and laid him down.

By this time all the party had collected on the shore, in astonished dismay. Gina Morven stepped forward.

"Do not let him lie!—lift him up! If he sink-a, his lungs are full of water—take his feet, and hold him upright-a." Since no one else had any other ideas, this was done, and a certain amount of water gushed from Eynsham's mouth.

"Somesing to lie him on, now—" Gina said, continuing to give orders as briskly as a sergeant-major. "Zis!" She snatched a bathrobe of Turkish towelling off the shoulders of the astonished German professor, and spread it on the gravel—"Lay him on zis. Now" she said to Count Endre, "you work-a his arms up and down, so—and I press-a his sides." She showed the Hungarian the precise movements for reviving the partly drowned, combining them with her own rhythmic pressure on the ribs to bring air back into the sodden lungs. The rest of the party stood round, watching the white face, the closed eyes, the gaping mouth.

"Move-a! He want air!" Gina said, panting a little with effort

—applying effective pressure to a man's ribs is quite hard work. They moved aside. "Rosina, can you do zis, if I show you? We take-a in turns."

"Yes" Rosina said. She came and knelt on the harsh gravel beside her husband, and began to repeat Gina's movements. "So? That right?"

"Yes."

"But I think we ought to get a doctor" Rosina said, pressing away. "Where is the nearest *good* one?"

"I know! I go!" Anna Dolinsky said. "At Szekesféhervár—it is not far!" And abandoning her house-party she threw a bath-robe over her Bikini and drove off in one of the Dolinsky cars.

Reviving the half-drowned is a slow and arduous business. Count Dolinsky relieved Endre Erdöszy with the arm movements at intervals; Gina and Rosina took turns at the pressure on the ribs. At last—just as the carriage returned and a groom hurried over with an armful of blankets—David Eynsham opened his eyes; he gulped up a mouthful of lake-water. Gina, like lightening, raised him in her arms. "Be sick, David" she urged—he was, bringing up more water and the remains of his breakfast. She wiped him down with the unhappy German's bath-robe; then with Count Endre and Rosina's help he was wrapped in blankets. "Now, brandy!" Gina commanded.

"No, whisky" Eynsham said in a faint voice—they were his first words. "Better for—for—" his voice failed again.

Neither whisky nor brandy were available—Count Ernest hadn't thought of that; distractedly, he sent the waggonette galloping off again. But by Gina's orders Eynsham was lifted into the second Dolinsky car and driven back to the house, accompanied by his wife, Gina herself, and Count Endre, leaving the Dolinsky party and the others marooned by the pool; gloomily, they dressed in the bathing-hut, and waited for transport—there was only one light waggonette for twelve people.

"How is it that your wife knows so much about this 'First-Aid'?" Count Dolinsky asked Colonel Morven.

"Oh, she used to be an Olympic swimmer—knows everything"

84

the Colonel replied. "But your wife did a good job, pulling him out. But for her, he was a goner." The Military Attaché was well aware of the Dolinskys' political views, but at the moment he felt quite warmly towards Countess Anna.

That lady, with the doctor, arrived at the same moment that the car bringing David Eynsham pulled up at the front door; Count Endre and the chauffeur carried him upstairs and laid him on the bed, where Rosina pulled off his wet bathing-trunks, and wrapped him afresh in dry blankets from Lucilla's room; Count Endre meanwhile went and fetched whisky.

"He asked for this" he said to the doctor, pouring out a glass with very little soda. "Eynsham, here is whisky!"

"Good" David said feebly; as Endre raised him up his wife held the glass to his lips, and he took a good gulp—and then another, and another. "That's better—that's enough" he said. They laid him down again, and the doctor began asking questions— Count Endre answered them at first, describing the seizure in the pool; Gina meanwhile had somehow mustered some hot-water bottles, and was carefully putting them round the sick man, outside the blankets.

While the doctor was making his examination—pulse, blood-pressure, and so on—both he and Rosina noticed that David Eynsham kept putting his right hand over to his left arm, and stroking it. "This hurts?" the doctor asked in Hungarian, his only language.

"Yes, hellishly," Eynsham replied in the same tongue, surprising the earnest little man in pince-nez.

"Ah, so we can speak together! Excellent! And the pain goes down into the hand?"

"Yes of course; the two outside fingers. It's just a good old coronary. Endre, give me some more whisky, there's a good fellow. Doctor, I hope you've brought your morphine?"

The doctor had; and while he prepared his syringe, and Eynsham took some more whisky from the glass—"The gentleman is medical man?" the doctor asked Count Endre.

Eynsham answered him.

"No, but I've had this thing before. Ah, that's fine!" he said, exhaling deeply with relief as the needle was plunged into his arm. He lay relaxed and quiet, waiting for the morphia to do its blessed work.

Rosina could not follow any of this except the word "morphine." "Endre, what have they been saying?" she asked anxiously, in a low voice. "What's wrong with David?"

Her husband heard, and again it was he who answered, in the slow tones engendered by the morphia as it began to take effect.

"Coronary thrombosis, Rosie. I had one in Ankara, while you were bringing Lucilla out at home. I didn't tell you, because your worrying wouldn't have done me any good, or you either. And don't worry now—*Unkraut vergeht nicht!*"

At this point Lucilla ran in; the party left at the pool had at last been brought back.

"Daddy *darling*, what goes on?" She bent over her Father and kissed him. "Are you all right?"

"Yes, poppet. In fact I feel lovely—but now I want to go to sleep." His eyes closed, gently.

"Are the Dolinskys still there?" Rosina asked Lucilla.

"Yes—having drinks. Not much of a party!"

"Then stay with your Father. Endre, keep the doctor till I come back—I shall want you to interpret."

"Mummy, *do* get out of that wet suit!—you'll catch your death." Rosina was still in her discreet little bathing-dress; it was damp.

"In a minute." She put on a dressing-gown and a pair of slippers and went downstairs. A distinctly subdued company was having cocktails in the drawing-room; the Professor was wondering audibly to someone how he could get his bath-robe washed. When Mrs Eynsham came in she met a barrage of questions: "How is he? What does the doctor say? Is it grave?"

"Oh—thank you" Rosina said to her host, who came up to her with a filled glass in his hand. "He is better—he is resting" she told the others. She took a good long pull at the drink—never had a cocktail seemed more welcome; she realised suddenly that she was beginning to shiver. "I must go up again in a moment" she said to Ernest Erdöszy—"I do not want to delay the doctor. Where is the Countess Dolinsky?"

"She went to change." But at that moment Anna, dressed, freshly made up, perfect, came into the room; Rosina Eynsham, in her dressing-gown and slippers, her hair still wet and untidy from when she had pulled of her bathing-cap to hear David's weak voice, her face damp and haggard with anxiety, went straight up to her.

"I came down to say Thank you" she said. Her teeth were beginning to chatter as she spoke.

Countess Dolinsky put her hands on the Englishwoman's shoulders.

"He will be all right?"

"Yes, thanks to you—and for your bringing the doctor."

The Hungarian put her arms round Mrs Eynsham, and kissed her on both cheeks. "So now you forgive my 'practical joke'?"

"From today I'll forgive you pretty well anything."

Count Ernest, who like everyone else had watched this small scene, came up with a Martini for Countess Dolinsky—she waved him aside. "Later. I take her up; she should change." With an arm round Mrs Eynsham's shoulders she led her out of the room. Upstairs, helped by Lucilla, Anna Dolinsky got Rosina out of her wet bathing-gown in the bathroom; she dressed her in dry underclothes and a frock before she would allow her to go in to see the doctor. "He can wait—in any case he cannot go till I take him!" she said coolly. "Where is your cocktail? Oh, I fetch you another." She glided off.

Lucilla had changed at the bathing-pool, and was left sitting by her Father during the conference on the landing, after the doctor had taken the patient's pulse once more. "You *sit*" Anna said, pushing Rosina down onto a walnut settee, and giving her the cocktail she had brought up. The doctor proceeded to give his verdict in Hungarian to Count Endre, who translated it for Mrs Eynsham. It was a coronary thrombosis; one could not tell how severe till an electro-cardiograph could be taken in Budapest, but it would be unwise to move the patient for ten days at least. He would call again in the evening, and give more morphine if necessary. Then he asked Countess Dolinsky if he could be taken home? "I have other patients."

"In a moment. Take him down to have a drink" she told Count Endre. To Rosina she said, in English, in a lowered voice—"I should get your husband up to Budapest as quickly as possible, and let Mendze look after him. He is a really *good* heart specialist; this man is not much more than a vet—isn't that how you call it?"

Mrs Eynsham was all for getting back to Budapest, and the best doctors. She didn't want to put the Erdöszys to the inconvenience of illness in their house—and there were those lists of parcels that she had undertaken to do, and the first knitting-party was to be on Thursday. In fact there and then, at Terenczer, began for Rosina the business of being torn between her husband's illness and the needs of the prisoners-of-war which was to be her staple diet, a diet of extreme discomfort, for a long time to come. In this first instance there was no conflict—after luncheon she got Colonel Morven to telephone to the Legation to arrange for an ambulance, with a nurse, to come down and collect David the following morning, and herself rang up Dr Mendze and booked a bed in his favourite nursing-home (in Hungary, so oddly, known as a *Szanatorium.*) David slept, happily drugged, all the afternoon; they roused him to take toast and bouillon with an egg beaten up in it about 8, and soon after the little doctor came and gave another injection of morphia; he pronounced the patient's condition fairly satisfactory—"But he must be kept still—he should not move."

Count Endre again acted as interpreter during this interview. How odd it was, Mrs Eynsham thought, as she hastily changed into an evening dress for the usual late Hungarian dinner, that the two people in this new country whom she had least liked or respected hitherto should be the very ones who had most helped her today—Anna Dolinsky and Endre Erdöszy. Margit Erdöszy

88

had sent her maid to sit with Eynsham during the meal. "She has had her supper, and he can tell her anything he wants, so luckily," she said as they went to have coffee—"Do sit quiet a little, Rosina. I will try to get the English news—" and she switched on her enormous radiogram.

During the War the B.B.C. often deliberately arranged a certain time-lag between actual events and their reporting of them. The Battle of Britain had been going on for some time; but it was in that quiet comfortable room on the edge of the Forest of Bakony that the three English people present—Colonel Morven, Mrs Eynsham, and Lucilla—first heard the announcer say, in his unemphatic tones: "In the heavy raid on the London docks some days ago, in which four hundred German planes took part, the enemy lost one hundred and three to our twenty-six."

"But they are fantastic, these Spitfires!" Count Ernest exclaimed.

"Quiet—let's hear" Colonel Morven said abruptly; they heard of the first bombing of Buckingham Palace. When the news was over— "No, but really the King and Queen should go away" Margit said.

"Why?" Lucilla asked. "I think they're where they belong."

"Quite right" Colonel Morven grunted, with a baleful glance at the German professor.

David Eynsham stood the journey to Budapest fairly well, and it was an infinite relief to his wife to have him safely installed in the Augusta-Szanatorium, in a pretty room overlooking a garden, with highly-trained nurses running in and out, and the excellent Dr Mendze in attendance. The electro-cardiograph showed that the coronary had been tolerably severe, and bed was decreed for at least four weeks. However David being David, besides flirting off-handly with the nurses, who all adored him, he was soon insisting on having boxes of papers sent down to the nursing-home.

"For two hours a day, this I permit" Dr Mendze said. "To fret is also a bad thing for the heart. But not more, of work.

Visitors—all he wishes. A distraction." It suddenly occurred to Rosina to mention the pink corners on the palms of David's hands which she had seen in the mirror at Terenczer.

"So—you noticed this? When?"

"Just the evening before." She described what had happened.

"Yes, in some cases this can be a symptom—not always."

What startled and rather horrified Rosina was the diet on which David was put. To lessen the load on the heart his intake was reduced to 800 calories a day, instead of the average 3000. In terms of food this meant a raw tomato and one wafer-thin slice of toast for breakfast, with a cup of milkless tea; a minute piece of steamed fish, some green vetegable, and a little stewed fruit at mid-day; a rusk and a finger of cheese with more milkless tea at tea-time, and two raw tomatoes and a wafer of toast for supper.

"Aren't you starving?" she asked him anxiously.

"No, I feel fine—especially as he lets me have a whisky at night—that's supposed to be a vaso-dilatory. Quite like your prisoners, aren't I?" he said grinning. "I bet they're getting more calories than I am!"

Relatively at ease about her husband for the moment, Rosina applied herself to the prisoners—when she wasn't running down to see him, taking packets of tea, flasks of whisky, books borrowed from the staff, and such papers as drifted in from time to time. In Central Europe in 1940 the odd copy of *Time and Tide* or the *New Statesman*, brought casually from Istanbul by a King's Messenger, was a boon beyond all price.

The first knitting-party, three days after their return from Terenczer, went off all right. Numbers of ladies came, said whether they would knit socks or gloves—some said they could only manage scarves in idiot-stitch—(they didn't call it that; Mrs Starnberg did) and were supplied with wool and needles. After which they drank the Minister's excellent coffee, and went off highly contented.

At the second party, a week later, the atmosphere was a good deal less rosy. It is astounding how knitting can befool women not bred up to it; some of the end-products brought back by their creators left Rosina aghast. Scarves seven feet long and four inches wide, or barely two feet long and eighteen inches across. "But Mrs Watlington, they don't want *shawls*" Mrs Eynsham said to a woman who brought one of the latter type to the table where she sat listing the objects received.

"It somehow seemed to spread" Mrs Watlington said abjectly.

"Well it won't do—it won't go round one's neck. Look." She demonstrated. Then with a pair of scissors she snipped the wool at the casting-off end, and began to pull the useless thing undone. "Would you take it down, and roll up the wool, and try again?"

"But I spent *hours* over it" Mrs Watlington wailed.

Rosina was not in the best of tempers that morning. When she had hurried down to see David before the knitting-party she heard that he had had a bad night, and Dr Mendze said that he was doing too much work— "He will not restrict himself to two hours."

"Well *you* fight it out with him—I can't" Rosina had said, distressed. "Can't your nurses take his papers away when he's done enough?" Hence she was unduly harsh with Mrs Watlington.

"We can't afford to waste wool, you know" she said. "It costs a lot, and it all has to be brought in from outside. Try again— *eight* inches wide, *four* feet long. Yes, Mrs Starnberg?"

Mrs Starnberg, followed by several discouraged ladies, brought up to the table five or six pairs of socks of which one foot was a full three inches longer than the other.

"I wondered if you could pass these, Mrs Eynsham?"

"No I can't" Rosina said flatly, after examining them. She plied her scissors again, and pulled out wool from the over-long feet. "They must be done to the correct length, ten-and-half inches." Two or three of the ladies murmured protests.

"But don't you *care* what our men get?" Rosina asked. "Personally I think the best is good enough for them—but only just."

The ladies retreated, abashed; and after two or three weeks quite tolerable articles were produced.

The knitting business soon spread. The Dutch Legation asked for supplies of wool, and organised a small but highly efficient knitting section which produced excellent garments very fast indeed. Old Countess Táray, Pista's mother, called on Mrs Eynsham to say that many Hungarian ladies wished to knit for the British prisoners, if they too could be supplied with the unobtainable wool; she undertook to distribute this if it could be brought to her house "discreetly"—not in a car with the C.D. (Corps Diplomatique) number-plate. So wool was taken after dark, by taxi, from Rosina's small yellow house in the Verböczy-utca to the huge Táray palace in another of Buda's beautiful golden streets. By the end of September the British Prisoners-of-War Relief Organisation was despatching to Germany, weekly, 250 pairs of socks, some 50 pairs of gloves, 10 to 15 pull-overs, and numbers of scarves and Balaclava helmets—Mrs Eynsham got the Minister to cable to Istanbul for a further half-ton of knitting-wool. (One little English lady regularly produced four faultless pairs of socks every week—when she ultimately reached her hundredth pair the Minister, prompted by the omniscient Mrs Starnberg, formally presented her with a huge box of chocolates.)

For the care of the knitting devolved more and more on Mrs Starnberg. Rosina Eynsham had other tasks. There were those lists. Horace Wheatley devised a system by which all parcels despatched to any camp had to be listed, and given a number, with their contents, under the date of despatch; he also told Mrs Eynsham that she must insist on an acknowledgement from the British *Vertrauens-mann*, "the man of confidence" in each camp, to whom all parcels other than individual ones had to be consigned. Rosina therefore spent hours writing to *Vertrauensmänner*, mostly rather illiterate sergeants in Stalags, telling them that parcels Nos. 86 to 101, containing so-and-so, had been despatched to them on such a date, and would they please say if all had been received, containing the stated amounts of clothing, cigarettes, dried fruit and food? Owing to the British blockade

92

Germany was itself desperately short of the things being sent to the prisoners; but from the Hungarian parcels, at any rate, there was surprisingly little pilfering—thanks to the overwhelming respect attached to labels bearing the symbol of the Red Cross.

The little English group in Hungary was of course intensely concerned about the state of affairs at home. The Battle of Britain had begun early in August—German air-raids on London, on the ports, on Coventry and other industrial towns; sad little notices in the "Deaths" column in *The Times* that Sir Malcolm and Lady Buggins and Miss Jane Buggins had died "suddenly, in London"—discreetly, no address was ever given, but their friends realised that the Bugginses and their pretty house and daughter had been blown to glory. Nevertheless by late September it was clear that the Germans had failed in their attempt to subdue England from the air, and the Bulletin published the official figures which gave the reason why—since the 8th of August Germany had lost 1,867 planes against England's 621. The Hungarian papers also gave an account of the bombing of the Queen's apartments in Buckingham Palace—"fortunately her Majesty escaped without injury."

This last item produced a tremendous impression in Central Europe. At a *jour* packed out with even quite half-hearted Hungarians, who with their habitual courtesy came to offer congratulations on the Queen's escape, Pista Táray, freshly returned from Vienna, related to delighted groups a scene which he had himself witnessed at the Opera there on the evening after the news broke. Frau Emmi Goering, the Field-Marshal's wife, had transferred herself and her children to Austria to be safe from the increasingly severe R.A.F. raids on Berlin; and on that night, "blazing with diamonds and dripping with silver foxes" as Pista said cattishly, she took her seat prominently in the front of a box. As soon as she was observed the reckless Viennese audience began to swing to and fro in their seats, chanting loudly—

"Emmi, die Königin von England ist in *LON-DON!*"—stamping their feet to emphasise the last two syllables. The unhappy woman left, unable to face this particular music.

"Well, that was quite a change" the Minister said to Martha

93

and Rosina when they had repaired to the little boudoir to chew over the party. "Did you hear Pista's story, Martha?"

"Yes. Very nice too. No whisk for me, H.E.—I thought I'd flip down and tell David; it should give him a good night! Oh, and did Master Milton trouble himself to tell you about that gale having scattered all the German invasion barges? The B.B.C. have released that piece at last."

"I'm not sure that I approve of the way you refer to my Press Attaché, who is technically your lord and master" Sir Hugh said, skilfully evading the question—Geoffrey Milton had in fact not told him.

"I thought not," Martha Beckley said, answering the evasion, and causing the Minister to laugh. "Anyhow it's in the Press here today, so you'll get it in the excerpts. Good night."

Now that David Eynsham was in hospital it was an understood thing that after the *jours*, at least, his wife dined at the Legation, since Lucilla ate at odd hours, to fit in with her periods of monitoring. As she and Sir Hugh waited for dinner Anton, the butler, came and said that a lady wished to speak with the gnädige Frau Eynsham.

"I expect that's more things from the Hunk knitting-party— do you mind if I go down and see?" Rosina asked. It was by now quite dark.

"Of course."

But it was not socks knitted in secret by the Hungarians. At the foot of the stairs stood a small woman, heavily veiled, holding an envelope which she handed to Mrs Eynsham.

"I wished you to have this—I copied it out of the book for you. It is so *true*—as true as it was three-and-a-half centuries ago."

The veil made the speaker's face completely invisible, but Rosina thought she recognised the voice.

"Isn't it Fanny Derkheim?" she asked. "How kind of you."

"Oh please do not speak any names! I am not sure that *they* are gone yet, and now one can trust no one" the lady said nervously, glancing through her veil in the direction of the footman who was lingering to usher her out. "Good night." She hurried out through the glass door which gave onto the *porte-cochère*. Rosina, thoroughly mystified, took the envelope upstairs, and reported to Sir Hugh. "She was terrified of being seen by the *spotteurs* across the road, or that Hans would remember her name."

"Well what *is* this precious document?" The Minister asked, practically.

The envelope when they opened it proved to contain a typed copy of Schiller's poem about the Armada—"*Die Unüberwindliche Flotte.*"

"Oh, my German's so rusty, I don't think I can cope with this fast," the minister said, glancing at it hastily. "You'll have to make me a translation. Let's go and eat"—as Anton appeared at the door to announce dinner. And after a brief meal they repaired to the study; there, after coffee, while Sir Hugh read through papers from leather boxes, Rosina spent an hour translating Schiller's poem, scribbling it down on blue-green foolscap sheets, with the Lion and the Unicorn embossed on the top.

"Done?" Sir Hugh asked at length, throwing the last of the papers he had minuted into one of the boxes, and snapping the lid to. (One only has to *un*lock diplomatic boxes, never to lock them.)

"Yes, just. It's quite fantastic—I mean it's so *à la page;* the Armada and the Battle of Britain are so frightfully alike."

"Really? May I see?"

"Or had I better read it? It's just scrawled."

"Yes—read away."

So Rosina Eynsham read aloud to the British Minister in Budapest, in the year 1940, what the German poet Friedrich Schiller had written about England over 100 years before.

> "*It comes, it comes, the proud fleet of the Continent—*
> *Earth's waters shudder under it.*
> *With roar of guns, and new gods in the firmament,*
> *Lightnings and thunders pouring out of it.*

A fearful horde of mighty floating fortresses
The ocean never saw its like as yet;
'Lo, the Invincible' men say of it
As it approaches through the watery passes.
With what majestic silent tread
Trembling Neptune bears his burden on
With world-destruction in its heart and head
And still it comes, and every storm dies down."

"*Weltvernichtung*—what could be more like Hitler?" Rosina said, pausing in her reading.

"Don't interrupt yourself—go on" Sir Hugh said impatiently; he was listening with intense concentration, the German original in his hand. Rosina read on.

"Now it stands right against you, in your sight,
Fortunate island, mistress of the seas,
A galleon-army, fearful in its might—
Can even Britannia face such foes as these?
Woe to your sons, though with brave hearts endowed
Menaced by such a monstrous thunder-cloud!

Say, at whose summons was it undertaken,
That task that made you Queen of half the earth?
What spirit then, by tyrannous threats awoken,
Brought wisest institutions here to birth?
That mighty Charter, that made Kings as burghers,
And turned your commoners to Kings?
You had a genius for the simple things—
Bought, sold, sailed ships, as it becomes plain burghers;
Your fleet's achievements told the world your worth.
Whom may you thank? Oh blush, each other nation!
Your spirit and your soul alone wrought your salvation."

"That's true, you know" Mrs Eynsham interjected again. "Poor Hunks, poor Czechs—always wanting someone else to save them."

"Any more?" Sir Hugh asked, still rather impatiently.

"Yes indeed—right up to today! Listen—"

"Hapless! Look now on these fire-flinging monsters,
Look on the ruin which you must await!
The whole round Earth watches, aghast, your fate—
And all free hearts beat now in terror
And freedom-loving souls lament with horror
Watching the menace standing at your gate.

God the Almighty from high Heaven looked down
And saw your foes' proud flags against you waving,
Saw the abyss in which you must go down—
'Is this my England?' He cried, 'these perils braving?
Shall my one hero-race be blotted out?
Freedom's sole bastion be brought to naught?
Tyranny's last opponent, now and here,
Obliterated from this hemisphere?
Never' God cried, 'shall the heaven-minded few
Humanity's last guard, by wicked men be driven!'
God the Almighty blew
And the Armada fled to the four winds of Heaven."

There was a little pause.

"That's a very accurate translation" Sir Hugh said then. "A lot of it is almost verbatim."

"Yes—it's very easy to translate into English from German; much easier than from French. I made a mess-up in verse three, though; there were two lines I simply couldn't do."

"So I saw—and you had to paraphrase *der Freiheit's Paradies* in the last verse. But it's a good effort, Rosina. Well done. I think you ought to get it published."

"David would hate that."

"Would he? I wonder why? All the same I wish it could appear —perhaps in America. It is so amazingly à propos—at the moment England *is* "humanity's last guard" in this hemisphere—indeed everywhere." He mused. "Most peculiar, really, that old Schiller should have written this—it's really more prophetic than historical. Perhaps all poets have a touch of the prophet in them."

"Only in the sense of being timeless, wouldn't you say? This seems to me just an odd coincidence—apart from the extraordinary fact of a German having really seen what England is."

"Oh, there's nothing extraordinary about that. They have always admired and envied us; this war, and the last one, have both really been a sort of *crime passionel.*"

Rosina laughed, and got up.

"I must go home."

"Why?" His tone made her blush.

"Well really because I get a bit tired; there's such a lot of work."

"You do too much."

"Of course—who doesn't? And now is one of the few times when it's worth while doing too much, don't you think? So often people do too much over pure rubbish, like entertaining, or being superlatively dressed."

"You are always well-dressed" the Minister said, opening the door for her.

"Yes yes—the sales in Davies Street! But I never *work* at it." She paused at the door. "Oh by the way, I had said that Lucilla and I would go to the Weissbergers this week-end. If David is all right, I mean. If we do, *could* you slip down and see him, and ring me up? Martha says you aren't going away."

"A private secretary leaves one no private life!" Sir Hugh said with a small smile. "Yes—I should have gone to see David anyhow. Why are you going to the Weissbergers?—apart from their being 'good citizens'? Save the Children, and all that?"

"I like her; and they keep on asking us. And I want to consult him about finance."

"Oh, are you proposing to invest in Hungary? I shouldn't, just now."

Rosina laughed again.

"Don't be silly!—I haven't got a halfpenny to invest anywhere. But I want to raise money for the prisoners, and I think he might advise me. And they're *good* people."

"He will advise you very well—and they are, as you say, good people; some of the best." He kissed her hand. "Goodnight."

98

7

The Weissbergers, to whose country estate Lucilla and her Mother drove down on the following Saturday, were Catholic Jews; Jews by race, devout Catholics for three generations —a curious phenomenon, not unusual in Central Europe, rare elsewhere. They were a large clan: Baron Hermann was one of four brothers, all Barons—in Hungary to be a Baron proclaimed one also to be a Jew; the indigenous aristocracy were Counts, Markgrafs, or Princes, like old Willie Tereny. These wealthy Jewish families had been ennobled under the Dual Monarchy (the old Austro-Hungarian Empire) because of their enormous importance to the country's economy: such heavy industry as Hungary then possessed it owed entirely to their capital, skill and enterprise, and most of the lighter industries were also in their hands. They were good employers, hugely charitable, and great patrons of the arts—music, painting, and sculpture in Hungary owed almost as much to them as its industrial output did; in fact, as Sir Hugh had said, they were good citizens. And they were collectors—the house at which Lucilla and her Mother presently arrived contained not less than four superb Titians.

During the drive down Lucilla was rather silent. She knew quite well that Hugo Weissberger, the son of the house, was seriously in love with her—no question, here, of Endre Erdöszy's flirtatious nonsense. She had been relieved, at Terenczer, to "have it out" with her Mother about Count Endre, but she was dissatisfied with her attempt at explaining her attitude. It had been true so far as it went, but it was not the whole truth. Her engagement to Hamish had been so hurried—what engagements weren't, on the outbreak of war? She remembered that evening with a quite peculiar clarity: not only the room and the fire—because the Highlands are so often chilly even in late summer—lighting up the rather dull furniture and the bad portraits, but the dual quality of her own emotions, even then. She had met Hamish in London, at balls—he was a beautiful dancer —and had fallen rather in love with him, though always with certain reservations. Then had come this visit to his home, an old and rather ugly house in surroundings that couldn't be lovelier, a place of which he adored every inch, quite uncritically; there were also his parents, his Mother absorbed in her garden, his Father in birds and his herd of pedigree red-polls—Lucilla's reservations had increased, though her liking for Hamish had increased too; he was so nice to his Father and Mother. Suddenly the wireless became menacing: Molotoff and Ribbentrop signed a pact; the situation of mine-fields was given at dictation speed during the news, as a warning to shipping; then there were telephone calls for Hamish—he must rejoin his regiment at once. That night the old people removed themselves and left the drawing-room to the young pair; Hamish proposed, with a desperate urgency which Lucilla found hard to resist at such a moment, reservations or no—she said Yes.

Hamish, rapturous, after some rather overwhelming embraces suggested that they should dance to their betrothal; he pushed the rugs aside, hunted in the record-stand beside the gramophone, and put on the tune of his choice—that rather charming but very out-of-date waltz, "Always." As the mechanical voice chanted the words of the song, Hamish sang them close to her ear—

> "Not for just an hour, not for just a day,
> Not for just a year, but always, always, always."

And even in his arms Lucilla had felt a chill, a sense of fetteredness—fettered by this touch of the old-fashioned in Hamish, and his simple-minded seriousness. But what could she do, or say, *then*? She had just accepted him; they were engaged—for

100

"always"; her word, given at the moment when her betrothed was about to go off to fight, must stand—it still stood. But Hamish had refused absolutely to let the engagement be announced, or even to give her a ring. "I might come back with no legs, or no arms, or something—I won't have you publicly tied to a cripple" he had said. "Wait till I come back."

All the same, she could not help being sharply aware of the difference between her chivalrous lover and the lively, cultivated Hungarian young men who now swarmed about her, whether frivolous like Endre, or good like Hugo; Hugo had his serious side too, but his mind and his interests were so wide—music, pictures, literature, films—that there could be no sense of fetters with him. And during this week-end he would almost certainly propose to her. She would refuse him, of course, but she would like to go on seeing him.

Lucilla recognised quite clearly that she was rather man-minded, and was perfectly frank about it. One day Sir Hugh had asked her which she liked best, Emmi Weissberger or Oria Tereny?

"Oh, about the same—they're both *very* nice. I'm not frightfully interested in women, really; so many of them have pinhead brains. I don't mean those two—they're both clever. But I do like men." Sir Hugh had laughed out.

"Really, Lucilla!"

"What's wrong with saying so, if it's true? It doesn't mean that people are nymphomaniacs; it's just that they're normal," the young girl pronounced, in her cool clear tones. And the much older man, looking at her—as cool as her voice, and completely unembarrassed—realised that she was uttering a truth that his generation seldom admitted, but was none the less true for that. "In fact I like *you* tremendously" Lucilla had ended, "but of course one knows what a pitfall clever, older men are." She gave a youthful girlish giggle as she said that, and the Minister had laughed again, disconcerted.

And now here she was, committed to a week-end with the Weissbergers, facing a proposal from Baron Hugo, and *really*

101

in torment about her fettering old-fashioned Hamish, underfed and lacking clothing and cigarettes, a prisoner in German hands —and worried about her Father's illness. She had plenty of cause to be silent, withdrawn into her own thoughts, as the car sped through the pretty villages and flat fields of the Alfold, the great Danubian plain.

A very large house-party was assembled in the white house, long and low, where they arrived in time for luncheon; Johanna, the Baron's wife, in spite of her devotion to good works was gay and lively, and loved to entertain young people. The afternoon, however, was devoted to the good works aspect. The Baroness wanted Mrs Eynsham to see the school that they had added to and staffed for the village children; the communal bath-house that they had built for the peasants' use, and above all the factory where maize, the chief local crop, was processed into starch for the laundries of Budapest and Vienna, while the sticky dextrose was sent to the Bata shoe-factories in Czecho-Slovakia in the form of glue; to gum, it seemed, one part of a shoe to another part.

Baroness Weissberger expatiated on the factory.

"This is such a problem, where the local product is both bulky, and cheap, so that freight charges eat up all the profits. But starch and glue are not bulky, and are quite dear; so that problem is solved. And there is now employment, here in the village, so that the young people earn money while they live at home, instead of going to the city, and being un-natured. Do you say this so? I mean *dénaturé*—wrenched into a form of life that for them is false."

Rosina, gazing at dusty machines in big airy well-lit rooms, at vats full of the yellowish stringy dextrose, and at the cheerful young men and women tending them, asked how many people were employed?

"At present one hundred seventy-five, about—all who are available."

"Aren't they missed on the farms?" countrified Rosina enquired.

"Oh, Hermann arranged for this. The factory works on a ten-

102

months' year, so that the men and girls can be released for the hay-harvest, for the maize-harvest, for the vintage and for picking the mulberry-leaves—this is only the girls—to feed the silkworms at the end of the summer."

Rosina was impressed by this intelligent planning, which seemed to her quite admirable; she was thinking of her beloved Highlands, where the main crop, the wool of black-faced sheep, also cheap and bulky, was all freighted away at ruinous cost to be processed elsewhere.

"Does the ten-months' year pay?" she enquired.

"Yes, well enough; there is always a profit. It would be larger on a twelve-months' year, but that would disrupt the village economy; there must be labour for the harvests. Hermann thinks he has found a solution, here—Rudolf and Alex and Tommie are all doing the same on their places."

"I think so too" Rosina said thoughtfully—"an ideal solution." She was struck by this recurrent theme among Hungarian country land-owners, about adjusting employment to local conditions being more important than making the extra $2\frac{1}{2}$ per cent, or whatever it was; she remembered Price Willie's refusal, for that very reason, to build big hotels at Devis. Why didn't other employers think thus imaginatively in terms of their employees' moral well-being? Oh well, there was Port Sunlight, of course, where the pretty workers' houses had so startled that set of Russian visitors—nothing would convince them that they were not the residences of directors!

At tea Mrs Eynsham observed that her daughter looked even paler than usual, and was extremely silent—she guessed, uncomfortably, at the reason, for young Baron Hugo too was noticeably abstracted, and took a seat as far as possible away from Lucilla at the big table. In fact Lucilla had passed a rather uncomfortable afternoon. She had not made up her mind which would be kinder—to stall Hugo by telling him of her engagement to Hamish, or to let him declare himself, and then say No; so often it seemed to do young men good, in some curious way, to allow them to strip their emotions bare, rather than cause them to leave these

103

decently stifled. However when Hugo invited her to a round of golf on the small private links, that seemed safe enough; she could postpone her decision till later—who would propose on a golf-links? Hugo would, and did. There were occasional seats for on-lookers beside the fairways, and at one point, throwing his clubs aside and taking hers from her, he led her to one, and holding her hands in his rather diffidently asked her to marry him. Could she bear to marry a foreigner? Did she mind his being a Jew? How would she feel about becoming a Catholic? "My children must be Catholics." And he spoke of the uncertain future for Jews in Europe—"Now, I can offer you *everything!*—but who knows what is to come?" It was all beautifully done—elegantly, considerately, though with a controlled passionate earnestness that left the girl rather shaken; but he also spoke very fast, there was no chance to break in. At last, still holding her hands, searching her face—

"Na?" he asked.

Lucilla found that solitary little syllable of enquiry quite heart-breaking.

"Oh dear dear Hugo, I can't" she said, tears coming into her big grey eyes.

"Why not?"

"Because I am engaged, *fiancée*, already."

"Not to Endre?" he asked, a flash of anger in his pale hand-some face—Hugo was a fair Jew, and over six feet tall. He dropped her hands as he spoke.

"Goodness no! To an Englishman—I mean he's Scotch—a soldier. He's a prisoner-of-war in Germany" Lucilla said inco-herently. "Oh Hugo, I am so sorry about this."

He looked at her ringless hand in surprise; then, with an obvious effort, tried to pull himself together.

"I think beautiful girls who are *fiancées* should wear a special costume, to indicate their status" he said, trying to speak lightly, but not altogether succeeding. "In our villages here they do this. It is more fair."

"Oh much more fair" she agreed. "Only one would feel rather

104

silly going round saying to every young man one meets—'I'm engaged, you know.' I mean, they might not be interested." Somehow she could not explain Hamish's objection to her wearing a ring just then.

He laughed at that, unwillingly.

"You never thought *I* should be interested?" he asked.

"Yes, I did" she replied frankly. "In fact on the way down I was thinking of telling you before you got a chance to propose —I never dreamt you'd catch me while we were playing golf!"

At that innocent admission the young man laughed again.

"Oh Lucilla, no one is like you! You are so true." (He meant truthful.) Then he turned sad again. "This makes it still worse to lose you" he said, and covered his face with his hands.

Lucilla let him be for some moments. At last she said—

"Well, there it is, Hugo dear. You see there's nothing to be done. If you were a prisoner in enemy hands you wouldn't much like to get a letter saying—'I've met another charming young man, so our engagement is all off,' would you?"

He took his hands from his face.

"Am I, to you, a charming young man?"

"No—that was a silly expression. 'Charming' usually means professional womanisers, like Endre. You are frightfully *nice;* something quite different, and much more important. But nice or charming, I can't marry you, Hugo, because if the Germans don't starve him to death I'm going to marry Hamish."

"Haymish" he repeated. "What a curious name. I never heard it before."

"It's Scotch—it means James."

"And you love him so much? No, I should not ask that. Of course you do." He was silent for a moment or two—so was Lucilla; she could think of nothing to say.

Hungarians are almost completely lacking in those English ideas of "not meeting" when a man has proposed and been refused.

"At least I shall often see you, and talk with you" Hugo said then. "That will be something."

"Of course—so long as you *know,* and it doesn't upset you."

"Upset, please?"

"Make you unhappy."

"To see you? This must always be a happiness, for me. But unhappy I think I shall be, always. Always" he repeated.

The reiteration of that word, reminding her of the night of her engagement, and the young man's sad sincere face, caused the girl to burst into tears.

"Oh don't! Let's go home. Oh, I am so sorry."

"Now I have 'upset' *you.* Forgive me—I am selfish."

"No you're not! You forgive *me.* Bring my clubs." She got up and walked hurriedly away, crying and wiping her eyes as she went.

They sat down thirty to dinner that night, and thirty to breakfast on the following morning—at 10, after the devout Weissbergers had attended early Mass. Breakfast on Sunday in those big comfortable country-houses was something to remember. The hot freshly-baked snow-white rolls sprinkled with poppyseed, and the loaves of fresh rye-bread, with its odd malty taste; cold home-cured baked ham, spiced and tender; home-made paté de foie gras and, in the autumn, a huge raised game pie with partridge, pheasant and hard-boiled eggs set firm in a strong jelly inside the decorated crust; cheese, and best of all *Hasenpastete,* a great oblong block of hare mousse, softened with pork fat and strongly flavoured with herbs and garlic. In fact an Elisabethan English breakfast, including beer (as well as coffee) for those who had been out riding since 6 a.m. (The Weissbergers, being very rich, still had real coffee, in spite of the British blockade.) Rosina Eynsham tucked into the *Hasen-pastete,* and secured the recipe from her hostess.

Later in the morning she had a long talk with Baron Hermann about the parcels for the prisoners-of-war. Like everyone else he asked if the British Red Cross was not contributing?

"Well not yet—they seem to have their own ideas. But they're not getting their parcels through, not *one,* so far—and meanwhile those wretched men are cold and half-starved, and our parcels

106

are reaching them, sometimes within a week or ten days. So we want to send all we can." She went into details—for one thing, how could she get all that Yugo-slav flannellette made up into shirts and pyjamas? Was there a firm who would do it?

His reply, careful and thorough, gave Rosina a frightening glimpse of what the Nazi attitude meant to the Jews of Central Europe. No, not a large firm; her order was not big enough. "But many of the smaller Jewish concerns are closing down; their owners are trying to get away while there is still time, so numbers of expert seamstresses and shirtmakers are becoming unemployed. Consult Baron Schönheim; he is in a big way, but he is concerning himself with their welfare, and I am sure he will arrange it for you. It will be a boon to those women and girls, who are mostly Hungarians; *they* have nothing to fear but the loss of their wages." He paused, and she looked at him in dismay. What exactly did *he* fear, this short bent man—Hugo and Emmi got their height from their Mother—who looked more like a don than an industrialist, with his square lined face and intelligent eyes? "But if the Red Cross does not help," he went on, "excuse me, but how will you finance all this?"

"Well, that is a worry. So far we've been just begging, and the officers' relations send cheques, of course. But naturally we are sending to the men as well, and their relations don't have cheque-books."

"It is strange that the English Red Cross does not finance you. I hear that they are sending their parcels to Lisbon, hundreds of tons of them, where they lie on the quays, immobile."

"Good gracious, why on earth to Lisbon? And how do you know that?"

He smiled finely.

"I have my sources of information! They hoped to get them on from there to Switzerland, across Spain and France; but at the moment the Spanish railways are fully occupied with getting out their crop of citrus fruit, their oranges and lemons—so nothing moves."

"What absolute nonsense!" Rosina said angrily—the prisoners

were becoming an obsession with her. "Why can't they send their parcels to Salonika or the Piraeus, and let them come on through here? Or else send *us* some money to buy the things we can get, and send on to the camps with no delay at all?" This was the first she had heard of that miserable and futile mistake, sending Red Cross parcels to fester on the quays at Lisbon, and it made her furious—as it made England furious when it became public property.

The Baron smiled again.

"You said they had their own ideas! Not very wise ones, I fear. But since they will not help, please let me do a little." He opened his notecase and gave her 2000 pengoes, rather over £200. "Schönheim will give you money too, as will my brothers —and many more, especially if much of it is to be spent on employing Hungarian labour. In any case, here in Hungary we all wish to help England—she is now the only defender of freedom in Europe."

Just like Schiller, Rosina thought. She thanked him warmly. "You *are* good! I didn't come here to beg, you know—I really wanted your advice." She paused. "Shall *you* be able to get away, if the worst comes to the worst?" she asked impulsively.

"We hope so. We have something to offer. But do not let us think of the worst. Shall we take a look at the garden?"

Rosina longed to know what the Weissberger brothers had to offer, and how they hoped to hear when "the worst," whatever it was, would come in time to make a getaway—but obviously she could not ask him. Anyhow Jews, like the Roman Catholic Church, always knew everything. (Sir Hugh, an agnostic, had for some months now been having *The Tablet* sent out by bag, because it gave so much more information than most other English papers.)

But she marvelled at the way these people, so menaced, continued to carry on such a gay and lively existence, to all outward appearance quite untroubled. On the Sunday evening everyone danced to the gramophone; even Baron Hermann steered Rosina

108

and then his wife round in whirling Viennese waltzes. Presently someone asked for the czardas—"Endre dances it so beautifully." But Hungarians would only dance the czardas, in those days, to "live" music, and gypsy music at that, so a servant was despatched to the village to bring the gypsy band up from the inn. There was some whispering apart among the young men; then Hugo said—"We must send for a girl too. None of you can match Endre in the czardas." And he and two or three of the others left the room.

There ensued a considerable pause, during which some of the young people did half-hearted fox-trots to canned music, while their elders talked. Eventually the gypsies arrived, three small dark-visaged men equipped with a fiddle, a viola, and a flute—they took their seats in one corner of the big room on chairs provided by Baron Hugo; then Count Endre appeared, leading the village girl by the hand. Her appearance shocked Mrs Eynsham. A flaring blonde, her strong features heavily made up, her bosoms boldly accentuated under the peasant dress —utterly unlike the decorous maidens normally to be seen in country villages. However in spite of rather thick ankles she danced the czardas most beautifully, as Count Endre did; the intricate steps and the restrained movements of the two bodies were as perfect as a poem, as closely-wrought as a sonnet—towards the end everyone began to applaud, in involuntary delight. Suddenly Endre threw restraint to the winds; he lifted the girl up in his arms, twirled her round in the air, showing her frilly knickers, and clapped her smartly on the bottom before, panting from his exertions, he set her down.

"No, but really Endre, this is wrong" Johanna protested. "You must not treat her so. Who is it?" she asked her husband.

"Unknown to me" the Baron said, looking vexed, while the blonde girl curtsied, smirking, on all sides.

"Oh yes, dear Baron, you know 'her' quite well" Count Endre said. He went up to the girl, tore off her blonde wig, and ripped open her blouse—a couple of tennis-balls fell out from an ill-

109

adjusted brassière, and without the wig, seeing his sleek dark head, everyone recognised Dickie Werckheim, a rather youthful boy cousin of the Weissbergers.

"This is what took so long, to dress him up" Endre explained. "But he made a lovely girl, no?"

"You went to my theatrical trunk!" Baroness Johanna said reproachfully.

"Yes, and to your dressing-table! You have no rouge left." She smiled politely.

"Did this amuse you?" Hugo asked Lucilla later.

"As a joke not much—no. But I loved watching them dance —they were fantastic, together. I do wish I could really dance the czardas."

"Nicely, you do; but *really*, no. For this one must begin as a child, I think."

The Minister had telephoned to Mrs Eynsham before the dancing began, and given her a good account of David; on their return to Budapest next morning she drove straight down to the nursing-home after dropping Lucilla and the luggage at her house, and recounted to her husband such of the small events of the week-end as she thought might amuse him. He laughed drily at the czardas episode.

"*How* Hungarian! For such a highly civilised nation they have the most elementary sense of what is funny. Endre's idea, of course?"

"I think so—he and Hugo and Dickie all went out together." Then, unwisely, she mentioned her guess that Hugo had proposed to Lucilla and been turned down.

"She didn't tell you?"

"No—it was their faces."

"An incredibly silly idea of young Hamish's, not to let it be announced," David Eynsham said impatiently. "As high-minded as you like, of course, but utterly unpractical. However, no one has ever accused Highlanders of commonsense!"

"Would people out here have known, even if it had been in *The Times?*"

110

"Of *course*. How little you know, Rosina."

"Yes, I'm afraid that's true" his wife said, gathering up her handbag and gloves, and bending over the bed to give a kiss which, she sadly realised, David could quite well have done without—only she could not have done without giving it. "Is there anything you want?"

"Yes—whisky, and some more thrillers; try the Consul—I know he reads them. And gaspers."

"David, I brought you a hundred on Friday!—and I know Dr Mendze only wants you to smoke ten a day."

He grinned at her.

"I give them to the nurses! You send all that down, like a good girl." He waved at her gaily as she went out.

After lunch—blessed Bertha had of course unpacked everything; the dressing-table looked as though she had never left her bedroom—Mrs Eynsham went round to the Legation. The desk in her little office was piled with communications from the camps in Germany. One of the Stalags, with nearly 18,000 British prisoners, requested 500 mouth organs as soon as possible—"and any food, clothing, and blankets that you can send. We get nothing from home." Another camp, apparently very cultured, wanted instruments for "an orchestra of 50," and specified the instruments—"and any sheet music you can find. It will keep the men occupied if they can practise." Yet another card begged for water-colours and/or oil paints for two artists—all asked for blankets and clothing, as well as food. And there was a flood of letters from frantic wives, mothers, and even grandmothers, enclosing cheques and imploring that food and clothes, and "something—anything—to smoke" should be sent to the beloved Tom, or Dick, or Harry. "He writes that his brother-officers are getting parcels from Budapest" several of these distraught women wrote. "I have sent pounds and pounds to the Red Cross, but nothing seems to happen. *Could* you help? I am really in despair—he has been a prisoner for just on four months, and none of the parcels I have paid for seem to have reached him."

These letters made Rosina very angry, remembering Baron

111

Hermann's story about Lisbon. Hastily she endorsed all the cheques, telephoned down to the Chancery for a typist, dictated a letter to her bank, asking for all to be paid into her current account; and then dictated another one, saying that something should be sent to Tom, or Dick, or Harry within a few days. "Forty-eight copies of that, Miss Maudsley—I will write in the names, and sign them. And make me a list of the names and addresses, and the amount of each cheque, will you? I shall want that for the files." She glanced at the calendar on her desk. "There's a bag going out tonight, isn't there?"

"Yes, Mrs Eynsham."

"Well these must all make it. Can you manage?"

"Oh yes, Mrs Eynsham. I don't care how late I stay, to get these off."

"Good girl! Nor do I!" Rosina said cheerfully.

"Oh, we all know what you do, Mrs Eynsham, raising money and all" Miss Maudsley said enthusiastically, rather to Rosina's dismay—she disliked adorers.

"Splendid" she said. It was something if adorers would work overtime without complaint. "Right—take all this downstairs." When the girl had gone she asked for the Minister's study on the house telephone—rather to her surprise he replied; she had half expected him to be out, shooting or playing golf. "Who is that?" his voice asked, non-committally.

"Me" Rosina said foolishly.

"Oh my dear—where are you?"

"In my office. May I come along?"

"Do."

"Nice week-end?" he asked when she sat down. "Did the Baron play?"

"Oh yes—he gave me two thousand pengoes, and put me on to Baron Schönheim, who he says will find me girls to make shirts and pyjamas out of all that Jug flannel. But he told me a frightful story"—she repeated the tale of the parcels being sent to Lisbon. "Do you think it *can* be true? It seems so dotty to try to send them through Switzerland, when parcels on from there are held up for *weeks* because of the R.A.F. raids on all

112

the Rhineland railways. Mademoiselle O. told me about that the other day; she said the situation was quite desperate, even for the invalid foods and medicines."

"Alas, I'm afraid anything can be true of the Red Cross" Sir Hugh said sadly. "Its personnel are devoted people, but very few of them have much training in administration, and you see they are not under any Government department, so they are not accountable for their actions to Parliament."

"Then who *are* they accountable to?"

"Only to public opinion—and that moves slowly. But it is beginning to move—Morven hears there are going to be some very awkward questions in the House of Commons next week."

"Who to, so?"

"The Secretary of State for War, since soldiers are his pidgin; but of course he won't be able to answer them—only express a pious hope that the prisoners will soon get some parcels. He can't compel the Red Cross to act rationally, or prevent them acting irrationally."

"What would *you* say was the rational action for them to take?" Rosina asked, again thinking of the Baron's remarks; she distrusted her own views where her emotions were involved.

"At present, pour money in here, where all the resources of Egypt, Turkey, and South-East Europe are available, and there is rapid access to the camps; and let you and my wretched staff send the stuff on!" he said, smiling a little ruefully at her. "And ship those miserable parcels to that Serbian port next door to Fiume; they could come here by rail and go straight on into Germany. In fact Morven says that a Yugo-slav ship-owner has offered some of his ships for this very purpose."

"And haven't they been accepted?" Rosina asked, staring.

"Oh no—not yet. They probably won't be, till it's too late. God knows how long we shall be here—but *now*, we could help; this is the ideal route, since the R.A.F. isn't bombing the Austrian railways."

"But *why* can't they see that?" Rosina asked, fuming.

"Age; inexperience; and a preoccupation with the past. Many of the devoted old gentlemen in Grosvenor Crescent are retired

Generals; it's fixed in their minds that in the first World War Switzerland was the place to send parcels through, because it was a neutral country contiguous to Germany, with an open frontier to the South—Italy; so Switzerland it must be. What they have omitted to register is that in this war Italy is an enemy, and France occupied by the enemy—so parcels still have to go via Geneva, although, *for the moment,* Hungary occupies the position that Switzerland held from 1914 to 1918."

His stress on the words "for the moment" struck a chill into Rosina's heart. Of course they would get out somehow, whatever happened; diplomats always did. But what would become of David if they had to "walk to Jerusalem," wheeling that pigskin bag with the drinks and spare clothing in Countess Pongracz's old garden-basket? Had she better lay on an invalid chair for Lucilla to push her Father down through the Balkans in?

"Min dear, how long do you think we *shall* last here?" she asked.

"I have no idea. You're thinking of David, of course. But he seems much better—Mendze is pleased with his progress."

"Yes, naturally I'm thinking of him—he's not likely to be fit for 'escapes and hurried journeys' for a good long time." She paused. "But I'm thinking of the prisoners too. They're getting *nothing;* I've just been reading the most horrifying letters. What happened about those quilts? So many *Vertrauensmänner*—and relations—ask for blankets. Could you possibly telegraph to the wretched Red Cross and ask when they will cough up the money to buy the quilts? They're terribly good value at sixteen bob, and it's getting late in the year."

"Yes, I will." He went across to his desk, opened a drawer and consulted his notes, and wrote rapidly; then he pressed a bell. "That do?" he asked, handing her the draft telegram.

"Yes, fine—you've even given the dimensions! You see they'll make perfect sleeping-bags—and we've bought up all the large safety-pins in Budapest *and* Sofia *and* Belgrade!"

Martha Beckley appeared in response to the bell.

"Hullo, Rosina. Do any good at Schloss Weissberger?"

"Yes, a lot. Two thousand pengoes, and no end of advice about

114

begging and seamstresses. If you could come in for supper to-night we might concert some plans."

"Not *for*—I will after. How *good*. Two thousand!"

"When you two young ladies have finished your private conversation, I should like to give a telegram to my secretary" the Minister said, with his sidelong smile. Rosina said—"Oh, so sorry"; Martha, in a cold flat tone, said—"Yes, Your Excellency?"

"None of your lip, Martha. Here you are"—he handed her the sheet of paper. "For the Red Cross, per the Foreign Office—and I think it had better be in code, innocent as it is."

"Very good, Sir. I'll send it off at once."

"Less of your 'Sir'; that's lip too, as well you know, between you and me," Sir Hugh said cheerfully.

"I didn't think there was anything between you and me, least of all lip, or lips" said Martha Beckley as she left the room.

"Oh what a splendid girl! I thank God for her every day" the Minister said fervently. Rosina Eynsham was laughing. "Why do you laugh?"

"It always amuses me to see Martha slapping you down. But I agree—she is God's gift to anyone. How soon do you think we shall get an answer to that telegram?"

"Heaven knows—the old gentlemen in Grosvenor Crescent are apt to take their time. However I addressed it to His Lordship personally, and headed it 'Urgent.' We'll see."

The reply did not come for over a week, and was highly unsatisfactory when it did. The Germans, the British Red Cross stated firmly, would never allow quilts to be sent to prisoners-of-war; it was far too easy to conceal compasses, or even small maps in them; the whole idea was impossible.

This obstructiveness made Rosina quite furious; she was nervy anyhow, between overwork and anxiety over David, and Martha had told her of the bitter questions (and futile answers) in Parliament about parcels for the prisoners, reported by the wireless —something which did *not* appear in the Bulletin. In her little office she asked the telephone operator to get her a friend at the American Legation; America was the "Protecting Power" for Allied prisoners-of-war, and members of the Embassy staff in Berlin were already detailed to visit the camps in this capacity.

"Oh Howard, listen. Is it *really* impossible to send quilts to our prisoners? Could you find out? Look"—she put her problem. "We use Hungarian Red Cross labels, of course. How soon can you get an answer? Honestly, I don't believe they know a thing in London!"

"Relax, Rosie. It won't take long to find out; I'll call you back the moment I hear. Don't kill yourself. How's David?"

In just under two hours the American rang back.

"Rosie? Good news! I got onto Perce in Berlin, and he went right round to the Ober-Kommando Wehrmacht. Will you take this down?—got a pencil? Good. In quotes: 'If the quilts are in bales or parcels bearing Hungarian Red Cross labels, and are sent across the frontier at Hegyeshalom'"—he spelt it out— "'they will be accepted by the German authorities, and forwarded to the camps immediately.' That do you?"

"Oh, marvellous! Bless you, Howard."

"I'll send you on the text of the order when I get it from Perce. But this should fix your old Red Cross."

"Infernal old Red Cross!" Rosina exclaimed. "Howard, I can't thank you enough." In her excitement she went straight across the passage to the Minister's study and tapped on the door, a thing that normally she never did—she either telephoned, or sent a servant to ask if His Excellency was at liberty? He was, on this occasion, and she showed him, glowing, what she had scribbled down at Howard's dictation. "*Now* they'll be able to sleep warm this winter" she said triumphantly.

She was mistaken. Sir Hugh prudently waited for 48 hours till the text of the German permission had come; then he sent another cable to the Red Cross, quoting this, and requesting that funds should be made available for the immediate purchase of 44,000 quilts for the P.O.W.s. But the old gentlemen in Grosvenor Crescent did indeed take their time; it was not till the spring of the following year that permission and funds were given— for the purchase of 10,000 quilts, for 44,000 men. Corporal Fraser and his like had to spend their first winter in German prison-camps under "the one thin blanket."

116

8

The little Prisoners' Relief Organisation Committee met once a week. It was always a slightly tedious affair to Martha and Mrs Eynsham, who both felt it rather a waste of time to listen to Eleanor Wheatley letting off bitcheries at Gina Morven, who hit back, to dear Hugo prosing, and to the general diffuse inconclusiveness. But soon after her return from the Weissbergers Rosina duly made her report, and read out several of the Camp letters.

"And have you seen this Baron Schönheim?" Mrs Wheatley asked.

"Not yet—I only got home two days ago, and I've been busy buying the instruments for the orchestra for that Stalag. They don't seem to have mouth-organs here; Stalag XX wants five hundred. Some will have to go down to Belgrade."

"What makes you think they have mouth-organs in Belgrade?" Mrs Wheatley asked pertly.

"I rang up Sir Monty, and they have millions, it seems. But who does the Committee wish to go aboard Baron Schönheim?"

"You, of course" Horace said. "Shut up, Eleanor"—as his wife opened her pretty doll's mouth to speak. "Yes, Gina?"

"I could go to Belgrade and fetch zese mouse-organs. Mrs Eynsham ees busy, and her husband so sick."

"Good, Gina" Martha Beckley said. "That is approved, I take it?" Martha kept the Committee's minutes. "And that Mrs Eynsham tackles Baron Schönheim?" She made rapid notes.

"There's one other point" Mrs Eynsham said. "The most terrible letters keep coming in from the camps; I haven't read them all to you. But no one is getting anything except from here, and Mrs Campbell's air parcels from Estoril—tiny ones, of course; and it seems that the Red Cross pays no attention to anything but public opinion. So if anyone knows influential people in England, I think it would be a good plan to write to them, and ask them to rouse up the Red Cross, and also to send money direct to us, who *can* get stuff in."

"Letters by bag take eight weeks now" Colonel Morven said gloomily—"wandering round by the Cape and Khartoum."

"I know. But Martha has had an idea about that. Tell your friends to address their letters with—we hope—their cheques, to you at 1 Verböczy-utca, Budapest; put *no* stamps on, and send them in a covering envelope addressed to our Ambassador in Lisbon. He'll send them on by ordinary European air-mail."

"How do you know he will?" Eleanor Wheatley wanted to know.

"Because she rang him up and arranged it" Martha Beckley said impatiently. "Don't be so tiresome, Eleanor. A cheque has gone to cover his stamps, too. And you all send *your* letters, also in two envelopes, the outside one addressed to the British Ambassador, British Embassy, Lisbon. They'll probably get through in eight or nine days."

"That's *smart!*" Colonel Morven said. "I shall write to Regimental Headquarters at once, and ask for funds."

"I shall write to the Archbishop of Canterbury" Horace said, grinning. "He might make a speech in the House of Lords; if public opinion is what we have to rely on, that could help. Rosina, get me some flimsies made of the more tear-jerking letters, will you?"

"Of course—the best of ideas."

"You don't know the Archbishop of Canterbury, Horace, do you?" Eleanor asked.

"He confirmed me—that's quite enough. You write to your tedious old Uncle Lord Cuddesdon—he could make a speech too, though no one will listen to it; I believe he empties the

118

Chamber the moment he gets up to speak! Anyhow he might send us a few quid—he's hideously rich."

"Hideously mean, too" Eleanor said. "However, I'll try it on. He was in the Ox and Bucks in the Boer War, or the Crimean War, or something, so he might know what a soldier is." They laughed, glad that Mrs Wheatley was being co-operative for once; indeed the whole small group was fired with a fresh eagerness at the idea of conducting this campaign.

"Poor Gina—what a pity *you* can't write to anyone!" Eleanor Wheatley said presently, spoiling the pleasant feeling that had suddenly prevailed.

"I can! I do! I write to ze Pope" Gina replied with vigor.

"What can *he* do?" Eleanor was asking contemptuously, when Geoffrey Milton, the Press Attaché, lounged in. He was in theory a member of the Committee, but seldom graced it with his presence. "What can who do?" he asked.

"The Pope, for the P.O.W.s" Martha replied, cutting Mrs Wheatley short.

"My impression of this Pope is that he can do practically anything for anyone" Milton said. "I gather the Vatican already has a high-powered relief organisation mobilised; helping the French refugees, so far. But why should he bother with our prisoners? Isn't that up to the Red Cross?"

"It should be, of course" Martha said, "but they've fallen flat on their faces over this job, so far. Didn't you know? Tell him, Rosina."

"Yes, do help me earn my salary" the young man said, in a voice as melting as his huge eyes. "I know nothing."

"You'd better come along to my office and see the actual letters" Mrs Eynsham said. "Then you might create a press riot."

"Give me a précis."

She did, briefly but forcibly.

"*No* parcels at the camps yet, except ours? After four months? All roosting at Lisbon? How awful."

"Can't you get in an article, Geoffrey?" Horace Wheatley asked. "The Yanks in Berlin are visiting the camps—you've only

119

to see Howard and get the low-down on the whole thing, straight from the horse's mouth. Send one of your reporters round."

Mr Milton reflected—they all watched him.

"No" he said at length. "I don't think it will work."

"Why not?" Martha asked sharply.

"Oh, because the British Red Cross is an untouchable—in the upper sense! It's a sort of Holy of Holies, like the Monarchy."

"You must have seen the questions in the House" Horace said.

"Oh yes—quite nasty, and from what you tell me well-merited. But I still don't think the time is ripe for an article about it."

"Oh very well—let us all write our private letters" Mrs Eynsham said brusquely. "I've never had much faith in the Press, anyhow." She rose, gathering her papers and stowing them in a leather case. "Have we finished, Hugo? If so I'll go and get on with my work. The time is always ripe for that!"

"Let me drive you home—that's a huge brief-case for you to carry" Milton said as she walked out.

"What a home-taker you are!—if it isn't Lucilla, it's even me" she said, getting into his Chrysler; her bag *was* very heavy.

"Rosina, why are you so nasty to me?" the young man asked, as he shot off up the narrow street of golden houses.

"Oh, like begets like! I think *you're* nasty, and a coward too —otherwise you'd get an article into the press at home about this Red Cross nonsense, headed 'By telephone from Berlin.' But you only care about your career, not about those frozen starving boys," she exclaimed in exasperation. The car pulled up at her house, and she sprang out. "Thank you."

He leaned out of the window, his face sad as she had never seen it.

"Rosina, do you really think me a coward? Unworthy?"

"Yes of course. How could anyone think anything else, after your performance just now?"

"I'll think about an article" he said, and drove away.

The very next night Gina Morven travelled down to Belgrade; her husband telephoned to his opposite number there, and she was met, and put up, and taken round the town by a Yugo-slav-speaking lady to buy "mouse-organs"; there were plenty of these, but in small quantities, a dozen in this little shop, twenty in that—her task occupied two whole days. Five hundred mouth-organs take up a surprising amount of space, too, and are rather heavy; she returned in triumph with two enormous cardboard dress-boxes which were already beginning to burst at the corners. Horace and Mr Smith re-packed them in stronger cartons, weighing them carefully—no prisoners' parcels were supposed to exceed five kilograms, or roughly eleven pounds.

Rosina had come up against this difficulty over the instruments for the orchestra. A cello by itself weighs anything from eighteen to twenty-five pounds; packed in a wooden crate for transit it was far over the permitted weight—the postal and railway officials protested. Dismayed, she consulted Sir Hugh.

"Ring up old Willie—he will fix it for you somehow" the Minister said. "Rather a good idea, a camp orchestra. Have you got them any music? That will weigh tons, too."

"I haven't begun to try—I'm rather stupid about music. I've got all the fiddles and so on—the instrument-makers have let us have everything at twenty-five per cent below cost price."

"Beautiful people! Let me have a go at the music. I'll talk to old Madame Buday—she plays a Strad herself, and used to run a small private orchestra—I expect her attics are full of tattered scores."

Prince Willie also thought a camp orchestra a good idea, and amusing. "I am coming up on Monday, and will see you. Probably for musical instruments there will have to be export licences; but I can see the Old Boy. It will all arrange itself; don't worry. How is your husband?"

Then there was Baron Schönheim to see. Rosina went to his house after dark, in a taxi—she suggested this herself, to his manifest relief. She found an enormous pale, fair man, with a heavy careworn face; he was much more open about his fears for the future than Hugo's father had been. "I can only expect the gas-chamber, if the English leave and the Germans enter here" he said—and Mrs Eynsham, horrified, heard for the first time how Polish Jews were already faring at German hands in Auschwitz. "But while there is time, let us do what we can" he said. "I am glad that you can offer work to some of these unemployed Hungarian women. I shall send one of my managers to arrange this, and collect the material. Must he go to the Legation?"

No, to her own house, Rosina told him; and the garments when made up could be returned there—she wrote down the address.

"Ah, excellent." Then, like Baron Hermann, he opened his note-case; but he gave her 4000 pengoes.

"Oh Baron, this is too much!" She was quite overwhelmed.

"Nothing is too much for England—our only hope! I have spoken to my friends; they will send also, but with no name, probably—it is safer so."

"But then I can't thank them."

"They do not want thanks." Then he asked her if she had any notion of how things were going? "Do the Americans come in? England cannot do all, alone."

Rosina said she had no idea. "No one over here can ever guess what the Americans will do, can they? I mean they're always so busy electing a new President, or arranging pensions for War Veterans from 1918, or fussing about educating or not educating the Negroes, or just hating all colonial countries—they're quite out of touch with the real world, don't you think?"

He gave a gloomy laugh.

"This is true—lamentably true. But perhaps one day the 'real world,' as you call it, may hit them."

"Oh do you think so? That would be splendid. Anyhow thank you a thousand times for all your help. Could someone get me a taxi?"

Next morning a small furtive-looking Jew arrived at her house, and carried off all the Yugo-slav flannellette to be made up into shirts and pyjamas. And day after day envelopes with typewritten envelopes now arrived at the Eynshams' house, enclosing Hungarian bank notes ranging from one or two thousand pengoes down to ten, or even five; none ever gave a name or address—the most usual covering note, if there was one at all, said: "From a friend of England." The generosity of this Hungarian response—for many who were not Jews openly gave large sums, after some skilful begging on Martha Beckley's and Gina's part—touched the little group of English people deeply.

Prince Willie duly called on Rosina. "I have seen the Old Boy, and everything is arranged for your band! All you have to do is to send a list of your crates and their contents to the National Bank, and they will give the export licences. We do not mind sending away violas and trombones!—if it were food or clothing it would be more difficult. The shortages here are getting very serious."

Rosina thanked him. "Everyone is so *good*." When he had gone she hurried down to the various musical-instrument shops and told each to send her a list, in triplicate, of all cases, with the weight and contents of each. Being down in Pest she seized the chance to look in on David. She found him in tremendous spirits.

"Mendze says I can come out at the end of the week, if I go fairly slow. Such a boon—I get bored in here."

"Darling, how *good*."

"That means we can go to the Hortobagy week-end after next after all, and get some duck, and please God some geese too. I rang up Hugo just now, and told him to confirm the rooms at the czarda. He thinks the geese will still be in."

"To the Hortobagy?" She was all astray.

"Rosina, you're losing your grip! We arranged ages ago that Hugo Weissberger was to take us down to the Hortobagy to shoot that week-end, and all stay in the pub—he, and Endre, and you and I and Lucilla. I want Lucilla to see the Hortobagy; there's nothing else like it in the world."

"But that was before she and Hugo"—his wife began.

"Oh, bother their love-affairs! Hugo won't mind—he's all on. You'll enjoy it too, Rosie—there are mirages, something you've never seen. You come down on Friday and pack for me, won't you?"

"No, I'll send Erich—he'll do it much better than I shall" Rosina said firmly. She was already wondering how she was going to manage to get through her work for the prisoners with David in the house, needing a lot of care, and on her way out she got hold of Dr Mendze.

"Will you give me, *in writing*, exactly what my husband's régime is to be at home?"

"Madame, I can tell you. Breakfast in bed, which he must not leave before 9.45 a.m.; dinner also in bed—he should be between the sheets by 7.30. And two hours rest in the afternoon."

"Well put it in writing, please." Then she asked about the expedition to the Hortobagy.

"Oh, for this let him relax the rules a little! What one enjoys does one good. He is really better, much better; but he must avoid *great* exertions—and of course any mental stress or anger can produce a recurrence. I had a patient, an old man, who died of a thrombosis because he lost his temper!" Dr Mendze said laughing.

"Oh dear! Lots of little things irritate my husband" Rosina said anxiously.

"Little things do not matter. But I shall warn him against giving way to irritation over anything."

Rosina, driving home through the elegant streets of Pest, more beautiful than ever in the misty autumn sunshine, then over the Danube on the Ketten-Brücke, and up the broad winding road to Buda, where the trees on the slope of the Bastion glowed golden, hoped fervently that Dr Mendze's exhortations would prevent David from getting irritated—she had her doubts. She stopped at the Legation to go in and collect her mail; she could read it at her solitary luncheon. In the corridor she encountered the Minister.

"Where are you racing off to?"

"Home to lunch."

"Why not have it here?"

"Because I must go through all these"—she held out a fat bundle, round which she had slipped an elastic band.

"Well at least come and have a drink first, and tell me what goes on." He opened the door into his study. "Sherry, or a Martini?"

"Oh, gin—just a plain gin and It. Don't do anything elaborate; there isn't time."

"You're in a regular fuss" Sir Hugh said, as he handed her her drink. "What's it all about?"

"David's coming home, on Friday—and I know he'll go and do all the wrong things, and get ill again" she said distressfully.

He lit a cigarette for her before he spoke.

"Yes, I can see that that is going to be worrying for you. But it's splendid news, all the same," he said. "He must be much better. And I suppose Mendze will tell him what he may and mayn't do."

"I've said I must have that in black-and-white. But you know what David is—if there's an emergency, or a rush of work, he'll ignore everything anyone says."

"Yes." He smoked in silence for a few moments. "He ought really to go home, of course" Sir Hugh said; "but honestly I should find it very hard—well really almost impossible—to manage here without him, with all his specialised knowledge. You wouldn't believe what he has put through, even from his bed."

"Oh I would. But anyhow I know he wouldn't go. And he couldn't go alone—and how can *I* go?" Rosina said incoherently. "No one else has the *time* to do what I do—and with him at home I don't know how *I* shall find the time. Oh dear." She was near to tears.

"Have another drink" Sir Hugh said, and re-filled her glass. "And take it all gently—though I know that's easier said than done. Tell me, how much have you got in hand in the way of funds?"

"I can't say without looking—and I only enter the amounts under dates; never with names, even if there are names. But something like thirty thousand pengoes. Why?"

"Never mind—you'll hear why later. I gather your Committee is sending vitriolic letters home to those in high places."

"I hope so. I expect mine will be much the most vitriolic!
God, when *can* I do them? Tonight, I suppose."

"Get a report on conditions in the camps from the American
Embassy in Berlin, who visit them, before you write—that will
carry much more conviction" Sir Hugh said.

"Good idea." And even before she sat down to a belated lunch
Mrs Eynsham telephoned to her friend Howard at the American
Legation and asked him to ring up Berlin and ask for a report.
"We want to put a rocket under the Red Cross" she explained.

"Are those poor toads *still* getting no parcels?"

"From home? Not a single one! Only from us, and some by
air from a splendid woman in Lisbon—privately."

"It's damnable. O.K., Rosie, I'll rustle them up in Berlin, and
tell them to hurry—or at least send the reports from their last
round at once."

"Oh fine. Bless you."

Mrs Eynsham spent the afternoon in her little office, checking acknowledgments of parcels received against lists of those
sent, and sending lists of further parcels despatched. She went
home to supper late, and tired; to her surprise and pleasure
Lucilla, exceptionally, was there to share the meal, and she told
her of her Father's return at the end of the week, and of the expedition to the Hortobagy.

"Yes, isn't it lovely? I'm *longing* to see the Hortobagy. Hugo
says it's quite entrancing."

"How did you know? Did your Father ring you up?"

"No, Hugo did." No embarrassment. "Martha's so incredibly
nice—she's given me from mid-day Friday to mid-day Monday
off for that week-end. It's a longish drive, it seems."

Mrs Eynsham was more concerned with the prisoners and
their needs than with the Hortobagy.

"I thought I'd write to Uncle Jim" she said presently, "and
ask him to beat up the people in Argyll to send us cheques for
the P.O.W.s. After all, lots of them are in the Argylls."

"Pure waste of time, if you ask me" Lucilla said. "Uncle Jim

126

won't send you *much* money, if any, and he'll find some splendid excuse for not taking any action. He loathes *doing* anything."

It was 1.30 a.m., after having drafted replies to numerous *Vertrauensmänner* and distracted English relations, that Mrs Eynsham, in spite of Lucilla's discouraging remarks, got down to her begging-letter to Uncle Jim, General James Cowall—who was really only a cousin, but was always called "Uncle" by the Eynsham children. She reported the piteous state of the officers and men of the Highland Division in the prison-camps, and the total failure of the Red Cross to get any parcels to them. "But *we* can, from here—our parcels reach them in under a fortnight. Do *please* ask the V.s, and the W.s, and the X.s and Y.s and Z.s, and anyone else you can think of, to send *us* money; not to the Red Cross." She gave instructions about posting cheques to the Embassy in Lisbon per the Foreign Office, and also gave some figures. "A parcel of 4 kilos of tinned food, chocolate and cigarettes costs 15 shillings; that leaves half-a-kilo for books, clothes, a pipe or whatever, and another half-kilo for the packing, which costs a little extra; but there is no freight or postage, as the parcels all go through the Hungarian Red Cross, *free*. So one can send a man a weekly parcel for 3 months for a tenner— enough to keep him going. But we must have money to buy the stuff, quickly. They are so hungry. *Please*, dear Jim, *do* do what you can. Let people give you their cheques, made out to me—or say what they will give—and then send me a wire—'Rosina Eynsham, Prodrome, Budapest,' saying—'300 coming' or '600 coming' or 'a thousand coming,' and I can begin buying. We have to get a lot in from outside—this country is pretty short itself." She ended with eager enquires about mutual friends. Then, well after 2.30 a.m. she went to bed.

Alas, Lucilla was quite right, as the young so often are. Far from asking his neighbours in Argyll to contribute, all the General did was to send Rosina's appeal on to his old friend Lady Otmoor, who lived in London, and request her to discuss it with the Red Cross! In due course he sent her answer on to Mrs Eynsham, via Lisbon.

"My dear Jim

I have visited Lady R., Mrs T., and Miss N.—rather like Dickens' Great Circumlocution Office!—but they are all very capable ladies. And it boils down to this. No one is allowed now to send Money out of the Country, Defense of the Realm Act; but of course Rosina has showed *you* a way! But the Red X. are having parcels sent from Canada, the Balkan States, Lisbon, and other parts. Rosina's parcel is the same weight as that sent by the Red X, but of course not nearly as *good* a parcel, and costs 15/– against Red X. 10/6. Of course Rosina's parcels might suplement" (Spelling was not Lady Otmoor's strong point) "what is being sent by the Red X."

Fortunately this exasperating missive did not reach Mrs Eynsham for 3 weeks, otherwise her letters complaining of the Red Cross's failures would have been even more vitriolic. How did the "capable ladies" in Grosvenor Crescent decide that her parcels were inferior to theirs? Did *they* send paté de foie gras and smoked goose-breast, with their high fat content? Spam and tinned sausages, more likely. And "supplement," when *no* Red Cross parcels were arriving from England. Also what "Balkan States" were sending parcels for the British Red Cross?—and where to? She was draining them dry herself. "Lies, lies, lies!" she said angrily—and she was not wrong. Dear Lady Otmoor's letter was a classic example of what very capable ladies, when assailed, *are* capable of.

However well before this deplorable letter arrived, David came home, in the sunniest of moods at being back in his own house, in his sunny bedroom looking out onto the golden trees on the Bastion slope; to his wife's infinite relief he kept faithfully to Dr Mendze's time-table, and sank contentedly into bed at 7.30 p.m.—she always went in to supervise his supper, and took coffee with him after it, gossiping over the day's events. And then, exactly a week after his return, they all went down to the Hortobagy.

9

This peculiar region lies to the east of the Tisza, the Danube's big northern tributary—an immense, open, tree-less plain, geometrically flat, unfenced and uncultivated; the salt-petre in the soil prevents the growth of any crop save grass, on which tens of thousands of horses, sheep, cattle and pigs grazed in huge flocks. There were no houses or villages save round the periphery; the whole vast area, some fifty miles long by thirty wide, was empty save for the live-stock and the men who tended them, and criss-crossed in every direction by rough earthen tracks used by the animals. It was studded all over by shallow blue lakes to which, in autumn, ducks and geese came flighting in; but it was so featureless, land and water so mixed up, that those who came to shoot always had to take a guide to lead them to any given mere.

In the heart of this strange place stood the *czarda,* or inn, on which the shepherds, swineherds, cowherds and horse-masters, the *Czikös,* who lived too far from the out-lying villages to ride to them, relied entirely for supplies; they both ate there, and bought their food and tobacco. This was the czarda's *raison d'être,* but there were a few bedrooms for the odd sportsman who came after duck and geese. It was a long white one-storey building, in front of which, on that Friday evening, the Eyn-shams' car drew up. There was no sign of Hugo and Endre, who were to have gone on ahead to arrange everything; but David had been coming there since boyhood, and was greeted warmly by the landlord, who showed them their clean simple rooms. Five minutes later the other two hurried in. "We had a *deff*ect!" (This was the invariable Hungarian phrase for a puncture or any

129

sort of break-down.) All agreed that it was too late to go out after duck that night; it wasn't, but they were thinking of David Eynsham's fatigue after the long drive from Budapest. However they strolled about in the low evening sunshine, admiring some splendid grey bulls with horns a yard across, penned in wooden enclosures—there was to be a sale next day. Rosina wandered off by herself to a small pond behind the inn, in which a purple heron was wading; in the half-bare willow-boughs which over-hung it some extremely ugly birds, a sort of buff egret, were al-ready going to roost; occasionally one plunged like a kingfisher into the water, and came up with a fish in its powerful beak.

When she returned to the czarda the others were already having drinks in the garden, where a few late flowers still bloomed under clipped trees; dung from the cattle-pens had made some degree of cultivation possible here. A she-ass and its colt were wandering between the tables, pushing their grey heads and soft moist muzzles over the shoulders of the guests, trying to reach the salted apricot-kernels which were served with the local vermouth. "What a sweet place this is," Rosina said happily, observing with satisfaction that David was drinking his own whisky.

"I told you you'd like it" he said. "Come and have a drink."

"I'll just wash first—I won't be a minute." What she really wanted was to unpack David's things, get out his hot bottle and so on; this she did rapidly, and then unpacked her own—in the small czarda they had to share a room, and she didn't want to fret him by fussing round when he was in bed. This done, she went to wash in the bathroom; someone had filled the basin, and the donkey and its child were drinking from it—more de-lighted than ever, Rosina shooed out the pretty intruders and washed her hands.

"Eleven and a half minutes" David said when she re-appeared in the garden, where a splendid crimson glow from the western sky gave a deeper hue to the yellowing trees, the late flowers, and even to the faces round the table. "You said one."

"Ah, but I had visitors, and I had to show them out." David looked surprised; suppressed giggles on Endre's and Lucilla's

130

part gave them away. "These children had put the donkeys in the bathroom, I fancy" she said laughing. "Yes, just Vermouth, Hugo, please."

For a small country inn in the remotest part of Hungary the food at dinner was surprisingly good—strong thick bean soup, a *real* goulasch, and wild duck from the meres roasted to a delicate pink tenderness, with fresh salad from the garden, aromatic with chives and tarragon; spiced apples, roasted before the fire on wire strings completed the meal. Halfway through it the gypsies appeared, and began to play. Before the advent of the Russians in 1945 practically every country inn in Hungary had its own gypsy band, slender dark men with faces rather like parrots; hence the name of the national dance, for which the inn gypsies produced the music to which peasants habitually danced when the day's work was done—the inn was the *czarda,* the dance was the *czardas.* The Hortobagy gypsies played and sang the "Hortobagy Song," which describes that unique place; Endre translated the words for Lucilla and Mrs Eynsham. The donkeys were again with them throughout the meal, stepping neatly between the close-set tables and thrusting their pretty heads between shoulders, now demanding bread; they were freely fed. Rosina thought she had never eaten a meal in more delightful circumstances.

Indeed that week-end on the Hortobagy was a halcyon interlude for all of them—strange, almost magical, with a sort of enchantment lying over it, as the *Fata Morgana,* the will-of-the-wisp, is said to hover over the meres, luring men to their death. They went out after dinner into the warm still night and watched a full moon rise in splendour over the plain; the sweet breath of the great cattle in their pens came to them as they walked—from the lighted inn, faintly, the sound of the gypsies' fiddles threaded the darkness, delicate strings of sound. Presently—quite early, to his wife's relief—David Eynsham said he should go to bed; she went too, and fell asleep at once, in this deep peace. But before midnight—her little clock with its luminous dial stood by her bedside—she was wakened by a tremendous clatter of horses' hooves galloping outside, suddenly cut short;

131

men's voices; then silence. David had taken a sleeping-pill, and never stirred; nor did he when two or three times, later in the night, the voices and the sound of galloping horses were repeated. How strange!—but still under the enchantment of that wonderful peace she slept again at once, each time.

Over breakfast, which they ate in the garden in the warm autumn sunshine, the donkeys still in attendance, she asked Hugo about the noises in the night—the two young men had been up and in the hides before dawn, and had brought back two brace of wild-duck and a couple of geese.

"Oh, those were the Czikös and the shepherds and swineherds; they ride in to eat and drink and sing, and then ride back again. Tonight you really must stay up and listen—they are marvellous. You might write a poem about them! We were up till half-past two this morning."

"You can't have slept much."

"Only two or three hours—but here this suffices."

"Mummy, they really are something out of this world! You *must* stay up tonight" Lucilla said, urgently. "Daddy quite likes sleeping alone, and you can undress in my room, and creep in. You *can't* miss it."

David Eynsham had breakfast in bed; when he appeared the party went off and drove about the Hortobagy in small low-hung carriages with two horses, better suited than cars to the earthen tracks. They visited some of the Czikös, the horse-masters who presided over the huge droves of horses; these men wore a most peculiar costume—full loose knee-length breeches of blue cotton, like Zouaves wear, a short tunic, and a round black felt hat with an up-turned brim, for all the world like the hats worn by Manchu coachmen under the old régime in China. Rosina, who as a child had been in Peking, where her Father held an appointment in the Chinese Customs Service, pointed this out to David.

"Of course" he said—for once not impatiently. "They're Magyars—and Magyars come from the Far East. They *are* practically Manchus."

132

One young Czikö showed his skill with the lasso, flinging a loop of rope from a considerable distance round a given horse and bringing it, kicking and helpless, to the ground. He invited Lucilla to try her hand; in her jodhpurs and shirt she looked so pretty, whirling the rope, but she was not very successful—she did better riding one of the graceful creatures, on which the Czikö threw a blanket for her.

They wandered far and wide over the great plain, the Puszta, in which the shallow lakes shone like blue enamel, with pallid clayey margins; they saw the tiny pointed wigwams, built of willow-boughs, in which the swineherds and cowherds and Czikös sheltered at night from the cold.

"And the shepherds?" Rosina asked.

"Some have shelters—more, not. They build fires, and they wear exceedingly thick coats—you will see tonight," Hugo told her, as they walked back past a flock of sheep so huge that it covered two or three acres with white rounded fleecy bodies; they were being moved, very slowly, to a fresh grazing-ground. Suddenly Mrs Eynsham came to a dead stop. "Oh, *what* is that?" she asked, gazing sky-wards and gesturing with her hand.

Away to their right, suspended in the pale blue arch of the heavens, hung a complete picture of a village—houses, streets, trees, a big church—but all upside down!—the trees were as dark a green, the church as white, the roofs of the houses as warm an Indian-red as on earth.

"Oh, the mirage!" Hugo said. "How fortunate we are to see it. I am glad for you."

"But why is it upside-down? I thought mirages looked real, I mean the right way up—so that they deceive travellers in the desert."

"I cannot tell you—the Hortobagy is not a desert, and here the images are always reversed."

"Anyhow it's quite exquisite" she said, staring entranced. "What a magical place this is."

"Yes, the Hortobagy is full of magic" the young man replied, seriously.

133

Well before sundown the whole party drove out again and took up their stations in hides by three of the larger meres, to await the wild geese and duck when they flew in at dusk. David Eynsham had equipped his family with what Hungarians used to call "Polish coats," long full-skirted affairs of sheepskin, the leather tanned to a soft suede on the outside, the fleece clipped close and short within, and fastened down the front with frogged loops of leather. A sheep's skin is practically waterproof, and Hungarians habitually wore these coats for the rather damp procedure of goose-shooting; the Enysham ladies soon saw why. David insisted on having a hide to himself; Hugo took Lucilla to another mere, and Count Endre escorted Mrs Eynsham to one still further on. The hides were merely round holes some four-and-a-half feet deep and less than six feet across, dug out in the stiff damp clay, with a narrow bench of sticky earth left on one side, facing the water, to sit on. Cramped in one of these, sitting knee to knee with Count Endre, Rosina could not but think of her Lucilla sitting in a similar damp hole, in equally close proximity to Hugo. But somehow she could not worry much; the enchantment of the place was strong on her as the vast simplified pageant of the sunset began, over the great empty plain—with distant lowing of cattle, the baa-ing of thousands of sheep, and the shrill whinnying of young horses being rounded up for the night. Oh, here was beauty and reality and peace—for a little while, for these few hours, let them forget the unhappy prisoners, the mistakes of the Red Cross, the menace overhanging Europe, and take what God sent! For the moment utterly happy she peered out of the hide at the blazing sky, the reddened waters, the bronze tone of the sunset-stained pastures on all sides.

In their hide half a mile away Lucilla and Hugo were discussing much the same idea.

"Are you happy, now, at this moment?" the young man asked.

"Yes, completely. It's so beautiful. Are you?"

"Yes. I shall be still more happy if we get some geese! But Lucilla, is this not curious, how one can live one's life on two

134

different levels at the same time? You endure fear and horror, don't you, about the bombing of your country, and what your prisoners suffer?" (He did not mention Hamish). "And I endure fear and horror too, at what will happen to my country—and my family—if the Germans come here. And yet this evening we can be happy, waiting for wild geese! I find this strange."

Lucilla considered.

"No, I don't think it all that strange" she said at length. "People have got to *live*, and we're given things to live by—for you and me, tonight, it's this place, and the sunset, and presently, with luck, some geese." He laughed. "No, but that's part of it, Hugo; shooting geese is a piece of the compensation you happen to be given for your back-ground terrors. Accept it—don't you think one ought to accept what one's given?"

"Yes, I do think so" he said, after a moment's pause. "One should accept the lightness of heart that comes, even when there are what you call 'back-ground terrors.' We both have them—and both for our country. But you are the better off. Your country is *committed*—mine is not."

"No—I think your Government are being lunatics about that" the girl said, but with no harshness in her voice. "They chose the wrong side in the last war, and lost Transylvania; what do they expect to happen if they choose the wrong side again this time?"

"I fear they will lose everything, whichever side they choose! Between the Germans and the Russians is not much of a choice!"

"But the Germans and the Russians are allies."

"Nonsense! This can never last—they are natural enemies. This Ribbentrop-Molotoff pact is merely a cover for treachery, on one side or the other. Poor Europe—how the clouds darken over her! We small States—we, and the Poles and the Serbs, and even the Rumanians—have our civilisations; as the Prussians and the Russians have *not*. But we lack military strength; we must be crushed by one or other of these huge, barbarian powers."

"Oh, don't!" she said, and put her hand on his. "I can't bear the thought of it, Hugo. But what can *we* do?"

135

"England? Nothing!" the young man said bitterly. "You gave a guarantee to Poland, yes—and what has happened to her? Invaded on one side by Germany, on the other by Russia; swamped, crushed. America could help, if she could ever begin to understand Europe; but this she cannot do. England and France and Belgium, the names she knows best, are 'colonial powers,' and so anathema—Mr Roosevelt has never heard of *Russian* 'colonial expansion' in Central Asia, and the cruel oppression of the small nations there. Pah!"

"I hate all this" Lucilla said quickly, sadly. "Just now, and here. I know it's all true, and *frightful* for you. And I started it—my fault. But just for now can't we stop, and go on taking what we are given?" This brief spell alone in the hide with Hugo suddenly seemed to her to have importance, and a sort of beauty; it was a thing too precious to be wasted on criticising America or Russia or Germany, or even the impotence of England—there were other times for those things. "Can't we?" she repeated.

"Yes; we will. Forgive me." Her hand was still on his; he took it and pressed it gently.

Suddenly out of the sky overhead came a most curious sound, really indescribable: very light, something between quacking and chattering, the talking of geese as they fly in onto a lake in the evening—utterly different from the loud honking of their high migration flights. "Here they are!" Hugo exclaimed under his breath, dropping Lucilla's hand abruptly; he raised and cocked his gun. During their conversation the light had faded, and stars were coming out in the pale sky; the great birds, skeining down onto the water, were only shadowy shapes in the near-darkness. "Perdition!" Hugo muttered; "one sees nothing! Keep your head down!" he hissed at Lucilla, who was craning her neck up to see the geese; as she crouched down, half-laughing, he leaned round backwards and fired—once, twice.

"Both! And both over the land!" he whispered, as he jerked the empty cartridges out of his gun, and re-loaded it. The sound of his shots had disturbed the birds coming in close to them—

other reports, from a distance, told them that Eynsham and Endre were also getting some sport.

"The duck should be here in a moment" Hugo whispered, peering into the darkling sky. "Ah yes, here they are! Damn!—they are coming in from the far side."

Lucilla could just make out the V-shaped formations flying in between her and the faint stars; the duck came in silence, till they landed with a little splash on the water. Hugo waited, and chose his moment well; his next two shots dropped a couple of duck close inshore. "I can get these easily" he said, still in a whisper; he was wearing waders under his sheepskin coat. "Are you cold?"

"No, it's fun. Exciting."

They waited a little longer; Hugo managed to shoot two more geese before it became too dark to see anything at all. Then he took Lucilla's hand and helped her up out of the hide, and switched on a powerful torch.

"I'll get the duck first. Ah, I see them." He waded into the shallow water and came back with two dripping feathered corpses. "Could you perhaps carry these? Now we must find the geese."

Lucilla, carrying the two wild-duck by their cold scaly legs, followed Hugo as he walked about, throwing the light of his torch over the rough coarse grass. This was all part of what they were being given—his satisfaction, and her share in it. But he could only find three geese. "That last one was flying fast—he may have planed some distance" he said. "The shepherds can have it!"

"You don't think it's wounded?" the girl asked, concerned.

"No" he replied abruptly. "We should hear it flapping about if it were. Stand still—let us listen." They stood; she watched the young man, tall, laden with birds, profiled against the first golden glow of the moonrise; the silence was absolute—the last birds had come in onto the mere. Then, in the distance, they heard the sound of the creaking of wheels.

"The others are going back—we must go too" he said. But for a moment he did not move. "You said we should take what we are given" he said then, slowly. "I am being given much, tonight."

Lucilla had an urgent desire to say how much *she* had been given, too. She had been more touched by his complete detachment and avoidance of any physical approach, cramped as they had been in the hide, than by the most passionate words he could have spoken. But she resisted the impulse—poor Hamish! She wouldn't, though, tarnish the gift with some inadequate phrase —she said nothing at all as they walked to where their little carriage waited. But as they drove back to the inn, over the darkened Puszta dotted, now, with the red gleams of the shepherds' fires, she murmured—"It's *beyond* beauty."

Dinner, accompanied by the gypsies' music and the pretty intrusiveness of the donkey and its foal, was late that night; the moment after coffee David Eynsham said he should go to bed. He had shot four duck and two geese, and was well content. "You stay up, Rosie, and hear the shepherds and Czikös sing— it's something you'll never hear anywhere else. You won't wake me if you don't spend ages fussing over your face."

"Mummy's going to undress in *my* room; and she never fusses over her face, not to any extent" Lucilla told her parent repressively.

"Feminine solidarity! 'Night, my poppet" David said, kissing his daughter. "Hugo, you translate the songs for them, won't you? You know them better than Endre."

When he had gone to bed the others left the small restaurant where they had eaten, and after taking a turn out-of-doors in the moonlight they went and sat down on trestle benches in a huge barn-like room which Rosina had not yet seen. At the further end were four large tables, each set for twenty or thirty—here, Hugo said, was where the people of the Hortobagy came and ate. "One set rides in, and eats, and then rides back to let their companions come." He went on to explain about the four tables.

138

"Each category—is that how you say it?—sits together; they do not mix. That table on the right is for the shepherds; they are counted the grandest. Next come the Czikös, then the cattle-keepers—and this table nearest us is for the swineherds, who rank the lowest of all."

"Poor swineherds!" Lucilla said laughing—she was very happy that night.

"Well pigs, as animals, are obviously less noble than cattle or horses" Count Endre said—"though they cannot possibly be sillier than sheep! Mrs Eynsham, do you like beer? It is rather good here, and we must spend a long time drinking."

Mrs Eynsham said that in that case she would rather go on with coffee, and switch to beer later; Lucilla followed her example.

About eleven, preceded by a clatter of horses' feet outside, a group of Czikös came in, in their exotic dress; they hung up their cloaks and Manchu hats on pegs on the wall, sat down at their own table, and proceeded to make a hearty meal, dipping bread in their bean soup and gulping down goulasch. They were followed by a dozen swineherds, who did the same at their humble table; and then by a number of cattle-tenders. Last of all in stalked several shepherds, wearing quite fantastic garments: white woollen coats heavily embroidered in black, but so thick and stiff that they merely *stood* them on the floor behind their table; the loose skirts crumpled down a little, but the tops stood up, nearly four feet high.

"This is what I spoke of" Baron Hugo murmured to Mrs Eynsham. "With such coats, they hardly need shelter; they can sit and keep watch in the open; for sheep it is better so."

Mrs Eynsham's eyes, absurdly, suddenly filled with tears. Here under her very eyes, today, in the twentieth century, was the reality that lay behind that most well-loved of Christmas hymns:

> "While shepherds watched their flocks by night
> All seated on the ground" ...

139

Where else did shepherds do that? Certainly not in the Highlands—if the Angel of the Lord came down anywhere in Europe
nowadays he would come to the Hortobagy, she thought, where
earthly "glory shone around" all the time, so far as she had seen.

Presently, over their wine, the various groups began to sing—
in turns, one table at a time; Hugo translated. For the most part
they were rather sad ballads, about cruel girls who betrayed
devoted men, or parted lovers—one described a shepherd watching a falcon sitting solitary in a tree: the bird had lost its mate,
so had he. But in spite of their melancholy the airs were beautiful, and of an almost Gregorian severity, and the men's voices
strong, filling the room with sad noble sound.

"They really sing splendidly" Rosina said to Hugo, when one
after another the tables emptied, and the singers galloped off
into the night.

"Their songs make love in Hungary out to be a very gloomy
thing" Count Endre said laughing. "Really we are rather gay
lovers."

"Love-songs are so often sad; I suppose happy love, like a
happy woman, has no history" Mrs Eynsham said, a little repressively. "But I was surprised that there were no drinking-songs—
they're such a feature of German and English folk-song."

"Forgive, but you and the Germans are both Teutons, races
for which drinking is an end in itself; we are Magyars, who drink
without noticing it" Count Endre said. "Have some beer, now—
the second parties will be coming in quite soon."

But Mrs Eynsham wouldn't have any beer. "I shall hear them
again tomorrow night. It's been wonderful."

The second day passed as sweetly as the first. The weather
held, the magic of the Hortobagy held: the inverted mirages
hung in the cloudless sky, they watched the great quiet flocks
and herds grazing on the boundless plain. Once near a large
mere, early in the morning, they saw an astonishing sight—a
flock of wild geese on migration resting quietly on the ground,
too exhausted to move; they covered nearly ten acres, though
set so close that they hid the rough grass. But when they went

out to shoot in the evening Lucilla insisted on sharing her Father's hide—"I want to see *you* shoot, Daddy." She did not want to risk a repetition of the evening before—it might be more, it might be less, but what she and Hugo had been "given" sufficed. And on the way back to her room the night before Endre had suddenly kissed her, as they walked through the garden, the only way of reaching their rooms; she was not going to have anything of *that* sort again from him. Other men in Hungary had kissed her before, and she had not minded; her sudden resentment this time sharpened an uncertainty already lurking in her mind about her feelings towards Hugo.

They breakfasted early on the Monday, David and all, before the long drive back; the gypsies, who usually lie in of a morning after playing late at night, were all up and dressed, and stood in the road outside the gate to play them off with a last rendering of the "Hortobagy Song"; the ass and her foal stood beside them. Rosina in her heart echoed the Minister's words, "A beautiful people."

Back in Budapest the outer world engulfed them all immediately: the Chancery David, the Bulletin Lucilla, the concerns of the prisoners Rosina. Martha Beckley came in almost the moment she reached her little office.

"Have a good time? So glad. Look, we have *some* funds in hand now, haven't we?"

"Yes. I shan't know how much till we've paid for having the shirts and pyjamas made up."

"Oh, they've come—they're all in the packing-room. Most *beautifully* done. Here's the bill; quite cheap, I think."

"Incredibly" Rosina said, after looking at it. "Yes, that will leave us quite a bit. I've paid for the mouth-organs and the orchestra. Why?"

"Oh, some merchants came to see me while you were away; the Dendrassys sent them, but I think the Min had a hand in it. They've got masses of most frightfully useful stuff—six-and-half tons of tinned sardines, and three or four of sultanas from Smyrna—just what we want, fats and sugar; but it's all on

141

Csepel Island, and it's the question of getting it out. I've told them to send samples and quote prices; but you will have to handle this."

Mrs Eynsham had never heard of Csepel Island, lying in the Danube below Budapest, except as the seat of the heavy industry promoted by the Weissbergers and their like.

"Why sardines *there?*" she asked.

Martha explained rapidly. Besides the factories, where loco-motives and rolling-stock were produced, the island had another function. Up the Danube, the great river-road from the South, a high proportion of its imports reached Central Europe; Csepel Island, furnished with quays and warehouses, was used as a sort of *entrepôt*, where goods were deposited pending further dis-posal. Those going up-stream to Austria, Czecho-Slovakia and Germany were shipped on free of duty; but anything which came out through the gates in the high wire fence to cross the bridge to the mainland, and be sold in Hungary, had to pay the full local tariff. "Pity to do that—and one oughtn't to, for Red Cross stuff. I'm sure you can fix it, Rosina. I've told the merchants to call on you tomorrow morning at eleven sharp, at your house. They're petrified of being seen coming here, poor devils."

"Jews, I suppose?"

"No, oddly enough, Hunks. But no one is safe here, today."

Mrs Eynsham found the samples when she got home after a rather long afternoon's work. Oflag VII C.H. had written to say that the Germans would allow them to have part of their yard flooded, so that they could play ice-hockey for exercise—to get exercise was one of the prisoners' main preoccupations. So could she send thirty or forty ice-hockey sticks, plenty of pucks, and thirty or forty pairs of skates and skating-boots, in assorted sizes? Here, Rosina decided, was where her Hungarian friends came in, and she dictated a letter asking for skates and skating-boots—"sixty copies, please, Miss Maudsley"—before driving down to Pest to buy the ice-hockey sticks and pucks, which she was given at the usual discount.

The sardines were very good—thick, tender, swimming in oil; each tin weighed just over a pound; the sultanas were plump, golden, and *clean*. Punctually at eleven next morning the merchants appeared. They explained about the duty on any goods leaving Csepel Island—"But for the Red Cross, if the lady could arrange it, it could come in duty-free, if it were consigned to the Legation. You have *franchise*." (*Franchise* is the technical expression for diplomatic exemption from paying duty on anything.) Mrs Eynsham told them that the samples were all right, but to their evident surprise she bargained rather hard over the prices asked; these were not high, but she wanted to save every penny. At last she told the men that she would let them know later, but meanwhile to reserve for her the whole six-and-a-half tons of sardines and one-and-three-quarter tons of sultanas—she had been doing some sums beforehand, and reckoned that this would provide quite a good little nibble for most of the 44,000, if a tin of sardines were shared between three. Of course the men ought to have that amount sent every week, but this was all they could afford at the moment. Pray God Uncle Jim raised some money!

There remained the question of getting the goods out. She debated with herself whether she should consult David about this, and decided against it; he had too much to do as it was, and she would get a better hearing from the Minister—who would have the final word in any case. She walked round to the Legation; on her desk, as well as the usual pile of appeals and cheques was a chit from Howard, enclosing the latest report from the U.S. Embassy staff in Berlin, who visited the prisoners' camps. It made gloomy reading. Against Oflag after Oflag, Stalag after Stalag, came brief comments: "Serious need of more clothing and shoes, cigarettes, soap." Soap! The Committee had never thought of that—Rosina made a note. "Warm underclothing, blankets, cigarettes." "Warm clothing, more blankets, underwear." "Blankets, socks, cigarettes." "Gloves, socks, clothing, Balaklava helmets, blankets." Blankets, blankets, blankets!—if only the Red Cross would answer about those quilts, and give

143

the money, every man in every camp could have a quilt within a few weeks. Anyhow here was superb ammunition for the letters to those in high places which she had not yet managed to get written—wise Min! After enquiring through Martha she went along the corridor to see him.

"I gather from David that the Hortobagy party was a great success" he said. "*You*, I may say, never came to tell me!"

"No. Such a huge back-log of letters. But it was heaven—such rest and peace."

"You look the better for it" he said. "But I fear you haven't come in just for a happy gossip; we never seem to have time for those now. Have you a problem?"

"Yes, as always! I *am* sorry to bother you so often."

"Don't be foolish. You know that you are never a bother, and *I* know what you are doing. Go on."

Rosina told him about the sardines and sultanas. "I gather you may have heard a murmur about them" she said carefully. "Can we have them sent here?"

"No. They won't be consumed by the Legation staff. This is a matter for the Commercial Department of the Hungarian Foreign Office. I think you had better arrange it by yourself—it will simplify things for me."

"But I can't!" Rosina was horrified. "How can I?"

"See old Willie about it. Tell him I said *you* must do it. Oh by the way, you've heard about the raid?"

"No—what raid?"

"The R.A.F., on Milan and Turin. They flew slap over the Alps, and did terrific damage. This will make a good party tomorrow, I fancy—the whole place is ringing with it. Quite a surprise for the Duce! Oh, and one other thing" the Minister added, "don't discuss your problem with Willie on the telephone—you will have to see him. Fairer to him."

Mrs Eynsham accordingly merely told the Prince when she rang up that she wanted urgently to see him. He was not coming up to Budapest for some time; she was bidden to stay at Siraly. David was so much better, and the servants so good, that she

144

decided to go—but she rang up Dr Mendze and asked him to keep an eye on her husband while she was away.

She arrived at Siraly just before All Souls Day, and on the first morning the Prince took her down to the garden, where all was bare and neat, the black empty beds ready dug to receive the blessing of the loosening frost—there were no flowers save in the green-houses, which were a scene of intense activity. The gardeners were busy tying evergreens and moss onto wire frames for wreaths of all sizes, three or four hundred of them; the head-gardener and his two immediate assistants were cutting white carnations and chrysanthemums and fastening them onto the green-clad wreaths, and then carrying them through into a cool house.

"Goodness, are these for Budapest?" Rosina asked. For once the Prince gave her his famous cold stare.

"No. These are for myself and my people. I always supply the wreaths for their families on All Souls. You will see."

And on All Souls Day she did see. After a thronged Mass in the village church the whole congregation, led by Prince Willie, carrying a wreath almost as large as himself, walked in procession to the cemetery, laden with wreaths, and deposited them on the graves; many of the women, kneeling, lit candles and stuck them in the ground, muttering prayers for the souls of the departed. It was something Rosina never forgot, this practical thought and care for the beloved dead: the Mass, the flowers on every grave, the murmured prayers, the candles flickering under a dark lowering sky. And there was such a *solidarity*, such a close link of affection between the Prince and his "people," his peasants and tenants—before he left they all came to kiss the *Durchlaucht's* hand, and thank him, and promise their prayers for him and his. How the Roman Catholic religion did *tie* people together, she thought—most of all the living, but the dead were tied in too.

Women never normally entered the Prince's study; it was a male preserve. But when Mrs Eynsham told him that the Minister had advised her to consult him privately on an extremely confidential matter, she was admitted to this sanctum—full of books, cigar-smoke, and leather armchairs. She there unfolded the problem of the stores on Csepel Island.

The Prince tapped his fingers on his desk, and considered.

"It is complicated" he said at length. Rosina's heart sank—he gave his little dry laugh at the dismay in her face. "No—I am sure it can be done, but there will have to be a formal agreement. Will the Minister sign this?"

"He said *I* was to do it" Rosina said unhappily. Oh dear—she did want the prisoners to have all those tons of sardines.

"Sir Hugh is a clever man!" the Prince said. "Well—yes—perhaps—everything will be sent under the aegis of our Red Cross." He pulled out a sheet of paper, and wrote on it. "Yes—'Parcels in Transit for Prisoners of War'—I think some formula of that sort will do. But I shall have to come up and see the Regent myself." He paused. "And who *will* sign on the English side?"

"Me, I suppose" Rosina said doubtfully. "Sir Hugh said I was to do it all."

Prince Tereny laughed consumedly.

"This will be something quite new in international relations! —a lady in a Legation signs a Treaty with a foreign government! Never mind; I daresay it can be made to work, in the very exceptional circumstances. I will arrange somehow to come up the day after tomorrow, and have a little talk with the Old Boy."

The "Old Boy," Admiral Horthy, Regent of Hungary, is another of the people to whom England, in the shape of her prisoners and their relations, owed more than she, or they, ever realised. This very unusual arrangement *was* made to work; Mrs Eynsham signed a document concerning the release of "Goods in Transit" from Csepel Island, to be consigned to British prisoners-of-war in Germany, bearing the labels of the Hungarian Red Cross. The Hungarians were "beautiful people."

10

Packing six-and-a-half tons of sardines was more than Mr Smith and the Legation staff could cope with—for one thing this amount couldn't be got into Rosina's dining-room. She consulted Baron Weissberger, who put her in touch with a little Jewish *expéditeur* called Hasler; he and his lorries, armed with a paper signed by Rosina, collected the crates from Csepel, and re-packed them in accordance with a list supplied by her of the amounts for each camp; she also furnished him with the requisite number of Red Cross labels, and Horace went down to Hasler's establishment and clamped on the seals. The Hungarian Red Cross now made a slight fuss; they were running out of lead!—somehow more lead was coaxed out of someone. When all this was duly reported to the Relief Committee Colonel Morven asked—"And what about the sultanas?"

"Well we haven't tackled them yet—I wanted to know what you all thought. Hasler's bill is quite moderate, but it all mounts up."

"How many sultanas are we getting?"

"One and three-quarter tons."

"That's nothing!" said the Colonel airily. "Let's do those ourselves—save money." This was agreed.

But a ton and three-quarters of sultanas—3,910 lbs, to be exact—in fact occupy quite a lot of space; after taking one look at the lorry-load outside her door Mrs Eynsham rang up Sir Hugh, and with his permission had them transported to the Legation and dumped in the wide inner *porte-cochère* or passage off which the Bulletin office opened, to be dealt with there. They were in

147

8-kilogram wooden cases, but these had to be opened, the contents weighed, and repacked in grease-proof paper bags to meet the 5-kilo parcel regulations. A couple of tables and a set of kitchen scales were brought down, and the whole Committee turned to pack; Anton and several of the servants were laid on to help. While this business was happily—if rather stickily—proceeding Sonia Marston strolled across the courtyard and watched.

"How convenient to have the Minister in one's pocket" she observed. "Servants and all!"

Rosina knew that this amiable remark was aimed at her, and bent her head over her work of tying up grease-proof bags. But Horace Wheatley, busy sticking labels on cartons and ticking them off on a list looked up and said—"Did anyone *ask* you to come here, Miss Marston?"

"No—I was in talking to Geoffrey, and I just came over to see what all the activity was about."

"Well now you've seen, perhaps you'll go away. We're packing food for British prisoners-of-war, if that is of any interest to you."

"Horace, I'm English!" the journalist said indignantly.

"Oh really? Good" Wheatley said, rubbing a small damp sponge over a carton and sticking a label onto it.

Colonel Morven, busy shovelling sultanas into the kitchen scales with a large flour-scoop, raised his great figure to its full height and said, with the utmost calmness—

"Clear off, Sonia. You're being tiresome."

"I shall see the Minister about this!" Miss Marston said furiously.

"*Which* Minister?" Wheatley asked, still plying his sponge. "The German, or ours?"

"Sonia, I told you to clear off" the Colonel repeated. "You'll only get a raspberry if you go to H.E." Gulping with anger, Miss Marston went away.

"Tiresome, silly creature" the Military Attaché said, as he carefully tipped another kilogram of sultanas into a bag. "Poor

148

girl. Wretched for her, though." He too knew about the girl's home background.

"She spent last week-end at one of those hotels on the Balaton with von Schaffhausen" Eleanor Wheatley said.

"Poor girl" the Colonel repeated.

A few days before this disagreeable scene Mrs Eynsham, in the small hours, had managed to draft several letters about the failure of the British Red Cross to get parcels to the prisoners to various highly-placed people in England, quoting the reports of the American Inspectors of camps—her letters were the more forcible since she had by then received poor Lady Otmoor's missive, sent on by Uncle Jim; she quoted this too. "It is all *lies* to say that the Red Cross are sending parcels from the Balkan States; I was down there myself earlier, and I have just telephoned to the Legations to check. *Nothing* is coming from there, except through us. Canada I don't know about, but as for Lisbon, the parcels are just sitting there—that I *do* know. If they can't help it, they can't; but I do hate untruthfulness."

These imprudent but forcible missives produced a certain reaction. Indignant and highly-placed mothers and even grandmothers called on equally highly-placed officials in the Foreign Office and the War Office. "She can *talk* to Berlin and Geneva on the telephone—can the Red Cross do that? Or you? And her parcels get there in a few days. Why doesn't the Red Cross send *her* our money?" The highly-placed officials were embarrassed.

"Rosina really *has* torn it this time" a friend in the Foreign Office wrote to David. "Lady C. called on the Secretary of State yesterday, and fairly beat him up. Can't you get her to softpedal? This sort of thing won't do you any good, you know."

David Eynsham was normally a man wholly devoted to his Service, and highly suspicious of all feminine activities, more especially those conducted by his wife; but this letter roused him to quite unwonted fury.

"I don't know what you are all thinking about in the Foreign Office" he wrote to his friend the Private Secretary. "Is it whitewashing the Red Cross? Here, where we *know* what is going on in the camps, we happen to be thinking about the British prisoners-of-war; some of them have lost two or three stone in weight since they were captured in June, from underfeeding. My wife, and the staff, are trying to *feed* them—something which so far the British Red Cross has signally failed to do in, now, nearly five months. If you think I care a tinker's.... about my career in comparison with helping these men, you are quite mistaken." He added—"I may say that we are now sending 2,500 five-kilogram parcels a month to Germany. If instead of trying to get me to quell Rosina, you would turn your attention to compelling the Red Cross to send *us* funds to do what we can do, and they, it seems, can't, you would be occupying your time better."

Eynsham showed both these letters to his chief—"I think you ought to see these, Sir." The Minister was surprised at this formality; he discouraged the use of "Sir" from his senior staff. When he had finished reading he looked up at his Counsellor with an unusually warm smile.

"Do you think any action is required from me, David?"

"Not unless you wish to take any, Sir. But I thought you ought to see my reply to X. before I sent it."

"Since I can't get at Master X. to give him a good clip over the ear, which is what I should like to do, I think your letter is the next best thing, David. Good for you—send it off. How are you feeling?"

"Oh, not too bad, thank you, H.E. This sort of thing doesn't help—Mendze says I'm not to get angry, but who can avoid being angry over all this?"

"Do avoid it—I need you here. And remember that I am behind you and your wife—and the Committee" he added carefully, "to the end—whenever that comes."

At the beginning of December 1940 the War Office in London suddenly forbade any further despatches of private parcels to officers or men in the prisoners' camps; everything had to be sent to the *Vertrauens-mann,* the British "Man-of-Confidence,"

150

for general distribution. In theory this may have been a good idea—"fair shares for all"; but it was a severe blow to the little Relief Organisation. Hitherto, since parcels for a high proportion of the officer prisoners had been financed by cheques from England, they had been able to devote all the money raised from local sources to meeting the needs of the men in the Stalags, and to such extras as the musical instruments, the ice-hockey sticks and mouth-organs. Now they could no longer do this, for the British Government took the quite extraordinary step of "freezing" all the Relief Accounts which most members of the staff had opened in their banks in London to receive the cheques from the distracted relations. Right or not, the thing was done in an ugly way, and caused the maximum of embarrassment—since people who had paid for parcels for their menfolk for months ahead had to be told that not only could Tom, or Dick, or Harry be sent nothing more, but that they themselves could not be reimbursed. Careless Rosina, too unmethodical ever to have thought of opening a separate account for the prisoners, scored here; all her cheques, including a most useful £300 from the Scottish Red Cross, had been paid into her private account, which could not be touched. David laughed delightedly when this came to his knowledge.

"Oh Rosie, who would ever have thought that incompetence could pay such a high dividend?"

She pulled his ears and gave him a kiss.

Lucilla was rather remote now from this part of her Mother's life. She spent most of her day and much of many nights in the Bulletin office; when she had a free evening she went out to dine and dance with her friends. She continued to see a lot of Hugo—his gentleness and affection were an extraordinary solace to her, and after that tranquil evening together in the hide she felt perfectly safe with him. She needed solace more than ever after the War Office decision. Sending a weekly parcel to Hamish, containing most of her own ration of Virginia cigarettes, had somehow put her right with herself, reassured her

151

divided heart; every time she smoked a distasteful Balkan one she thought of her fiancé, and felt that she was doing right by him. Now this fragile safeguard had come to an end.

"Mummy, is there *nothing* we can do? It seems so outrageous, when the Red Cross isn't sending anything whatever."

"No, darling, I'm afraid we can't do anything."

"Don't *you* think it outrageous?" Lucilla demanded.

"Yes. Worse; very silly. They've cut off funds that *were* available to feed some people, and aren't replacing them. How do they expect us to raise extra money now? Human feeling is human feeling—or psychology, or whatever they call it" Rosina said with her usual vagueness. "But it's no good expecting politicians to pay any attention to things like that—they think about votes, not about realities." Lucilla laughed and kissed her Mother, and went back to her work.

That night—it was one of her rare free evenings—Hugo and Emmi took her to dine and dance at the Parisian Grill with a party of young people. This restaurant, very fashionable, had a peculiar feature: a revolving dance-floor, which in its circuit passed behind the bandstand through a narrow shadowed space bounded by a curved wall, on which (feeling being what it was then in Budapest) young gentlemen were apt to scrawl political slogans with their partners' lipsticks, completing these on successive rounds. Sonia Marston was there that evening with a German journalist; when they got up to dance Hugo said to Lucilla—"Let us follow, and see if they write anything." They did—"Heil H . . ." was scrawled on the first round.

"What do we write?" the young man asked, as they emerged into the light again.

"God Save The King?"

"Too long. 'Hoch England!' I think. Where is your lipstick?" Lucilla got it out, and "Hoch England" followed "Heil Hitler" on the curved wall. By this time they were both rather excited, but Lucilla was taken by surprise when on a last round Hugo suddenly kissed her mouth deliberately, back-stepping to keep their place in the dark passage—she made a little startled movement. But the small episode told her some very unwelcome facts about her own feelings. She was not in the least angry with Hugo, being kissed by him was heaven; and his apologies when he was taking her home in the taxi made her realise that she loved him as she never had and never could love Hamish. When would Hamish ever have worried about whether one did or didn't want to be kissed?

She put up a front, of course, poor child.

"Yes, well you oughtn't to have done it, and you mustn't again" she said. "But don't worry—these things happen, I know." He kissed her hand.

"Then I may still see you?"

"Of course."

Shortly before Christmas rumours began to fly through Vienna and Budapest concerning the escape of several British officers from the Oflag where Hamish was confined—first by word of mouth, then in the Press; they were said variously to be making for Persia, for Palestine, for Spain. This last seemed highly improbable, since that particular Oflag was right up near the Polish frontier, and they would have to cross the whole of Germany and Occupied France to approach the Pyrenees; the obvious place for them to try to reach was Hungary, whence there was a certain amount of coming and going across "the Green Frontier," the long stretch of forest and mountain which was not watched sufficiently closely to seal it altogether. Geoffrey Milton ingeniously contrived to put out a counter-rumour—he was good at that sort of thing: "Reliable sources believe that the escaped Britons have reached Scandinavia by sea"—and this much more probable version was generally accepted.

A few days later something happened which emphasised Lucilla's feelings about Hugo more clearly than ever. She had been asked to a party at the Dendrassys, but had left it open— "I'll come if I can"—because Hugo had asked her to go with him to the Looping Bar; and to prove to herself that she was not afraid of being alone with him, after his kiss at the Parisian Grill, she said Yes. He was to pick her up at home about ten;

153

she dined with her Mother, dressed afterwards, and then sat waiting for the ring at the front door bell—Mrs Eynsham had gone back to her office in the Legation. Ten o'clock came, ten-fifteen, half-past ten—no sign of Hugo. At a quarter past eleven, furious with him for letting her down, she rang up Elsa Dendrassy and said that she would love to come, *now,* if it wasn't too late. Of course it wasn't, nothing used ever to be too late in Hungary; a taxi was sent for and she drove off, still fuming at Hugo. But as the cab spun down the winding road and across the Danube, strung with lights, over the Chain Bridge—the Dendrassys lived down in Pest—the young girl was disturbed by her own anger. Would she be so enraged if she were stood up by someone she didn't care tuppence about?

It was a question she didn't care to examine just then—where had she read that to be angry with a man was a warning signal? Oh yes, Helen in "Howards End," of course. But was it invariably true? As her taxi pulled up before the Dendrassys' house another pulled in in front of it, and Endre Erdöszy got out—he was late too, it seemed; they went up in the lift together. Presently he asked her to dance, and out of pique she began to flirt with him a little, lightly. Now when he kissed her in the czarda garden on the Hortobagy not so long before she had set him down very sharply indeed; at this new *démarche* on her part Endre tilted his long, permanently amused face back a little, and studied hers with a quizzical gaze.

"How we do blow hot and cold, don't we?" he said, looking more amused than ever as she blushed a little. "Can it be that we are rather a flirt, after all?—in spite of seeming so strait-laced?"

Lucilla, already upset, was so disconcerted by this direct attack that she forgot all discretion, and blurted out the fact of Hugo's defection—"He never even rang up!"

For the first time since she had known him the young man's face lost all hint of amusement; he turned deadly serious, and waltzed her out of the room into an open hall-way, brightly lit—it was empty.

154

"Where was he taking you?" he asked.

"To the Looping Bar. But why?"

"At what time?"

"Well, he was to call for me at ten, or a little before." She was startled by these imperious questions, and his unwonted manner.

"Listen to me, Lucilla. If *anyone*, however well you know them, should ask you where you were tonight between ten and, say, nearly half-past eleven, you must say that you *were* at the Looping Bar with Hugo."

Now something made her feel rather frightened.

"But—but why on earth should I?" she asked, uncertainly.

"Because it might mean the difference between life and death, for him." The band struck up again, and he started jigging her about in a slow fox-trot.

"Could you explain why?" she asked, in a very small voice indeed, as they shuffled round the empty landing.

"Not fully—no. But you are not too stupid to take a hint, I fancy" he said with a fleeting grin. "He does undercover work; so do I—and we are often called upon to do it at short notice, and cannot telephone. I was late here tonight, as you saw—and for a similar reason. But it is all for the Allies."

At this point Countess Dendrassy appeared in a doorway. "Don't forget that you have been in the Looping Bar" Endre muttered in her ear as he danced her over towards their hostess.

"Children, what are you playing at out here?" Elsa Dendrassy asked.

"A little privacy, Elsa" Count Endre said cheerfully. "But now we return."

Lucilla was puzzled by all this, and rather disturbed; but she had lived all her life in what her Father cheerfully referred to as "an atmosphere of hideous secrets," and she asked no further questions. When one or two of her subsequent partners enquired why she had come late she said carelessly—"Oh, I was at the Looping Bar with Hugo; but it was rather dull, so I came on here."

A couple of days after the Dendrassys' dance Dr Mendze rang

up David Eynsham and asked if he could come down to the clinic that morning for his weekly check.

"I'd sooner come at tea-time" Eynsham said—he was busy, as usual.

"I am afraid this does not suit me; please to come when I say" the Dr replied, very firmly.

"Oh very well" the Counsellor said coldly, after a glance at his engagement block—"I'll come at 11.15." Tiresome old man, he thought, breaking into the morning's work; however he went.

After making the examination with his usual care the doctor said—"Would you mind coming across to the Szanatorium for a minute? I will explain as we go."

"I really ought to get back" Eynsham objected.

"No, it is essential that you come." Out in the street—the nursing-home was barely two hundred yards away—the old doctor, safe among the hurrying and indifferent passers-by, said—"I have two English prisoners-of-war here; so they say. I want you to speak with them, to establish their *bona-fides;* something I myself cannot do. This is why I sent for you. I think they are two of those whose escape was reported. But I cannot keep them long—I would like them to leave this evening."

"How on earth did *you* get hold of them?" Eynsham asked.

"One of our agents went up and brought them down from the frontier—he has done much of this work for the Poles, also. I think you know him, young Weissberger?"

"Hugo? Oh yes—a good boy."

A nursing-home is a place where people can come and go unquestioned, if escorted by the doctor. In a chintzy room very like the one where he had recently spent so many weeks David Eynsham encountered two very tall men, most oddly dressed for British officers. Muddy trousers of shoddy cloth and windproof zip-jackets with fleece collars; on the bed lay two high sheepskin hats—the whole constituting a very fair reproduction of country winter dress in Central Europe. A few minutes conversation satisfied him that they were British officers: a Major Dougal Malcolm and a Captain Donald Campbell of Escairt,

156

both of the Argylls. "What was your Mother's Christian name?" he asked the younger man.

"Lorna, Sir."

"I thought so. Where from?"

"Kinlochruel."

"That's all right" Eynsham said to Mendze. "They're genuine. I'll send someone down to collect them tonight, at seven, with a taxi." He had already decided what must be done with the prisoners. But the Major wanted reassurance about David's *bona-fides,* after being bundled about from one foreign guide to another, across strange frontiers, and finally fetching up in what seemed to be a hospital.

"I beg your pardon, Sir, but might I ask who you are?"

"Yes of course—sorry. I'm Counsellor at the British Legation here; my name is Eynsham."

The younger man got up off the edge of one of the beds. "You're really *English?* How wonderful. Can't you stay a minute or two?" It was clear that he couldn't take his eyes off an Englishman.

"Not just now; I'll be seeing you later" Eynsham said smiling.

"Shall *you* come to fetch us?" the Major asked.

"Certainly *not*" Mendze put in, decisively. "This is a sick man, a patient of mine. He must not run about."

David, grinning, pulled an envelope from his wallet, tore off the flap, and wrote on it—"Go with bearer." He handed it to the Major.

"Whoever comes to fetch you will have a duplicate of that, so that you can compare the writing." He turned to the doctor. "Very good of you, Mendze—can't thank you enough. Now I must go. Good-bye—see you later" he said to the two prisoners, and went away.

Back at the Legation he had a brief conference with Sir Hugh.

"Yes, they'd better come here. The P.C.O. or one of his people can fetch them; the M.A.'s away today. What did Mendze say about you, David?"

"Oh going on fine, thank you."

157

"Good."

The Minister then summoned Martha.

"Can you fix up a couple of beds in those spare-rooms opposite the Bulletin? Without the servants helping?"

"I'm not sure—they're pretty crammed with what came out of the office. When for?"

"This evening."

"I'll go and look."

She was back in a couple of minutes.

"We could do it with Tom." (Tom was the English boxer night-porter.) "There's a lot of heavy stuff to shift."

"No, don't use Tom; get hold of Horace."

"Right—and get the radiator vent key from Anton, Min, will you, so that I can let out any air-locks. The chauffage hasn't been on in those rooms, and they're like a morgue. Will they want sheets? That will mean asking Minnie—she keeps the linen-room locked."

"Then we'll do without sheets."

"I can snitch some towels and pillow-cases out of the upstairs spare-room" Martha said, "and put bottles in the beds. But do get me that key pronto, Min."

He rang for Anton.

"Can you get food there without ordering it specially?" Sir Hugh asked.

"Oh yes, easily. I often have sandwiches and a thermos of soup brought to the office, and so does Lucilla."

Anton entered at this point, and was told to bring the vent key. "Does the Excellency's radiator not function?" the nice man asked, looking distressed. Sir Hugh gave him a cold glance.

"His Excellency likes his orders obeyed" he said very quietly. "Bring me the key."

"I'm not perfectly sure about Anton" he said to Martha, when the servant had gone. "It has been suggested to me that he is in the pay of the Gestapo."

"Oh well, they've got to look to the future, haven't they?" Martha said tolerantly. "We shan't be here for ever, p'raps not

158

for so long at all. Dear Anton! Look, Min—I'm sure your unexpected and furtive guests will be dying for eggs and bacon
for breakfast, but that we *can't* do; they'll have to put up with
milk and cereal and bread-and-butter."

He smiled his sidelong smile at her.

"Most complete and admirable of Marthas, that will suffice.
I don't need to tell you anything! Who will be monitoring tonight?"

"Lucilla and Phyllis."

"Can you stand Phyllis off and be there yourself?"

"Of course, if you'd prefer it that way."

Martha hastily cancelled a date for a film that she really wanted
to see, and spent a strenuous afternoon shifting furniture with
Horace Wheatley, making up sheetless beds, and filling and
re-filling hot-water bottles from the kettle on which the Bulletin
staff perpetually made tea. She sent Horace out to buy china:
bowls, plates, cups and saucers, spoons—"The servants will want
to take away everything they bring overnight, and then there'll
be nothing to use for breakfast. Oh what a worry!"

"No knives? Are the poor toads to live on slops?" Horace asked
grinning—he, like Martha, guessed what was afoot.

"Yes—slops and sandwiches!" Martha said with her brief
laugh. "Oh, and bring a tea-pot, Horace—Franz will spot it at
once if ours is missing."

From the point of view of concealment the prisoners' hide-
out could not have been better arranged. The door leading into
the suite was so far inside the arched passage (where the sultanas
had been unpacked) that it was impossible to see it from the
glazed corridors round the main courtyard, and most of its windows gave onto the garden, which ended at the very lip of the
Bastion slope, with nothing but air beyond. All the same, when
she had finished Martha closed all the shutters, locked the main
door of the suite, and pocketed the key. Then she went and did
a little of her neglected editorial work, after standing Phyllis
off; she also told the servants to bring two thermoses of soup
and two lots of sandwiches to her office that evening.

159

Precisely at 7 p.m. the Minister came down and tapped on Martha's door. "Give me the key" he said. "I'm meeting them at the garden gate."

This also could not have been more convenient to their purpose. A very small narrow street, which rejoiced in the name of Lilac-utca, led down on one side of the Legation to the Bastion; it was a blind alley, little used save by lovers for dalliance in the shadows. But a door in the high wall of the Legation garden opened onto it; and there, after unlocking it, the Minister stood in the dark, waiting. He heard a taxi pause up in the Verböczy-utca; then, silhouetted against the bright lighting there he saw two very tall figures, wearing high sheep-skin caps, coming down through the dimly-lit little street towards him. As they approached they walked more slowly, peering uncertainly about them in the darkness; when they came level with the door Sir Hugh said—"Good evening. In here," in a low voice. They followed him in; he re-locked the door and led them across the garden, through the passage, and into the room prepared for them.

There he introduced himself. "I am the British Minister in Budapest." And while they stood, blinking a little in the bright light, in the warm pretty room, he took a good look at his guests —their immaculately shaven faces were in strong contrast to their odd and rather shabby clothes.

"Well, I hope you'll be all right here" Sir Hugh said. "A bit cramped, I'm afraid. Delighted to have you. I mustn't stay now, or I may be missed; the Military Attaché will be seeing you tomorrow. You'll get some supper presently—rather scratch, I fear, but the servants don't know you're here, and *mustn't* know. That's why there are no sheets—so sorry."

"Is this really the British Embassy?" the younger officer asked, with a wistful eagerness.

"No, the Legation—not an Embassy in Hungary. Look, you can open one shutter on the garden side, there"—he pointed— "when you put your lights out. But when you're using the passage put one of those very *peculiar* jackets across the doorsill, so

160

that the light won't show. Bathroom and lavatory are first on the left; but don't use those between 7.30 and 9 a.m. tomorrow, when the servants are about. You can have baths tonight, all right."

"Can we really, Sir? How grand."

"Yes—but before eleven; the night-watchman starts his rounds then."

"Thank you—we'll do that. Frightfully good of you to have us."

"Not at all—so glad. Good night."

"Good night, Sir."

Martha was lurking at the door of the Bulletin office.

"Everything O.K.?"

"Yes. Here's the key. You can send their supper across any time now."

"How many are there?"

"Only two."

"I wonder what happened to the others" Martha speculated.

"I didn't ask—I must get upstairs again. Such a nuisance Morven being out shooting with the Regent, today of all days. You just feed them—I've told them about the shutters, and their baths."

Martha went back to the office, where Lucilla was monitoring the wireless on the bathroom stool. "Getting anything?" she asked.

"Radio Toulouse—nothing much."

"Well I'll take over now. Listen, Lucilla. There are two escaped British prisoners in a room across the passage."

"Goodness! Some of *them*?" the girl asked.

"I think so. Anyhow you nip across with that tray of sandwiches and thermoses that's on the table in the main office. Better take a look at the courtyard before you start."

"If they *do* come from there, they're bound to have news of Hamish" Lucilla said eagerly.

"I should think so. I think you'd better wait while they eat their suppers, and bring the tray back; we don't want more running to and fro than we can help. Here's the key; lock them in when you leave."

Lucilla found the tray, and went out to look at the courtyard. Lights shone in some of the Chancery windows on the ground floor, and all round the glazed corridors on the next storey; the whole space was brightly lit—it was quite empty. She unlocked the door of the opposite suite, picked up the tray, and took it in; she had to set it on the floor while she re-locked the door. The little passage was dark save for a line of light showing under one door; she tapped on this.

"Who is there?" said a voice.

"Your supper. Could you open the door?" Lucilla said nervously—when the door opened she picked up the tray and took it in, looking with the deepest interest at the two men in the room as she set it down on the table, already laid with Horace's crockery.

"*Ham* sandwiches, by Jove!" one of them said, lifting the cover of the Pyrex dish.

"Yes—do start. I hope you don't mind if I wait to take the tray back."

"*Mind!* I haven't seen an English girl for nearly a year! Are you the Minister's daughter?" the older man asked, as they both fell to on the soup and sandwiches.

"No, he's a bachelor!" Lucilla said, laughing a little. "My Father is the Counsellor." She perched on the arm of one of the chintz easy-chairs.

"No idea what that is. Does he give counsel?"

"I hope so—anyhow he's Number Two in the Legation." She was longing to ask about Hamish, but hesitated to do so while they were absorbed in their food.

"It seems incredible that we should really be in the British Legation" the younger man said. "Safe at last!" He was staring at her almost as greedily as he was eating his food. "I suppose you haven't such a thing as a tomato?" he asked.

"No. I'll try to get some tomorrow, but I doubt it."

"Donald is mad on vitamins" the older officer said, looking amused.

"Oh well, I believe the Min's chef might have some green paprikas in the frig—I'll see. They're practically solid vitamins!"

When they reached the stage of coffee, provided by Martha in her own thermos, it occurred to Lucilla to offer them cigarettes.

"Not *Players?* God Almighty! I began to think I should never smoke a real Virginia again" the younger man said, inhaling deeply. "Can one get them here?"

"We do—they come by bag." At last she put her question. "*Do* you come from Oflag XXX?"

"Yes. We were the lucky ones" the Major said, also smoking with intense satisfaction. "We had the rounds of the outer patrol taped to the second, and there ought to have been ample time for the five of us to get clear—we drew lots, of course, for the order we left in. But for some reason the patrol came round ten minutes earlier that night, and spotted the other three; they wouldn't halt, tried to run for it, and they were shot—Jock Campbell and Toby Graham and Hamish MacNeil, all such *good* chaps."

He went on to describe how they had seen this, waiting in the shadow of a small building for their companions to join them— "But then the alarm went, and we heard the patrol calling for the dogs, so we cleared off. There was nothing we could do for them —the guards switched on the search-lights the moment they heard the shots, and we could see that none of them was moving. It was a damned shame."

So there, in that over-crowded bedroom, Lucilla learned of her fiancé's death. She sat, rather white, holding the back of the chintz armchair tightly, while the two soldiers went on recalling their adventures, clearly enjoying this first opportunity of doing so safely, to an Englishwoman, on English territory. Oh, *poor* Hamish! But she asked no more questions; she tried to think of proper responses to make to their narrative: "*No?*" "Goodness!" "Not really?" she kept saying at intervals, and offering them more cigarettes. At one point, lighting another, the young Captain said—"I say, if you really have Players here, do you think we could buy a few?"

163

"Yes, I'll bring you three hundred tomorrow—I don't need them now." The "now" slipped out unthinkingly, in her increasing agitation; of course she hadn't needed them for Hamish since the hateful, hateful War Office had stopped her private parcels to him.

"Why not now?" the Major asked, innocently.

"Oh, I'm getting to like Balkans." But she must get away—she couldn't stand any more of this. She put her cigarette-case—a long folding one, a present from Hamish—on the table.

"I'll leave you those for tonight. I'd better take the tray back now. Will you wash out your cups in the bathroom? I'll take these bowls back for the servants to see." Her emotions were so confused that she was getting almost incoherent.

"Can't I take the tray?" the Major asked.

"As far as the door. Switch out the passage light while I have a look." He stood holding the tray in the darkened corridor while she unlocked the door and examined the courtyard. Most of the Chancery lights were out now, but the blazing upper passages still illuminated it, again perfectly empty.

"O.K. I'll take it now. Don't talk after eleven, or the night watchman may hear you."

"You couldn't stay a little?—or come back?" the younger man said, over the Major's shoulder. "It's so wonderful to talk to someone English."

"No!" Lucilla hissed, desperately. "Good night. Shut the door quietly."

"Can't thank you enough" the Major said. "Good night."

She slipped across the passage to the Bulletin office, opened the outer door, picked up the tray again, and started to carry it into the big room with the roneo machine, where it was always left on the table—she meant to go back and lock the two prisoners in. But in her distraught state she stumbled against a pile of Bulletins on the floor; the tray slipped from her hands and crashed to the ground. This small disaster overset Lucilla altogether; she sank down on a chair and burst into tears.

164

11

Martha Beckley, making shorthand notes on the stool in the bathroom, heard the smashing of crockery and muttered— "Damn. Silly little clot!" But she didn't leave the wireless, because she was listening to one of the really inspired things which the B.B.C. did during the War. That evening, December the 20th, 1940, was the first anniversary of the suicide of Captain Langsdorf, the Commander of the crack German "pocket battleship," the *Admiral Graf Spee;* wounded by British warships she had taken refuge in the harbour at Monte Video, but on Hitler's orders her Captain took her to sea and scuttled her—then, in Buenos Aires, he shot himself. That night, a year later, the B.B.C., in German, gave a brief account of the man, his career, and his end—"a good sailor, a gallant officer, whom a disgraceful order drove to his death. Though no voice is raised in his honour in Germany today, we in England, a nation of sailors, will praise him": and a male-voice choir broke into "Ich hatt' einen Kamaraden," the cherished theme-song of all the German armed services for fallen comrades. Even hard-boiled Martha felt the tears stinging behind her eyes.

"*Superb!* That will fetch them in Germany" she muttered. "I wish I knew who thought it up." Then it occurred to her to wonder what had happened to Lucilla. Was she afraid to come and confess that she had broken all the thermoses? She lowered the radio volume, and went along to the main office. There, surrounded by broken crockery and shivered glass, the girl was sitting at the table, her head in her hands; when Martha entered she looked up.

165

"I *am* so sorry. I don't know how it happened" she said.

"Are you ill?" Martha asked, a little frightened by the deadly whiteness of Lucilla's face, from which she had made no attempt to wipe off the tears.

"No, I was just clumsy. I *am* so sorry" Lucilla repeated, stupidly.

Martha could recognise shock when she saw it.

"Stay where you are" she said peremptorily. She went along to her own little office, where she always kept a bottle of whisky and some glasses for visiting journalists; she poured out a stiff tot, and added water from the tap in the bathroom, where the wireless was now muttering in Rumanian. Something must have happened—probably something to do with Hamish; the child was all to pieces. She picked up her packet of cigarettes from the soap-shell at the end of the bath, and took it along with the glass.

"Drink that up" she said. "Come to think of it, I'll have one too—nothing much seems to be going on, except that we've bombed the Ruhr, as usual." When she returned with her own drink Lucilla was obediently sipping at hers; her face was a shade less white. Martha gave the girl a cigarette, and lit one herself; but she had got to know what was the matter with far the most valuable member of her staff, and after a moment she asked straight out—"Did they give you bad news of Hamish?

"He's dead" Lucilla said, putting her glass down.

There is always an appalling finality about those two words.

"Good God! What happened?"

Lucilla told her. "But for that change in the patrol's time he'd have been here tonight, I suppose" she said, and once more wept, thinking of Hamish's kind dull old parents, in their ugly house, and what this news would mean to them.

"How absolutely bloody" Martha said. "Lucilla, you know how sorry I am."

"Of course. But please don't tell anyone" the girl said imploringly, "or people will go condoling."

166

"I won't. Now you'd better go off to bed. Give me the key—H.E. will want it tomorrow."

"God! I don't believe I locked the door" Lucilla said, handing the key over.

"I'll do that—you get to bed. Have you got sleeping-pills?"

"Mummy has."

"Well take two. You'll carry on first thing tomorrow morning, won't you?" Martha had a wholesome belief in work as an antidote to grief.

"Of course. But how awful about the thermos—yours, too! What are we to do?"

"Not to worry!—the Min has dozens. Now take those pills, and sleep tight." Martha gave her an unwonted kiss, and Lucilla slipped away across the now darkened courtyard; she heard the waste running from the prisoners' bathroom as she went, and cried afresh—when had Hamish last had a lovely hot bath? The very ambiguity of her own feelings added to her distress on his account.

Rumour can be a deadly thing—so can the press if suitably manipulated. On the following day, while the Military Attaché, a stenographer in attendance, was sitting in that over-full bedroom in the Legation questioning the two officers as to their capture, the conditions of their imprisonment, and the circumstances of their escape, and getting all their replies taken down in shorthand, the very air of Budapest, and the mouths of its inhabitants, suddenly became full of the actual names of the five officers who were supposed to have reached Sweden, including that of Hamish MacNeil. And a Budapest evening paper, the *Esti Ujság*, printed them in full—all spelt perfectly correctly, an unusual thing for foreign names in a Hungarian journal. Colonel Morven did not hear of this at once; even before getting his report off to the War Office he was busy having the prisoners measured for civilian suits and overcoats, and sending down to the town for these —the largest available sizes were a bit skimpy on those two tall Scotsmen, but they had to do. Meanwhile the Passport Control

Officer was getting the two men photographed and fudging passports for them in false names. "What shall we call them?" the P.C.O. asked.

"Smith and Brown?" the Colonel suggested.

"Oh no—they'd spot that at once. It must be something unfamiliar." He thought. "Freeman Hardy and Willis—let's call them Hardy and Willis; excellent English names." The M.A. laughed, and agreed to the use of the well-known shoe-makers.

The Minister did not hear the rumours either; he was preparing for a hurried journey down to Belgrade on the midnight train, with Horace Wheatley in attendance, as well as a clerk and a manservant, respectively called Hardy and Willis. There was no trouble in Budapest, but the Hungarian frontier police, already beginning to be linked with the Gestapo, started a fuss at the exit into Yugo-slavia; in the cold dark of the winter's morning Horace Wheatley, an overcoat over his pyjamas, came and tapped on the door of Sir Hugh's sleeper and reported. "They say the passports bear no entry visa into Hungary."

"Send them to me" the Minister said.

In the ordinary way Sir Hugh was apt to throw England's weight about very calmly and elegantly; but in this case he knew that he was playing on a bad wicket, and acted accordingly. When Horace ushered three men in neat uniforms into his sleeper he fairly bawled them out in every language he knew. Why should he, the British Minister, be roused from sleep by futile enquiries about his personal attendants? Unless their passports were stamped here and now, he would get out of the train and ring up the Regent.

This toughness worked. The frontier police crumpled, and presently brought along the two passports, duly stamped with exit visas. But Sir Hugh was deeply relieved when at Belgrade he took his two guests off the train, stowed them in the back of the Legation car, and handed them over to Sir Monty's minions to be shipped on to Egypt. Yugo-slavia had no love for Hitler's Reich; once there they were safe. He spent a pleasant day with his nice colleague, and he and Horace returned on the

168

night train to Budapest, arriving at 6.30 the following morning.

For Lucilla, however, those last forty-eight hours had been ghastly. Rumour and press alike penetrated into the Legation, and kindly members of the staff, infected with the pretty Hungarian habit of saying it with flowers, fairly swamped her with bouquets and pot-plants, accompanied by cards or little notes— "How marvellous that your young man has escaped! *So* glad. Much love." Lucilla opened these, one after another; as she read them her inner eye held that intolerably clear picture of Hamish lying motionless in the glare of the searchlights outside the barbed wire of Oflag XXX, as the Major had given it—"None of them was moving." Hamish was dead, and how was she to thank these dear people who thought that he was alive, since she couldn't possibly reveal *why* she knew that he wasn't? Lucilla had not been brought up in diplomacy for nothing, and didn't need to be told—no one *had* told her, as a matter of fact—that for the Head of a Mission to connive at the escape of prisoners was something that had better not be publicised. She scribbled little notes of thanks, tears running down her face as she wrote, sometimes spoiling the notes so that they had to be done all over again; usually she confined herself to such safe phrases as— "How dear of you! Thank you so much." But it was a torturing experience.

She debated with herself whether she should tell her Mother —she had no means of knowing that her Father had himself in-interviewed the two prisoners in Mendze's nursing-home; he was as discreet as she. She decided not to—she would leave it till after Christmas, which would account for the flowers anyway. White-faced, tight-lipped, she went about her work; the whole episode was so novel that it didn't occur to her that the Military Attaché would have interviewed those two Scotsmen, and have learned all that she had learned, and much more.

Colonel Morven, however, of course knew that Hamish Mac-Neil was dead, and was shocked and horrified by the mention of his name in the *Esti Ujság* as being safe in Scandinavia. As soon as was decently possible after the Minister had returned from Belgrade and eaten his breakfast, he presented himself in his chief's study, a copy of the paper in his hand, and unfolded the situation.

"How appalling!" Sir Hugh said. "That delightful child! Does she know?"

"I don't see how she can. I stopped Gina from sending her flowers, but everyone else is" the M.A. said, ungrammatically.

"How on earth do you suppose the *Esti Ujság* got hold of the names?" the Minister asked, studying the newspaper spread out on his desk. "There isn't a single mistake—extraordinary!"

"I'm afraid I can guess, Sir." Hugo Morven was not as stupid as he often appeared to be.

"That *very* disagreeable girl Sonia Marston?"

"Yes, Sir. She has von Schaffhausen completely under her thumb, now; and as he's rather high up in the German Legation, he could get the names of escaped prisoners from Berlin by telephone quite easily."

"But wouldn't he also learn which of them had been shot?"

"Oh yes!" the Colonel said bitterly, for once betraying some emotion. "She's done this quite deliberately, I'm pretty sure. You see she'd been living with Milton—at least everyone supposed so—for some time; then Geoffrey switched to Lucilla. Now Sonia's taken her revenge."

"Is she sleeping with this German?" the Minister asked, with his usual calm.

"Undoubtedly, I gather."

"Well, she'll have to go. What's her paper, do you know?"

"I'm afraid not. Milton would, of course."

"In the circumstances I don't think we'll bring Milton into this; embarrassing all round. I'll find out. But we can't have a British journalist out here sleeping with a German, and running in and out of the Legation. Thank you, Morven." This was a dismissal.

"But what are we to do about the girl, Sir?" Colonel Morven, like most of the staff, had a soft spot for Lucilla, so pretty and friendly, with her graceful good manners. "Oughtn't she to be told?

At any moment that creature may put out the news of the young man's death."

"I'll think about that one. Thank you, Morven" the Minister said again; and this time the Military Attaché accepted his dismissal, and went out. Sir Hugh pressed his desk bell, and Martha came in, shorthand-pad in hand.

"What agency does Sonia Marston represent?"

"The Global News Agency." Martha looked surprised.

"Good. Send this to the Foreign Office, will you? 'Sonia Marston, British subject, representing Global News Agency, known to be sleeping with member of German Legation Staff. Unsuitable for use intelligence purposes. Please get her recalled immediately. Transport easy via Athens but warn Embassy there not desirable character.'"

"Right" Martha said. How quickly the Min had found out!

"That nice child has no idea that her young man is dead, has she?" Sir Hugh asked then.

"Oh Lord yes, poor little one! I let her take those prisoners' suppers over the first night, and they told her everything, all un-knowing."

"How awful! And now she's being bombarded with flowers!"

"She's being quite splendid" Martha said. "I've kept her hard at it, on purpose—but I'm rather wondering what the next move is. Of course if we can get that wretched Sonia away within the next thirty-six hours it may be all right—otherwise I wouldn't put it past her to spill some final beans, in the opposite sense."

"Nor would I. What a creature!" He reflected. "Do her parents know?"

"David hasn't uttered—I haven't seen Rosina."

"Well I think I had better see the child. While they're encyphering that telegram send her up."

Lucilla, busy folding Bulletins, was surprised by the summons to the Minister, but also rather pleased—she liked him so much, and it would take her mind off her private troubles.

This it did not do—but the interview helped her all the same.

"Sit down there" Sir Hugh said. "Have a cigarette." He lit it for her.

"Lucilla, my dear, I am so sorry about all this" he said then. "It's bad enough that your fiancé should have been killed, but even worse that everyone should be congratulating you on his having escaped alive. I really can't say how distressed I am for you."

Lucilla stared at him with her immense grey eyes.

"How did you know?"

"Morven told me this morning, as soon as I got back from Belgrade. Of course he interviewed the prisoners, and heard everything. Have you told your parents?"

"No. I didn't like to; Daddy's still ill, and Mummy so overworked with the P.O.W.s, and Christmas just coming. But the flowers and all that have been a bit trying."

"I'm sure they have. I gather you have been behaving very well indeed." How much her Mother's daughter this girl was, he thought, as a faint blush came into Lucilla's pale cheeks at his praise. "Tell me—how soon, if at all, would you like the truth to be put out? It's a little complicated—the International Red Cross will learn in time, but that is usually a matter of weeks, of course; and officially, that is the only way we can hear."

"I don't think it matters. I've had it, anyhow. The only thing I'm worried about is Hugo" Lucilla said—"He's sent a square yard of lilies-of-the-valley in a copper dish, and he's coming to see me tonight. That *is* a bit troublesome." Somehow she felt it much more possible to talk about Hugo to the perspicacious Min than to anyone else.

"Who is Hugo? One of your local young men?"

"Yes—Weissberger."

"Oh, I know. A grand boy. It was he who went up to the frontier and fetched those two men down."

"No? Did he really?" she glowed.

"Are you in love with him?" Sir Hugh asked, watching her face.

172

She hesitated for a long time before she answered. At last—
"I'm sure I can trust you" she said. "Yes. Much more in love than I ever was with Hamish—that was simply one of those outbreak-of-war mess-ups. But I couldn't do anything about it then, and I don't see that I can do much about it now. It's too soon, if you see what I mean, for *me*—and anyhow everyone would find out if I got engaged to him, and it would make a scandal."

The Minister did not speak for some moments. He was thinking how sensible, and how public-spirited, this youthful creature was.

"Has your Hugo proposed to you?" he asked eventually.

"Oh Lord yes. He was frightfully cross when I told him that I was engaged, because I wasn't wearing a ring," Lucilla said with a funny little smile. "But Hamish wouldn't give me one, or let it be put in *The Times,* in case he should come back crippled in some way." Tears came into her eyes as she said that: dear Hamish, with his ideals and his chivalry and his dullness; and now he was dead and buried—where? Did they give Christian burial in Germany to prisoners who were shot escaping? She put this point to Sir Hugh.

"I've no idea; I'll find out. But I think you'd better tell your Mother about Hamish." Normally, of course, the Military Attaché would at once have told the Counsellor this, but in view of David Eynsham's fragile health it was possible that he hadn't.

"Do you think so? Very well, I will."

"Shall you tell Hugo? Do you mind my asking?" Sir Hugh said, as she hesitated.

"Not a bit. It's a help to talk about it; and it will all upset Mummy frightfully, whereas you don't mind in the least" Lucilla replied, with youth's practical candour. For perhaps the third time in his life Sir Hugh Billingshurst regretted his bachelor status; parenthood, which he had always regarded as an alarming and troublesome responsibility, might have been rather delightful in connection with a girl like this—he was a little hurt by her words.

"Do you think he knows you love him?" he asked.

"I hope not—I've been tremendously careful. But Hunks are so cute, you never know."

The older man laughed—then sighed.

"Dear child, I wish I could advise you. Hugo is perfectly reliable—if you want to tell him that Hamish is dead, you have my leave to do so."

"Thanks very much. I think I must see how it works out. My own idea would be to let it stand—but that means lying to Hugo, and I'd rather be on the square with him."

"I see that. Well, I leave it to you. Nothing can make this situation easy for you, but I should like to cut down your difficulties in any way that I can, my child," he said earnestly.

"Oh Min dear, you are sweet!" She sprang up and gave him a quick kiss. "*Thank* you" she said, and ran out of the room.

Back in the office, again tidily folding Bulletins, Lucilla considered what to do about Hugo. In the end she decided not to tell him that Hamish was dead; it would only cause more emotional disturbances, with which she really couldn't cope, she felt, just now. Perhaps she was being cowardly, but she just didn't feel equal to it—nor to telling her Mother; that must wait till she had got Hugo over. So when the tall pale young man arrived that evening she thanked him for the flowers he had sent, and said how wonderful it all was. But the effort was extreme.

"You look pale" Hugo said, concerned.

"I'm always pale, thank Goodness! I hate rosy English cheeks!" the girl said vehemently. "Look, Hugo, I am so frightfully sorry, but I must get back to the office. It was so good of you to come up. Give my love to your Mother and Emmi." She rose abruptly.

"You come to our Sylvester-Abend dance?" Hugo asked, rather surprised at this hurried dismissal, but rising too. ("Sylvester-Abend" is the Continental phrase for New Year's Eve.)

"Oh yes, surely. Didn't I write? I will—tell your Mother. Goodbye." She hastened him out of the house—once again she couldn't stand any more of this.

Telling her Mother about Hamish was easier than Lucilla had

174

expected. She put off doing it that night, and by tea-time next day, when she braced herself to the task, Rosina had already heard the news from the Minister. She had gone in to put some query about the prisoners, and when their business was dealt with he said—"Has Lucilla told you about Hamish?"

"No. What about him?"

Rosina, always vague, and at present wholly concentrated on David's health and supplies for the prisoners, had heard none of the rumours, and had politely brushed aside, indeed ignored, the vague congratulations of Mrs Starnberg and other ladies at yesterday's knitting-party—"How kind of you! But look, one sleeve of this pull-over is shorter than the other; it will have to be done again." Now, looking at Sir Hugh's face, his expression arrested her attention. "Has something happened?" she asked, at last anxious on her daughter's account.

"He's dead" the Minister said, repeating those two fatal syllables. "He was shot trying to escape. My dear, I am so sorry— I thought the child would have told you. She promised me she would."

"Well she hasn't" Mrs Eynsham said, after a short silence— she spoke rather brusquely. She had not consciously neglected Lucilla, only she and the child were both so busy that they seldom met, let alone had much time to talk. But if matters had reached the point when the Minister knew that her daughter's betrothed was dead, and she didn't, something was wrong somewhere, and it was probably her fault. (Rosina was dismally accustomed to things being her fault.) "As she *hasn't* told me, perhaps you will" she said rather bitterly.

"Rosina dear, don't be vexed with her—or with me! Your splendid child was only thinking of you and her Father, and not worrying you both."

"Well now please tell me."

Sir Hugh did—and also reported the account of the escape in the *Esti Ujság.*

"*Poor* Hamish!" Mrs Eynsham said. "He was such a nice boy, only so *borné*. I'm terribly sorry that he's dead, but I was ap-

175

palled at the idea of Lucilla's marrying him. Are you shocked?" she asked.

"Not in the least. Lucilla told me herself that she realised her engagement had been a mistake."

There we go again, Rosina thought gloomily. Lucilla had never admitted to *her* that she would make a mistake in marrying Hamish, but apparently she had made no bones about telling the Min this. Mothers weren't much good!

"Well thank you very much" she said, getting up. "When she *does* tell me, I shall know where I am. Does David know?"

"I'm not sure. He was the first person to meet Hamish's two brother-officers, down in Mendze's clinic—they would have no particular reason for telling him, and he hasn't referred to it. But you never know, with David."

You're telling *me!*—David's wife thought, but didn't say. "Well thank you" she repeated, and went home. Walking back along the golden street, glowing even in the cold winter sunshine, she thought sadly of what a dismal Christmas this would be for that little unit, her family, which meant so much to her—tomorrow was Christmas Eve, and they would all have to show up at a huge dinner-party for the staff at the Legation, and play games afterwards. Oh dear!

Lucilla came to her room after tea.

"Mummy, I've got something to tell you."

"Is it about Hamish? If so, I know."

"Who told you?"

"H.E."

"Oh. Well there it is" Lucilla said sadly. "Don't let's talk about it. The Min and I settled to keep it quiet—till after Christmas, anyhow. No need to cast a gloom."

"Darling, I am so sorry."

"Yes I'm sure. But let's leave it, shall we?"

"Certainly—much better. Bless you." She kissed her daughter's cool cheek.

"You see there really *isn't* anything to say" Lucilla said, half-penitently.

176

"My darling, I *know*. Don't worry; I'm the last thing for you to worry about."

Lucilla suddenly put her arms round her Mother, and gave her a warm hug.

"You're not a 'thing'—you're a good woman" she said, and went away.

Early on the morning of Christmas Eve Wheatley brought several telegrams to his chief. One, from the Foreign Office, said that the Global News Agency was recalling Sonia Marston immediately. "Good" Sir Hugh commented briefly. But later that morning the journalist came to see the Press Attaché.

"Do you know *why* I'm being recalled?" she demanded.

"I didn't even know you were" Milton said coolly.

"Oh, don't lie to me! You must have known."

"Never heard a word about it. But as to 'why,' use your head, Marston. There's a war on, you know, and even agencies have a way of learning things."

"How will you like it if I go and see your wife, and tell her about you and me?"

"She won't be surprised. Be sure to tell her about von Schaffhausen too, though, won't you? Because you and I are rather out of date." He rang his bell, and got up. "Get out of here, Marston" he said coldly. When the messenger appeared he told him to show Miss Marston out. The young woman had begun to cry. "Oh Geoffrey, where am I to go?"

"What does your cable say?" Milton asked. She took it from her bag and gave it to him.

"Proceed Athenswise" he read. "Yes, well Athenswise is the only way you can proceed, as things are. Now don't make an exhibition of yourself; dry your eyes and go. Good-bye."

"But my visas! Can't you get them for me?"

"No. Go to the Consulates—that's what they're for."

"Exit traitress, sobbing" Milton said aloud, after the messenger had ushered Miss Marston out—he had a taste for Shakespeare. But he used his local "sources" to ascertain that Miss Marston really had secured her Yugo-slav, Bulgarian and Greek visas, and was leaving on the midnight train—he reported this to the Minister shortly before the party began.

"Good" Sir Hugh said again.

The Staff party was a tremendous affair. Fifty-seven people sat down in the big dining-room, and partook of soup, five turkeys, spiced baked ham, and plum-puddings lit up with brandy; they pulled crackers over the almonds and raisins, and then repaired to the drawing-room, where Martha and Rosina organised guessing-games and charades. Martha was in despair over the dinner —the chef, who closely resembled Erich von Stroheim, had sworn that he knew how to make *Sauce Bred*—i.e. bread sauce; but he didn't—he had used rye bread and put it through a sieve, so that the turkeys were accompanied by a grey, rather slimy fluid tasting of treacle, as rye bread does.

"Oh don't worry, Martha. Everything else was perfect," Rosina told her. David had gone home to bed, but Lucilla was sticking it out nobly; she put a paper cap on the Minister's head, and with a quick movement managed to kiss Colonel Morven under the mistletoe before he realised what was happening, amid applause—this provoked a general out-break of manoeuverings under the bough, and much mirth.

"How I admire that child of yours" Sir Hugh murmured to Mrs Eynsham.

"So do I. I *reverence* her" Rosina said—an unusual tribute from a mother to a daughter.

12

Early in the New Year—1941—the Minister came into Mrs Eynsham's little workroom and put a telegram down in front of her.

"British Red Cross would be much obliged if Mrs Eynsham would act as their representative in Hungary. If she feels able to do so please let me know how many parcels from Hungarian sources she can send weekly. They propose she should send all to Camp Captain Oflag VII C/H. Red Cross would pay and you would be authorised to charge expenses per the Foreign Office."

Rosina looked up at Sir Hugh, bewilderment in her face.

"But how extraordinary! The Red Cross simply hate me, because of all the fuss I've been making." (From Lady Otmoor, via Uncle Jim, she had heard a good deal about the irritation in Grosvenor Crescent as a result of those letters of hers.)

Sir Hugh gave his low sardonic chuckle.

"My dear, don't you see? They think that if you become their representative it will shut your mouth. Of course they don't know you!"

Rosina laughed too.

"Well, I must think about it" she said. "Of course pure 'Hungarian sources' are drying up every week; but I suppose we could count Csepel Island as a Hungarian source, couldn't we?"

"I daresay you can get away with that, in the circumstances! Anyhow think it over, and draft me a memorandum for the reply. But it looks as though you might get some Red Cross money at last."

"Well I can't spend it all on VII C/H—we've pretty well clothed them already."

"Write it out" Sir Hugh repeated, and went away.

Rosina had never drafted a memorandum in her life, but she had read plenty of David's; after dealing with her current day's work she thought awhile, and then put pen to paper.

"(I) It will look rather bad if after all the telegrams from this Mission saying 'Red Cross is doing everything in a dud way,' the moment they say—'Very well, *you* do it and we'll pay' we refuse. Therefore I think we should accept."

"(II) Acceptance might have slight advantage that as accredited Red Cross agent one might be able to bring more pressure to bear on various officials here."

"(III) But when accepting, if we do decide to accept, we should make two points clear."

"(a) Position is now very different from when we started agitating for funds in September. Then we could have done an immense amount; now all we can promise is to do what we can for as long as we can. And will they pay for the ½ cwt. of chocolate every week from Sofia?"

"(b) While *food* is extremely precarious, we can produce a certain amount of clothing. VII C/H is already pretty well clothed, by us; are we free to send our surplus (70–100 shirts or prs pyjamas a week, and knitted garments) to other camps?"

The Minister studied this document when Rosina brought it to him.

"Quite sensible" he said, and drafted a telegram conveying Mrs Eynsham's acceptance, subject to her conditions and reservations, to be forwarded by the Foreign Office to the British Red Cross.

"Do beat them up about those quilts, too. We've *still* heard nothing" Rosina reminded him.

"I will."

The Red Cross reply, though not very precisely expressed, was generally favourable, and Mrs Eynsham became the British Red Cross Representative in Hungary—with, at last, some money be-

180

hind her and the Committee. This rather went to her head, and she fairly got going. She cabled an order to Yugo-slavia for several thousand yards of flannellette for pyjamas, and when this arrived she set the unemployed Hungarian seamstresses to work on it; she telegraphed to Cairo for another half-ton of knitting-wool for the use of the three working-parties.

She was impelled to these measures by the increasing tone of desperation in the prisoners' letters—some reaching her direct from the camps, some forwarded by distraught relations in England, who had somehow heard of the Relief Organisation in Budapest. A mother in Newcastle-upon-Tyne sent on a letter, dated December the 31st—"I am now wearing less than I do at home in summer"; a wife wrote from Hindhead—"My husband says 'Hungary has saved us in clothing and smokes' "—she added: "I send my husband vitamin tablets every week, and 200 Players once a fortnight; but none of them ever reach him. Do please go on helping." A Camp Captain reported that his men could not even take the wretched form of exercise of walking round the prison yard because they no longer had any boots—"and they can't walk barefoot in the snow, in twelve degrees of frost. Can you get them some shoes, or slippers even?—and can you think up any form of game?" And six other Camp Captains wrote soon afterwards in the same sense, begging for boots, or footwear of any sort.

These last requests sent Rosina down to Belgrade again, where soft Yugo-slav slippers, leather below and knitted wool above, were abundant and cheap. More, she thought of a game. On her childhood trips to and from China she had often watched deck-tennis being played on the P. & O. boats; for this all that was necessary was a string stretched between two uprights, and some rope rings, or teni-quoits. As usual she stayed with Sir Monty, who lent her his car and his German-speaking chauffeur to assist her quest. The slippers were easy enough, but the teni-quoits were more complicated. The kind clever Serbian drove Mrs Eynsham down to the small ships'-chandlers' shops along the Sava, the Danube's great tributary flowing in from the North-

West, where she explained to him in German what she wanted, and he translated into Serbo-Croat; she demonstrated herself how to pare down the ends of the strands of rope, to splice and bind them into a ring, and waited in each little shop, perched on a keg, smiling and smoking, till after several attempts a fairly smooth and satisfactory ring was produced. Then she ordered a hundred, to be delivered to the Legation within twenty-four hours, in all these humble establishments, and returned to dine with her host; the following night she travelled back to Budapest with over a thousand rope-rings, several thousand pairs of slippers, and innumerable boot-laces—another "want" in the prison-camps for those who still had boots.

On her return the Minister informed her that the Red Cross had at last sanctioned the purchase of 10,000 quilts, and the Embassy at Ankara had been instructed accordingly. "They know where to get them, I suppose?"

"Oh yes, I left the estimates and everything with her." ("Her" meant the Ambassadress.) "But why only *ten* thousand? That will leave more than three-quarters of the prisoners with none."

"Almighty God is not the only institution whose ways are past finding out" Sir Hugh said wryly.

"No but really, they must be dotty!" Rosina said, very much put out. "They've got packets of money from the miserable relations, and I sent on the American Inspectors' reports, *all* saying blankets were so desperately wanted."

"Well we must leave that. I've said you would divide them up and forward them if they were sent here. Can you?"

"Yes of course."

"How quickly do you suppose your Istanbul merchant can produce them?"

"He said about eight weeks, for the whole amount. Why?" she asked, a shade of anxiety in her voice.

"Oh, everything is going from bad to worse. The more successful we are in North Africa, the stronger the pressure Hitler applies hereabouts. I don't think Rumania can hold out much longer

182

—then we may have to accommodate their surplus staff from Bucharest."

"Well if they have some good strong men, who can help Horace and Hugo and Mr Smith to pack, that will be splendid" Rosina said blithely. But she was not feeling at all blithe—if Rumania went, yet another escape route would be closed, and the mouth of the sack become narrower still.

Her view of the dottiness of the British Red Cross was increased a few days later. Diplomats acquire friends everywhere, and during a spell in Berne Rosina had become very friendly with a wealthy and leisured Swiss bachelor, who admired her poems and still wrote her long, witty, and rather literary letters four or five times a year—she had had three since they came to Budapest; she had answered one. When her telephone rang one morning and Bertha said—"A call from Geneva"—she was delighted to hear his voice.

"Oh Melchior! How are you? Are you coming to Hungary?"

"No. I am quite busy here, doing some work for the International Red Cross. But I hear you are now the representative of the British Red Cross in Hungary, and there is something you should know."

"Tell away" Rosina replied, delighted to learn that she had got a reliable sleuth in Geneva.

"You will not believe it, but the British Red Cross have sent ten thousand pairs of *grey* flannel trousers for your prisoners! Naturally the German authorities will not accept them; for prisoners all must be khaki."

"What clots!"

"We hear that you are sending much clothing; this is why I telephone. *All* must be khaki."

"We've been having everything dyed khaki since last August, except pyjamas" Rosina replied crisply. "But a thousand thanks all the same, Melchior. Can't the Swiss get the trousers dyed? The men are simply frozen."

"I hope so—this is not in my hands. But is it not strange that the British Red Cross should ignore this fact?"

183

It was, very strange. After some reflection Rosina rang down for a typist and dictated a letter to an elderly General, also a friend of hers, who was, she knew, now high up in Grosvenor Crescent. She sent it by air via Lisbon, and after a few days received a reply which filled her almost with despair.

"It is not our business, or yours, to supply *clothing* for the prisoners" the General wrote. "Under the Geneva Convention the obligation to clothe prisoners adequately is on the Power which holds them. In the last war we never sent clothing to our prisoners."

There you were—the *last* war! Mrs Eynsham thought bitterly. The past, the past!—what about the present? Did no one in London realise the famine of woollens of all sorts in Central Europe, created by the British blockade? She sent a rather tart reply to the General, pointing out this situation: "You can't really expect the Germans to give our prisoners what they haven't got themselves. But if you *do* manage to get clothing for them, why not dye it khaki first?" Rosina was not a very submissive employee.

Her hand was strengthened by public opinion in England, which was steadily rising in criticism of the Red Cross. On January the 21st there were a number of questions on the subject in the House of Commons. One Member asked whether the Secretary of State for War could now make any statement as to the working of the Red Cross machinery for the despatch of parcels to British prisoners-of-war in Germany, and what defects in procedure remained to be remedied? Another enquired whether, to allay the disquietude of friends at home, he would take steps to arrange closer cooperation between the War Office and the Red Cross with a view to speeding up the delivery of food and clothing to the British P.O.W.s in Germany, treating it as a matter of the greatest urgency? Yet another enquired whether the Secretary of State for War could explain why it was that letters were continually being received from prisoners saying that they had received no parcels so far from the Red Cross Organization? And a further questioner asked whether the

184

War Office realised that for four months parcels had been ac-cumlating between Lisbon and Geneva?

The spokesman for the War Office replied to these questions as best he could. Yes, there had been serious delays in the trans-mission of parcels across the Iberian Peninsula and France. Yes, it was true—this in reply to another question—that no repre-sentative of the British Red Cross Organisation had gone to Lis-bon to look into the matter till December, but ships had now been chartered to convey the parcels from Lisbon to Marseilles, whence they would be forwarded to Geneva under the direct supervision of the International Red Cross. He ended by telling the House that during December 99,592 parcels had left Geneva for the camps in Germany. He did not mention—probably he did not know of it—the immense delay of parcels into Germany from Switzerland.

But the House was not quite satisfied. Rosina read with par-ticular satisfaction a question from one M.P. asking whether the Secretary of State for War had received the report from the United States Embassy in Berlin on conditions in Oflag VII, which had been asked for in the second week of December?—and whether he would publish it? (She suspected that this might be partly the result of those letters of hers.) The War Office spokesman replied that he had received a telegraphic summary of the report, but that the United States Government was not prepared, in the interests of the prisoners themselves, to agree to reports by United States officials on prisoner-of-war camps being published.

Mrs Eynsham saw the point of this decision, though she re-gretted it. She herself had had no difficulty in getting the texts of the reports of all the camps—indeed in those early days of 1941 she had several face-to-face conversations with the mem-bers of the American Embassy staff in Berlin detailed to visit the prisoners; they came down to Budapest to get a little sleep—the R.A.F. raids on Berlin were making the nights there a horror, as the Luftwaffe raids were doing to London. (But the London-

185

ers had no Budapest to go to.) What these kind, devoted Americans told her made Mrs Eynsham more reckless and determined than ever to do all she could, *while* she could—it couldn't be for long—for the prisoners. Bed-ticking—that had got to be procured somehow, or even sacking, to cover the straw in which so many of the men slept; straw harboured lice, the hideous insects loved it, it seemed. She procured mattress-ticking from the Hungarian Red Cross, and sent it all over Germany, regardless of the suggestion that she should confine her supplies to one Oflag; the men in the Stalags needed this form of help more, since officers were given mattresses.

During those obsessed days, when she knew that she was laying up trouble for herself, her husband, and the whole Legation, Rosina Eynsham thought constantly of Florence Nightingale, and found consolation in the thought. That great woman had been perpetually at odds with officialdom, perpetually slapped down—but she had stuck to it, and won in the end. She, Rosina, in her very small way would stick to it too, as Miss Nightingale had done, regardless of consequences.

Presently there arose the great question of the ham, one of the most lamentable episodes in a lamentable story. Some Budapest merchants offered Mrs Eynsham 300,000 pounds of cooked, boned, tinned ham—as usual from Csepel—at the extremely modest price of 3/4d per lb. She asked for a sample and tasted it—it was excellent; she could have immediate delivery, and with Hasler's help could get it to the camps within three weeks. The merchants' only stipulation was that it should be paid for in Swiss francs. £50,000 was a lot of money, but the Red Cross had vast reserves, and for this sum *every* prisoner in Germany could be sure of receiving slightly over six pounds of good, nutritious, fat-containing food in under a month. She hastened to Sir Hugh with the offer and her rather childish sums, done in pencil on a rough bit of paper.

"You see what it means" she said eagerly, while he studied her figures. "Absolutely *life*-saving, while their miserable ships are dodging the submarines between Lisbon and Gibraltar! And

186

anyhow the Belgians tell me that eighty per cent of the first lot of parcels were stolen between Marseilles and the Swiss frontier!"

"Is the stuff really good?" the Minister asked.

"First-class—I'll send some over. It's real ham, not gammon, in big oval tins. But I daren't order it without permission—I thought you might telegraph."

"I will" the Minister said. "I don't see how they can refuse an opportunity like this, in the circumstances."

They could, however, and did. The British Red Cross, claiming to be able to purchase ham more cheaply in Switzerland, turned the Csepel consignment down flat.

"Good God!" Colonel Morven exploded, when Rosina read this out to the Committee. "What a creature! Who is he? Not a soldier, anyhow."

"But zis is idyot" Gina said, indignantly. "We getta ze parcels to ze camps, zey don't! I sink fools."

However there was nothing to be done—the Committee could not possibly raise £50,000. "Well, the men must just go on starving—by the decision of the British Red Cross" Colonel Morven said, unspeakable bitterness in his voice. "I never dreamt they would come to this, with their past record of service. Anyhow we don't know what quality of ham theirs is—ours was good."

The Minister's prognostication about Rumania had been quite correct. Early in February the British Legation there was recalled, since the country was practically under German occupation; the Minister and most of the staff went home through Turkey, but one attaché and a couple of typists were sent up to Budapest to lend a hand to the over-worked personnel there. They came by car, and on the way ran over a Rumanian peasant who was reeling all over the road; they picked him up and took him to the nearest hospital. "What was so fascinating, Sir" the attaché said to Sir Hugh, when explaining their late arrival, "was that he was a hermaphrodite—the surgeon came out and told us. It seemed so fitting."

"Oh, why?" the Minister asked, amused.

"Oh well, so Rumanian. Before the Germans really took over the Army tried to brace itself up; an Order of the Day went out that no officer under the rank of Major was to be allowed to wear rouge!"

Sir Hugh laughed a great deal. But he realised that the string round the mouth of the sack was getting very tight indeed. There was only one way out now, south through Yugo-slavia; the small railway running up to the Russian frontier through Ruthenia had been closed owing to bombed bridges for some time past. He had already taken certain measures. Workmen had come in and dug a huge square hole in the courtyard, just inside the *porte-cochère;* in this one of the big oil companies had placed a tank holding thousands of gallons of petrol, and erected a pump over it; when the tank was filled the Legation had its own private supply of petrol. Now he chartered several lorries, and parked them discreetly here and there. He knew what had happened when the British Legation had to leave Warsaw in a hurry. Only one lorry, bought by the foresighted wife of a member of the staff for her private collection of modern pictures had been available to transport essential documents and safes; her pictures were left behind, the official necessaries had been taken—but the whole caravan of Legation cars, on their flight to the Rumanian frontier, had been dependent for petrol on the *caches* which this lady, a "wise virgin" if ever there was one, had organised along the route. Sir Hugh was not going to have anything of that sort happen; he ordered all the members of his staff who had cars to lay in a supply of 4-gallon cans, and fill them from the Legation pump. Hearing of all this Rosina Eynsham laughed a little—perhaps she wouldn't need old Countess Pongracz's garden-basket after all! But she still kept her pigskin bag of supplies in her bedroom, ready packed, to leave at a moment's notice; it had been there now for nearly a year—an uncomfortable year.

Mrs Eynsham had little time nowadays to get out into the country, to her the great restorer of peace and strength; but one afternoon fairly late in February her work was so well in hand

188

that she decided to drive out again to Buda-Örs. She felt that she needed to be restored: she was worried about both her children. Dick, after his escape from Dunkirk, had spent six months "drilling grey-haired sub-lieutenants with broomsticks over their shoulders," as he described it; bored with this, he had got himself transferred to the R.A.F., and was now on the point of becoming a Pilot-Officer, the most junior of officer airmen. But with the great shortage of pilots after the losses in the Battle of Britain, he wrote that he had great hopes of soon starting "ops" as a bomber-pilot—not altogether a reassuring occupation to his Mother. As for Lucilla, she was steadily becoming paler, thinner, and more nervy—her Mother suspected, as Mothers do, her attachment to Hugo, but lacked the courage to embark on the subject with her.

It was a mild day, pale sunshine from a pale sky, and a definite feeling of spring in the air, though patches of discoloured snow still lay under northward-facing banks. Mrs Eynsham left the car—her own, this time—in the usual place, and walked along the familiar track under the small pine-clad ridge; the sun already had power enough to make the surface muddy, though she could still feel what her Father used to call "the bone in the ground" beneath the sticky mud. The grass beside the track was withered and brownish after its long weeks under the snow; but here and there, in sunny sheltered hollows the aconites were beginning to open—some tight yellow knops, a very few fully out, staring like broad golden pennies at the sun; she knelt and picked them, delighted. Up among the dark pines to her right the tits had decided that it was spring; they were tzipping everywhere among the branches, busily seeking the last seeds in the pine-cones. In the little glens running up towards the top of the ridge, too rocky and steep-sided to be planted with conifers, the cloud-shaped bushes of *Cornus mas* bore a faint yellowish tinge; the buds of their absurd little tufts of flowers were already taking colour. Rosina wandered along, happily, and sat down on the rock where she always rested; inevitably, she thought of last year, of the terrible days of Dun-

kirk. There were no nightingales now, and the flowers were different—so were her private forms of anxiety: Lucilla and David
added to her concern about Dick. But, as always, Buda-Örs
brought her peace.

Peace never lasted long in Budapest in those days, though.
She told the chauffeur to drop her at the Legation, and went up
to her little office to see what fresh work had come in. On top of
the usual pile of acknowledgements and requests from the camps
was a pencilled note from Bertha, the telephonist: "The Gnädige
Frau was called from Geneva; she shall call back at once. It is
highly urgent." A Geneva number was given.

Rosina put the call in—while she waited she went through
the acknowledgements from the *Vertrauensmänner*, and ticked
them off on her typed lists. Bother—two Stalags had failed to
acknowledge twenty-five parcels each. Those tiresome old sergeants!—they never could be bothered to put pen to paper. She
began to draft telegrams.

"Apparently you have not received our parcels Nos. *XY 471*
to *XY 496* stop. Supplies so difficult here that in view of your
nonreceipt am cancelling all further despatches your camp.

Mrs Eynsham."

She was just recopying this, with different parcel numbers,
when her telephone rang.

"Hullo? Oh, Melchior—how nice! I'm sorry I was out before.
What goes on?"

"A quite incredible nonsense! The British Red Cross has at
last decided to send some underclothing to your prisoners—
shirts, vests, pants. They buy these from your Middle East Command in Cairo."

"But how wonderful! How many?" She at once thought of the
lamentable shortfall of the quilts ordered.

"About forty thousand. But it is not wonderful at all—how do
you think they propose to send them?"

"Well either to Salonika or the Piraeus by sea, and on up to
us—the railway's still open."

"*Tout au contraire!* They insist that this clothing shall be sent

190

to Genoa, and from there to Geneva, to be forwarded to the camps."

"But that's quite *mad!*" Mrs Eynsham exclaimed, aghast. "Genoa's in Italy, and Italy has been enemy territory since last June, eight months ago. What *can* they be thinking of?"

"Who can conceive? This is why I telephone. I told you it was a nonsense! But can you perhaps do something?"

"I'll try. Dear Melchior, thank you so very much for tipping me off—you *are* kind."

"I am more exasperated than kind, I fear" the Swiss said. "How are you? And David?—and *la belle petite?*"

"All quite all right" Rosina fibbed briskly. "I'll let you know what happens. Bless you for this."

She rang off, and imprudently hastened along to the Minister's study without telephoning first to find out if he was free. He was not—at his "Who is it?" she said "Me," and went in; a lean man, with a lined clever face, rose as she entered—she recognised Count Teleki, more renowned as a geographer and naturalist even than as his country's leading statesman.

"You know the Prime Minister?" Sir Hugh said, rising also.

"Yes indeed. I hope Countess Hanna is better?" she asked, as the Hungarian kissed her hand. "I see you are both busy—I'll come back presently, if I may," she said, embarrassed at her *gaffe.*

"Do—I will ring you up" the Minister said. "Some trouble about the prisoners, I suppose?" He turned to Count Teleki. "Mrs Eynsham—and indeed all our staff—work incessantly on getting supplies to our prisoners-of-war." The great man nodded. "So I hear."

"Your Excellency, as the representative of the British Red Cross in Hungary, I should like to take this opportunity of telling you personally how grateful we are for all the help your people are giving us" Mrs Eynsham said, rather formally; she was a great one for seizing chances. She glanced at Sir Hugh, and seeing approval in his face she pursued her theme. "The generosity of your shop-keepers has been beyond belief—for the prisoners they sell us everything at cost price, or even less. And I should like to thank *you* for the agreement about goods in transit from Csepel Island; this has meant so much for our men, and it must have been a Government decision."

The lined severe face relaxed into a smile.

"Thank you, Mrs Eynsham. What you say makes me very happy. Of course you have good friends"—now he smiled finely, and Rosina knew that he meant Prince Willie—"but this can surprise no one! Au revoir." He kissed her hand again, and Rosina hurried out of the room.

She had despatched her telegrams to the two peccant Sergeant-*Vertrauensmänner*, and nearly finished logging up the receipts for parcels from the more reliable ones, when the Minister rang through. "Come along now, if you're free."

In his study Rosina began by apologising.

"I *am* so sorry I burst in—I won't again."

"Well it is wiser to make sure first. But in fact I'm glad you came. You did well—he was so pleased by what you said about Hungarian help. Where do you get your inspirations?—for you were all astray when you came in and saw him." He grinned rather mockingly at her.

"The Holy Spirit, if at all" Rosina said. "I pray every morning for help in everything I do—but I'm not sure that I always listen very carefully to what I'm told!"

"You really are devout?" Sir Hugh asked, a little incredulously.

"No, only *croyante,* up to a point—I couldn't call myself devout. But I do really believe that it is in God that 'we live, and move, and have our being,' so it seems silly not to ask His help about our daily jobs" Rosina said briskly. "Especially as Our Lord told us to ask for whatever we wanted—'ask, and ye shall receive.' *He* ought to have known what He was talking about."

Sir Hugh laughed at that.

"I envy you your faith" he said. "But now, tell me what made you burst in."

"Oh, such a frightful thing." She repeated what Melchior had told her about the underwear from Cairo.

192

"How incredible!" the Minister said. "This must be put a stop to." He went over to his desk, and began to write on a sheet of paper.

"Are you telegraphing to the Foreign Office?" Rosina asked, curious.

"No, to the Ambassador in Cairo. He will deal with it much more quickly, and we can't afford any delay if we are to get the stuff up here and across the frontier in time."

During the ensuing weeks "the Athens Underwear," as it came to be called, developed into a positive obsession. The Ambassador in Cairo fairly easily persuaded Middle East Command to ignore the instructions of the Red Cross in London to despatch this vital consignment through enemy territory, and instead to send it to Budapest via the Piraeus. But there were hitches and delays; first no ship available, then difficulties with the Greek railways; later a hold-up at the Bulgarian frontier. The Minister took an active part in all this, cabling repeatedly to Cairo, then to Athens—where at last, on March the 13th, 294 bales and six cases were reported to have been put on rail.

"Shall you and the Committee be all ready to ship the stuff on the moment it comes?" he asked Rosina. "It looks as though it may be a pretty close-run thing."

"I hope so. I rang up Geneva and got the latest figures from the Red Cross there for the numbers of men in each camp—the Boches *will* keep switching them about from one to another, so tiresome!—and we've allocated amounts for the camps on that basis. I'm getting lists typed out to send to each 'man-of-confidence,' and we're getting labels stencilled. Oh by the way, I hope it's all right, but I got onto Pista about persuading the railway people to relax the 5-kilogram rule for this bulky stuff, and for the quilts, and to let it go through in units of up to 100 kilos."

"What did Pista say?" Sir Hugh asked. (Pista Horthy, the Regent's son, had recently been made Head of the Hungarian State Railways.)

"Oh, he was *so* nice and helpful! But he told me to talk to the

National Bank and ask them to have the export licences ready, *with* the weights and contents, so that there wouldn't be any hold-up or delay."

"Did he now?" Sir Hugh looked thoughtful as he asked the question. "H'm. And have you done that?"

"Oh yes, of course. Dr B. is such an angel—he's mad on Palestrina, and sings beautifully!—I often go there, and I love his wife. I sent him a list this morning, and he rang up and promised to have the licences ready to hand over the moment the stuff comes in."

"Well that's all you can do. Now we must just wait, and hope it comes in time. *You* might pray that it does, since you're such a pray-er" he said with his sidelong smile.

"Oh I *do*, all the time!—even when I'm walking along the *utca* between here and home. Walking is a very good time for praying, I think" Rosina said airily. Then her face changed. "Min dear, how bad *is* everything? Do you think we shall be able to stick on here till we get all this stuff through? We *must*," she added urgently.

"Rosina, I can't tell you, because I don't know. But Bulgaria is practically in German hands now, as Rumania is already; when the Boches come in here is anybody's guess."

"But if they come in, how do we get out?" Mrs Eynsham asked, thinking of her sick husband.

"God knows!" the Minister said.

194

13

Budapest during the early years of the war was still such a small and closely-knit community that everybody knew everybody, and met them, at least on large formal occasions. Countess Anna Dolinsky, rabidly pro-Axis, was naturally on close terms with the German Legation staff, including von Schaffhausen, and in time she learned that not all the five British officers whose names had been published in the *Esti-Ujság* had reached Scandinavia, but that three of them had been shot while escaping, including Hamish MacNeil. From Eleanor Wheatley—careless, and such a little snob that nothing could make her prudent about her contacts in Budapest society—she found out that he had been engaged to Lucilla Eynsham, an open secret in the British Legation. But nothing ever escaped observation in the small capital. "The night has a thousand eyes, and the day a million!" an attaché had once bitterly misquoted—and the fact that Lucilla was so often seen dancing with Hugo Weissberger had been duly registered. The Dolinskys, with their Nazi proclivities, did not see much of the Jewish Weissbergers; but at a big party, to which all Budapest inevitably had to go, Countess Anna, seeing Hugo's tall figure in the crowd, went over and spoke to him.

"How sad that your little friend's fiancé has been shot."

"Countess, you perplex me." (His perplexity was genuine, but he was at once on guard.) "Who is my 'little friend'?"

"But of course the lovely Lucilla. Do you not constantly dance together?"

Hugo played this light, though his mind was immediately full of that scene on the golf-course at his home.

195

"One dances with as many pretty girls as one can! But who is this famous fiancé, and why has he been shot?" He spoke casually.

"He was a British officer called MacNeil, a prisoner-of-war, and he was shot while trying to escape" the Countess said inexorably.

Hugo Weissberger's emotions were as mixed as Lucilla's had been when she learned of her fiancé's death; but like her, he concentrated on preserving an outward façade.

"How terrible, if she really was engaged to him" he said, with careful incredulity. "She wears no ring."

The act he put on was convincing enough to irritate Anna.

"Oh well, if you don't believe me ask in the British Legation. Everyone there knows that they were *fiancés.*"

"Tiens! And how interesting that *you* know that he is dead" Hugo said rather recklessly. "I remember the name, now that you say it; surely MacNeil was one of the five British officers who were mentioned in the *Esti-Ujság* as having escaped to Scandinavia? But you know better it seems."

He was so angry with Anna Dolinsky, and so upset by this news that he might have given himself away completely if at that moment one of the old Hapsburg Archduchesses had not come waddling up to them. "Oh my dear Anna, how are you? You never come to see me and August. Ah, Baron Weissberger, and how are you?"—as he bent and kissed her hand. "Still making railway engines? So useful—one must have these things today, and I hear you even export them. Dear Anna, I wish you would come to luncheon with us one day."

Hugo seized the opportunity to escape. He was in complete disarray. If Lucilla's "Haymish" was really dead the situation was quite different; he might have a chance—anyhow he must talk to her about it. But he didn't trust Anna Dolinsky—not many people did; he must make certain. He walked uncertainly through the large crowded rooms; in one of them—propped against the wall—huge, monolithic, making no attempt at social

196

intercourse—he observed the British Military Attaché. Ah!—him
he knew; he went over at once.

"Good evening, Colonel Morven."

"Oh good evening, Weissberger. Glad to see you. Ghastly,
aren't they, these shows? I mean, they mean well, of course; but
this standing about in crowds is frightful, to me—though my
wife loves them."

"Yes, they have their boring aspect. I wonder if I might ask
you a question?"

"Ask away, my boy" the Colonel said benevolently. He knew
quite well that it was this young man who had escorted the two
officer-prisoners over the frontier and down to Budapest.

"Is it true that an officer called MacNeil was shot while he
was trying to escape?"

"Who told you that?" the Colonel asked sharply.

"Countess Dolinsky. Of course she is very pro-German—I
wondered if it was true."

"Yes, it's true all right. God help the poor chap's parents!"

"Yes indeed" Hugo said.

"When did she tell you?"

"Just now. Thank you, Colonel."

"Thank *you* for what you did for the others" the Colonel said.
"They're safe in Cairo now—we got a signal."

"This is excellent. Good night."

"Good night, Weissberger."

Hugo scoured the big rooms looking for Lucilla, but it was
one of her nights on duty; he saw Mrs Eynsham in the distance,
and avoided her—this was between Lucilla and him, alone. He
left early—early for Budapest, that is, namely about midnight—
and on reaching his parents' house he rang her up at home. He
knew that the Bulletin monitoring stopped at 11.30, and guessed,
rightly, that she would still be awake—in fact she answered the
telephone; David Eynsham had had an instrument put beside
every bed in the house, as well as in the living-rooms.

"Hullo? Who's that?" she asked in Hungarian.

197

"Me—Hugo" he replied in English.

"Goodness, what a time of night to ring up! What's the matter?"

"I must see you. At what time, tomorrow?"

"Wait while I get my diary." A pause. "Is 5.30 too early? I must be back in the office at 6.15."

"No, I come then. Thank you." He rang off before she could say anything else.

Lucilla wondered rather why Hugo should be in such a hurry to see her; why hadn't he made one of their usual assignations to dine and dance? She was totally unprepared for what took place when he arrived, punctually at 5.30, the following day. Hugo for his part was wishing that he had managed to find out if Lucilla knew? Colonel Morven was really his only contact in the Legation besides Lucilla and her Mother, and he had shied away from asking him, as he had avoided meeting Mrs Eynsham —in either case it would have been something of a give-away, and the good boy had all the devout lover's shyness. But as he drove up to Buda in the blue early dusk, at the bends in the road seeing the lights beginning to come out along the Danube and in the big streets of Pest—the beautiful city putting on her evening diadem—he regretted his caution, and that he had come so ill-prepared.

Since her Father and Mother were both at work in the Legation, Lucilla received her young man in the pretty drawing-room, where the usual Hungarian idea of tea was set out—tiny sandwiches of ham, cheese, and caviare on the table beside the big English tea-tray, with its monumental Victorian Eynsham silver: teapot, and jugs for milk, cream, and hot water.

"Ah, there you are. Don't wait, Erich, we will serve ourselves" she said in German to the hovering manservant, whose training had led him to believe that it was his duty to hand those plates of sandwiches to host and guest alike. Reluctantly, he withdrew, and Lucilla began to pour out tea—the beauty of the movement of her hand and slender arm wielding the massive teapot made Hugo's heart turn over.

198

"No tea, thank you so much. I came to talk with you. I bring bad news." She abandoned the teapot.

"What is it?"

"Your Haymish is dead, shot. He was trying to escape. I thought you ought to know this." He blurted it all out, not in the least as he had meant to say it, carefully, feeling his way.

"I do know it" the girl said.

"Since when?"

"Oh, for quite a long time now. Those prisoners you brought down told me—they didn't know about him and me, of course."

"They told you?" The young man was staggered. "But—but when I sent you flowers, and came to see you, you knew this already?"

"Yes" Lucilla said flatly. "But I was rather upset, and I'd only just heard that you were in on the job; I simply didn't want to talk about it then."

He looked both startled and hurt.

"This is extraordinary!"

"No it isn't, Hugo. Everyone was sending me flowers and congratulating me, and I just had to say 'Yes, yes' to them all— and it seemed easier to say 'Yes, yes' to you, too. I did think of telling you"—she remembered her conversation in the Minister's study—"but when it came to the point I funked it. I'd had all I could take, just then. I'm sorry I lied to you."

He digested this explanation in silence for some moments.

"I think I understand" he said at last. "It must have been terrible for you—all those flowers, and having to keep silent. Only to *me!*—since you knew that I knew about the prisoners. How did *you* know that?"

"The Minister told me."

"Why should he tell you?" he asked sharply.

"Because he knew that I was engaged to Hamish, and when the M.A. interviewed those two officers they told *him* that Hamish had been shot, so he—H.E., I mean—thought I ought to know, and sent for me to talk about it; and he mentioned that you had brought them down."

Hugo considered this rather revised version of Lucilla's conversation with Sir Hugh; he apparently accepted it.

"Nevertheless it is strange" he said presently. "All these weeks we meet, and dance, and talk—and you say nothing!"

"No, nothing" Lucilla said, setting her mouth obstinately. The young man looked half-exasperated—then he suddenly gave her a glowing smile.

"Oh, you English! Who can ever understand you?"

Lucilla was rather glad of the tea-table with its massive array of silver; it was sort of rampart between her and this eager creature. He rose—then sat down again.

"Well now, let us be rational" he said. "The prisoners we can forget; they are safe in Cairo—so Colonel Morven told me last night. So we should speak about you and me. When I asked you to marry me before you told me that you were affianced; but now your betrothed is dead. *Requiescat*" he said. He crossed himself, and paused.

"So you are free" Hugo pursued. "Now there is no question of being false to an imprisoned lover. You know that I love you—could you ever love me?"

Lucilla waited for a moment. Then—"I do love you" she said.

The young man stared at her.

"Truly?"

"Yes, truly." She got up from behind the rampart of the tea-table, and went over to where he sat on a sofa and gave him a long deliberate kiss.

"Oh, du mein liebstes Herz!" He held her away from him and studied her face. "Since when?"

"Oh, a long time now. I think really since you were so nice in the hide on the Hortobagy" the young girl said reflectively.

"How was I nice?"

"Not squeezing my knee, or trying to kiss me! Anyhow you *were* nice."

"It was hard to be" he said, smiling.

"I know—that's why you were nice to be *nice*" Lucilla pronounced, making him laugh. Then his face turned sad.

200

"But dearest, what do we do? At this moment I can offer you a reasonable amount: wealth, two beautiful homes—my parents would make a flat for us at Derekegyhaz, and we could have another in Pest, or a house up here in Buda, if you preferred that. But who knows what comes, and when? If the Germans came here I may be beggared, as so many Poles have been."

"Yes, I know." Lucilla knew a lot of beggared Poles. "And of course if the Germans come in, we go out. No, I don't see a lot of future for you and me, Hugo; these aren't the sort of days for making plans. But"—she paused. "*I* feel it's something to know, and acknowledge, that we love one another" the girl said, slowly. "Love is much more important than houses, or money, or horrible wars that destroy plans and houses, and try to destroy love itself. They can't do *that*—love is indestructible." She paused again. "So I suggest that we should just be happy in knowing that we love one another, and wait for what comes."

He took her in his arms. "My darling! You speak eternal truths."

"Don't exaggerate, Hugo! That's just *fact*. Look, I must fly now. But we'll simply go on seeing one another, and being happy, for as long as we can, won't we? Oh, I do love you so much!" She gave him a long eager kiss before she ran off to get her coat; he drove her back to the Legation for her evening work on the Bulletin.

The Bulletin didn't actually last much longer. It had never been posted or circulated; people had to collect it, or send for it, either from the Legation or from the Consulate down in Pest. But when some men from the Secret Police went so far as to seize from their messengers, and confiscate, the two copies addressed respectively to the Regent and the Prime Minister, Sir Hugh felt that the time had come to close down. He sent a formal and severe protest to the Foreign Ministry, though in fact he knew that they could not help themselves. The German pressure on Hungary was becoming extreme. Members of the Chancery staff who had been encouraged to take flats over-

201

looking the West-Bahnhof reported long trains full of tanks, tracked vehicles, and guns passing through, their shapes clearly recognisable under the waterproof covers, bound for Rumania, or perhaps ultimately Bulgaria. The Serbs suddenly and recklessly got tough with Germany; they threw out Prince Paul, the Regent, whom they suspected of playing ball with the Nazis, and put the youthful King Peter on the throne. This display of independence infuriated Hitler; it was obvious that some form of action against Yugo-slavia would be taken before long. Then the sack would be closed, finally and completely. In view of all this the Minister caused Martha to send out the last edition of the little paper which had brought truth into the heart of Central Europe for so long, and despatched the girls who had worked on it back to England "Athenswise," the only route available, while the going was still good.

When the Bulletin went out of action Lucilla suddenly found herself with a lot of time on her hands, after her months of unremitting work; but Horace Wheatley was glad enough of extra help in the Chancery in the complicated three-man business of decyphering and encyphering telegrams. All the same, she was much more free than she had been, and when Hugo could get off in the afternoon he would drive her out into the country for an hour or two. Spring was beginning: the ice on the Danube was breaking up, and big floes drifted down on the current; the sun had more power, the air was balmy, full of the scent of growing things; thrushes and blackbirds began to sing outside David Eynsham's windows in the trees that clothed the slopes of the Bastion, filling him with delight and reassurance—he had always felt birdsong to be one of the most definite evidences of the goodness of God. Birds sang too in the forests where Lucilla and Hugo wandered hand in hand, or knelt on the dark soil, which gave out a woody fragrance, to pick snowdrops and woodanemones—sometimes they sat on a fallen trunk, and listened, and kissed; they were very happy.

But Mrs Eynsham could pay little attention to the spring that year, after her one drive to Buda-Örs when she picked aconites;

she was working a fifteen-hour day, till 1.30 a.m., with breaks for meals, and her thoughts were elsewhere. She was troubled about David. He seemed to her to have gone back since he left the nursing-home; she heard his panting breath when he walked upstairs, the outer corners of the palms of his hands were often a brilliant pink; he was working much too hard, and he wouldn't stop. One morning, when as usual he was having breakfast in bed, the window open to the soft air—like all heart subjects David could not endure closed windows—he said: "Listen to that cock-blackbird—he has such an individual song. There!—now!— 'Oh you pretty-pretty-pretty-pretty *biird!*' Isn't he lovely?" He mused. "I wonder sometimes how many more springs I shall hear blackbirds singing?"

Rosina's heart nearly stopped. He had never spoken like that before.

"Oh, for ever so long" she said, automatically. "But darling, don't you feel well?"

"Well enough. It's only that one sometimes wonders. I wish I knew whether there will be blackbirds in Heaven; I shall miss them frightfully if there aren't—always supposing that I get to Heaven."

"You *will*—and in Heaven Our Heavenly Father will give everybody everything that they want" Rosina said confidently. "If you want blackbirds, you'll get blackbirds—unless you find, there, that you want something else more; then you'll get that."

"What else could I want more?" he asked, looking at her in surprise.

"Oh, Angel-song—which you've never heard!—or the Beatific Vision."

"You're very certain" he said after a pause—his smile was relieved and contented.

"Yes, I am; quite certain. Darling, I must go now. You'll be sure to rest properly this afternoon, won't you? Promise?"

"Yes, I promise, my dear. What a funny old believing Christian you are, aren't you?" His mockery reassured her a little.

"It always seems to me so much funnier *not* to be a Christian, when it's there" she said, with her usual careless use of words.

"Just put the tray on the trolley, would you?—since like Christianity you *are* there!" David said, grinning. "And give me my slippers." She did as he asked, and handed him his dressing-gown; when he pushed his long lean shanks out from under the bed-clothes and stuffed his feet into his slippers she noticed that his ankles, and even his insteps, were swollen and puffy, a thing she had never seen before. She repressed a question, but when she got round to her office she rang up Dr Mendze, and reported this phenomenon to him.

"Last night, when he had been up all day?"

"No, this morning—he'd been lying flat in bed all night."

"Did they pit?" the doctor asked.

"I'm sorry, I don't understand."

"When you pressed your finger into the swelling, did it leave a depression? This is pitting."

"I never touched his feet—and I never said anything. Oh, does it mean something bad?"

"I will see him" Mendze replied, non-committally. "Thank you for giving me this information. It can be useful."

"Well do please telephone to me when you have seen him— here, at the Legation. I'm here most of the day." Troubled and anxious, she nevertheless concentrated her attention on the prisoners-of-war. The first card on the pile on her desk was dated February the 25th, 1941—it had come rather slowly. After thanking the Relief Organisation in Budapest for socks, gloves, a pull-over and a scarf, the writer added: "I have had nothing from home yet but *one book!*" There was a letter from Melchior in Geneva, which had come very fast. "Do do all you can" he wrote. "The parcels situation here is really *desperate.* So many are pillaged in transit through France, and those that *are* full— well, the delays in getting them accepted by the German railway authorities are endless—and Heaven knows how long it takes for them to reach the camps."

In Budapest there was desperation too—as to whether the quilts from Istanbul and the "Athens underwear" would arrive

204

in time to be sent on to Germany. A cable from Ankara reported the despatch of the quilts to Budapest on March the 10th; another, from Athens, stated that the underclothing from Cairo had been entrained there on the 13th. The little Committee waited, and packed, all they could do; the knitting-parties knitted furiously, and gloves, socks, scarves, pull-overs, cigarettes from Athens and pyjamas of Yugo-slav flannellette were steadily despatched, week by week, together with Hungarian smoked goose-breast and Yugo-slav tinned goulasch.

The quilts came through fast—Horace and Rosina furnished the good Herr Hasler with lists and camp labels, someone was sent hurrying round to the National Bank with duplicate lists to collect the export licences, and an emissary of the Hungarian Red Cross personally escorted the consignment up to the frontier, and saw it safely across. (Years later returned prisoners called on Horace and Rosina in London, bringing with them the stained, torn, dirty quilts which, they said, had saved their lives during four bitter winters in Germany.)

But the "Athens underwear"! Day after day passed, and still there was no sign of this vital consignment. The Minister cabled to Sofia, and learned from the Legation there that it had passed through Bulgaria and was now in Yugo-slavia—telephoning had suddenly become difficult: "It is regretted, but we cannot get the connection." Everyone knew what that meant—calls from Legation to Legation were simply not being put through. On March the 28th the Minister sent an urgent cable to Sir Monty in Belgrade: "Underclothing ex Cairo for all repeat all prisoners known to have reached Yugo-slavia. Gor God's sake get it into Hungary before frontier closes." He had the best of reasons for believing that Hungary's southern frontier might be closed at any moment. Then they all waited again.

Erich, the Eynshams' excellent manservant, never on any account disturbed his mistress in her bedroom; he sent messages by Bertha, the maid. But on the morning of April 3rd he tapped on her door, and when she called "*Herein!*" came in, with a distraught face.

"Gracious Lady, the Count Teleki Pál is dead."

"Dead? The Prime Minister? But how? He was not ill."

"*Meine Gnädigste,* he shot himself. His valet is my friend; he has telephoned to me. He found him in his bed, and the revolver on the floor. I thought the Lady should know—and also I wondered if I should tell the *Gnädiger Herr?*"

"No, not yet" Mrs Eynsham said instinctively. She knew how fond her husband had been of Count Teleki. "But Erich, *why?* It seems so extraordinary."

"Most gracious, the Germans are here; they came in at dawn. If the Lady allows me to open the windows she will hear them."

"Yes, open up." Not suffering from heart, Rosina only slept with a crack of open window at the side of the house; when Erich opened the big ones which gave onto the Bastion a deafening roar came into the room—the hideous noise which tanks and tracked vehicles make passing over cobbles.

"How frightful! Shut the windows again, Erich. Are you sure they are Germans?"

"Oh yes, *meine Gnädigste.* I sent Janos down to see when the noise began." Janos was the house-boy.

"But where are they going?"

"South—to destroy the Serbs! May God rot this Hitler!"

Mrs Eynsham at once thought, naturally, of the prisoners' underclothing, still presumably in Yugo-slavia—but she also thought of her husband.

"Well if the *Gnädiger Herr* asks, tell him that the Germans are here. But do not speak to him of Count Teleki—I will tell him this."

As she spoke the telephone by her bed rang.

"Yes?" she said, lifting the receiver.

"Here the Hungarian Red Cross—is it Mrs Eynsham?"

"Yes" Rosina said impatiently. "What is it?"

"*Sieben Wagonen* of clothing for the British prisoners-of-war have just arrived at the Keleti Bahnhof. What do we do?"

"Oh, accept them, of course. I will arrange for their transmission to Germany. Have you a representative at the station to sign the papers?"

"We send one. Who collects the goods?"

"Hasler, as he did the quilts."

Pondering hurriedly, she decided to get onto Hasler before going to tell David about Count Teleki's suicide—if it was true; but she trusted Erich. She got the little Jew at once—Hungarians are early risers—and asked him to send to the Keleti Station to collect seven truck-loads of clothing for the prisoners.

"Lady, I do not think that I can do this."

"Why not?" Mrs Eynsham asked sharply, vexed. Here, thank God, was the Athens underwear at last—it *must* go on at once, especially if the Germans were already in Budapest.

"Lady, I can get no benzine for my lorries; the Germans have taken over all the pumps."

Rosina wondered whether she dared to tell the little man to send his lorries to fill up in the Legation. No—if the Germans were really here they themselves would have to get out, and might need every drop. "Have you no horse-drays?" she asked.

"Ah, this I could arrange."

"Well arrange it."

"But Lady, I dare not undertake the packing at my place. I am Jew, so under suspicion. Where do I bring the clothing?"

Again Rosina pondered. If the Legation was leaving there would be frenzied packing, burning of cyphers, and so on. All the same she quickly took her decision; the soldiers must have their vests and pants.

"Bring it here" she said.

"To the *Gnädigste's* house?"

"No no—to the Legation. The Rote Kreuz are sending a representative to the Station to receive the goods, and they have my instructions to hand them to you."

After she had rung off it occurred to her that she must warn the Min that all this stuff would be coming to the Legation, but before doing so she telephoned again to the Hungarian Red

Cross to confirm that Hasler would be collecting the clothing and bringing it to the Legation. Oh goodness!—of course someone would have to go to the National Bank to collect the export licences; she must get out the letters of request, and the lists. She rang for Bertha and ordered her breakfast at once, while she began to dress—the maid lingered.

"Is it not terrible that the Count Teleki is dead? Such a *good* man. And the Germans here, in our city! Will the gracious Lady and the gracious Herr remain? Oh, what will become of us?"

"Bertha, bring my breakfast. We speak of all this later" Rosina said. She was already thinking about how much "pay in lieu of notice" they ought to give their kind staff. But she *must* ring up the Min. She had pulled on her stockings, and after clipping them onto her suspender-belt she went over to the telephone; but at this point David walked in in his dressing-gown, and sat down on the foot of the bed.

"Teleki Paul has bumped himself" he said.

"Yes, I know. What a frightful thing" Rosina replied, pushing her feet into her knickers, and pulling her petticoat over her head.

"Who told you?"

"Erich—and that the Huns are in." She sat down at the dressing-table and began to comb her hair and arrange her face. "It's all appalling" she said, watching her husband's face in the mirror; it looked drawn as well as distressed. "Who told *you?*" she asked.

"Janos."

Oh—well Erich might have prevented that, she thought. She turned round on the dressing-stool and faced her husband. "Darling, you know how sorry I am."

"This *good* little country" David said, deep sadness in his voice. "Why should it all be mucked up, just to satisfy a house-painter's ambition?"

"Why indeed? Hateful Hitler!" As she spoke she thought of the Weissbergers, and all the other Jews who had deserved so well of Hungary—including poor little Hasler.

"Why are you up so early?" Eynsham asked then—the thought of Hasler had caused his wife to turn back to her dressing-table and go on attending to her face.

"The Athens underwear has come! Isn't it wonderful? So I must go and cope."

"What on earth is the Athens underwear?" Eynsham asked.

"Oh darling, you're like the worst English Judge! Never mind —it's clothes for the prisoners, and it's *come*, and I must get it pushed on before we leave." She went to a wardrobe, took out a dress and a hat, put on both, and then reached a fur coat out of another press.

"I must fly. Bless you, darling. Go back to bed and have your breakfast." A hasty kiss, and she went out. She slipped into Lucilla's room. Her daughter was still fast asleep, she had been dancing with Hugo till all hours—nevertheless Rosina stirred the pretty sleeping figure.

"M-m-m-m?" Lucilla muttered.

"Darling, when you're awake, start sorting your things and do some packing. Did you hear me?"

"Yes. Why? Have the Huns come?"

"Yes. Be a bit selective—I don't know how much we shall be able to take."

"I must take my books!" Lucilla said, suddenly sitting bolt upright in bed.

"Well I hope you can. Anyhow get going."

"Where are you off to?" Lucilla asked, rubbing her eyes, and observing her Mother's fur coat and pretty matching hat. "Aren't you going to pack?"

"Yes—the prisoners' underwear! I'll see to my things later. But do get yours done; then I can have Bertha."

Still Mrs Eynsham had failed to warn the Minister that the Athens underwear was coming to the Legation. She thought of using Lucilla's bedside telephone, but didn't; she would be there in two minutes—heaps of time! But she was detained in the hall by Erich, by the cook, and by the old gardener, all bewailing Count Teleki's death, and asking if the *Herrschaften* would be leaving? She condoled and pacified as best she could: the *Herr Gesandtschaftsrat* would make all proper arrangements when the time came. At last she left the house, and hastened along the pretty golden street—too late. As she approached the big yellow palace which housed the Legation black flecks of burnt paper filled the air, landing on her coat, and puffs of pale smoke were billowing up into the sky behind—ah, they were burning the cyphers already! When she turned in at the *porte-cochère* she found it completely blocked by a huge horse-dray, piled with bales of clothing; it had been piled too high, and was stuck in the arched entrance like a bung in a barrel—by the glass door leading to the staircase the Minister stood, fuming.

"Ah! Is this some performance of yours?" he asked as she came up to him—he had never spoken to her so harshly before.

"Yes. It's the Athens underwear. I had to have it sent here, because Budapest is full of Nazis today, and Hasler is a Jew—he can't handle it at his place."

"You hadn't thought that we might be fairly busy here today ourselves?" he asked coldly.

"Hugh, don't be beastly! Of course I had, and I meant to ring you up—only then David came in, and all our servants were in such a tizzy." She spoke in Hungarian to the dray-men; the top bales were pulled off, and the big vehicle moved forward into the courtyard—she told them to dump the bales in the covered passage leading to the garden.

"And who, may I ask, is going to re-pack this stuff?" Sir Hugh asked, more mildly—he was slightly mollified by her having called him "Hugh."

"Me—and Hasler's men. I'm sure we shall manage."

"You really can't monopolise my staff today, you know" he said, still rather stiffly.

"I won't. I'll get Mr Smith and Lucilla" she said, hurt. As she was moving away Anton appeared, accompanied by a Hungarian policeman, very smart in his tall blue helmet.

"What is it?" Sir Hugh asked.

Anton explained that people in the houses near by were com-

210

plaining about the clouds of black ash, and the policeman had come to request that it should be stopped.

"Tell him it shall be stopped" Sir Hugh said, and walked through the courtyard and into the garden, where two rather makeshift incinerators had been erected on the broad path which led across the lawn; Horace Wheatley and Geoffrey Milton, in their shirt-sleeves, were tearing sheets out of cypher-books—so that they should burn more easily—and shoving them into one machine, while two Chancery clerks were stuffing files of official telegrams into the other.

"Good. Keep at it" the Minister said. He knew that the police protest had only been made *pro forma*, as a gesture, and anyhow the stuff had got to be burnt. He went back to his study and rang for his breakfast.

14

In her little office Mrs Eynsham presently telephoned to Mr Smith, asking him to come up and pack. "And if you can bring any helpers, do—we shall want all the pairs of hands we can get."

"Are you all off?" good Mr Smith asked.

"I expect so—no actual orders yet. But we *must* get this stuff through."

Very few people have ever seen seven large train truck-loads of goods spread out on the ground; they take up an enormous amount of space. And when Mr Smith, Rosina, and Lucilla cut open the 294 bales and checked their contents, to Rosina's dismay they found that these did not in the least correspond with the figures sent from Middle East Command in Cairo. They had been led to expect shirts, vests and pants; in fact there were *no* pants—only thousands of khaki shirts with no collars, *very* short white vests, and an enormous quantity of khaki socks, which made a complete nonsense of the lists so carefully prepared for the National Bank. Poor Mrs Eynsham, lists of the new quantities in her hand, eventually went to her office, made out fresh allocations, and then rang up Martha Beckley.

"Martha, the Athens stuff has come."

"I know. Marvellous!"

"Yes, but it's all wrong—they haven't sent what they said they were sending, so there'll have to be different letters to the Bank, for the licences. And the Min said I wasn't to use his staff today. So what do I do? I can't type."

"Oh, he's so upset that he was cross to you" Martha said. "He's been moaning about it all the morning. It was just that dray! Are you all ready? If so I'll send a typist up at once—and a messenger will go to the Bank."

The typist came up and Mrs Eynsham dictated fresh requests for export licences; then she went down to the courtyard again. Hasler's packers had now arrived, and under her and Mr Smith's direction they repacked the Athens underwear, while she and Lucilla and Mr Smith gummed labels onto the freshly sewn-up bales; there were 99 bales of socks alone.

"Pity they sent all these socks, and no pants" said Mr Smith, trying to wipe the gum off his hands on a rather dirty handkerchief. "We'd pretty well fixed most of the camps up with socks."

"We shall never know if this particular dottiness was the Army or the Red Cross, I don't suppose" said Mrs Eynsham. "Oh, do come and wash in the Bulletin bathroom—I expect there's still a towel."

"They're *all* total clots, if you ask me" Lucilla observed acidly, following her Mother and Mr Smith into the Bulletin rooms. There was a towel, not very clean, in the bathroom, but the huge wireless-set had gone, as had the roneo machine from the big outer office.

Packing up a Legation for a hasty flight is quite a business; it was not only for Mr Smith and Lucilla and her Mother that it was a long hard day. At 3 p.m. they went along the *utca* to have a belated meal at the Eynshams' house; as they left the Legation the official Humber drove out, taking the Minister to the Palace to take his formal farewell of the Regent. Horrible flecks of black ash still landed on their clothes as they walked—the burning of cyphers was going merrily on. Martha Beckley, who had lunched early, was hard at work with Minnie, preparing inventories of the linen, blankets, pillows, glass and china which must be left behind—in the care of the Americans, who, as so often, became the "Protecting Power." (When America came into the War after Pearl Harbour the Swiss, perennially neutral, took on this obligation—it might have been simpler to hand it all over to them in the first place.)

213

By ten o'clock that night the re-packing had been done; the fresh export licences had come from the National Bank, and first thing on the following morning Hasler's horse-drays began to cart the whole mass of bales across to the West-Bahnhof. There the railway authorities refused to accept them! A sort of creeping mobilisation was going on—the Hungarians, unable to defy the Germans, but threatened on all sides, were trying to put their small army on a war footing against any eventuality, and wanted their railways free. Mrs Eynsham, aghast at this contretemps, without consulting anyone rang up Pista Horthy, the Regent's son, who was head of the State Railways.

"Pista, we've been waiting for *weeks* for some underclothes for the prisoners to come from Cairo. It came yesterday, and we killed ourselves getting it re-packed, and the export licences and all—and now your people at the West-Bahnhof say they can't accept it! *Please* do something; you really must."

"How much is there?" Pista Horthy asked, in his faultless English.

"Seven truck-loads—I mean *sieben Wagonen;* not lorries."

"Where is it consigned to?"

"Hegyeshalom—that's where all our stuff goes through."

"Who has the export licences? You say you have got these."

"One of our messengers—he's with the stuff now. Dear Pista, do *please* let it go off."

"Don't worry, Mrs Eynsham—I will see that it goes. How is your husband?"

"Oh, not too bad, thank you. Give my love to Illi—when does the baby come?"

"Not for some weeks; she is very well."

"I'm so glad. But remember, Pista, I'm relying on you about this."

"Don't worry" the young man repeated.

However at that crisis in Hungarian affairs Mrs Eynsham didn't really rely on Pista Horthy, or anyone else. She went downstairs to the Military Attaché, and reported her conversation. "I would like to be sure that all that stuff really goes."

214

"My God, so would I!" Colonel Morven said. "I'll get someone to watch at the West-Bahnhof, and at Hegyeshalom too."

"Oh fine—and let me know."

Rosina with her one-track mind was concentrating on getting the Cairo clothing out to the prisoners; the Minister, and her husband too, were concerned with the graver problem of how they were to get out themselves, with their staff of fifty-four souls, when the time came. With German armoured divisions roaring down into Yugo-slavia the string at the mouth of the sack was suddenly drawn tight and knotted, finally and definitely; no way out there, by rail or by road. The Germans would of course have sent them in sealed trains across Europe to Lisbon, but Sir Hugh did not fancy this idea.

And then a mouse-hole was discovered in the sack whose neck was tied so tightly—mice have a way of nibbling holes in sacks. That little railway up through Ruthenia to the Russian frontier was suddenly found to have been opened again three weeks earlier; the bombed bridges had been rebuilt, and there was a way clear through to Moscow, via Lwow, Tarnopol, and Kiev. To reach England by that route meant going round the world —across the Trans-Siberian railway, oversea to Japan; across the Pacific, across America, across the Atlantic; the Minister suggested this route to the Foreign Office, who concurred—he and his staff should return via Moscow and America.

There were also the Allies to be thought of, the Belgians and the Dutch—they must be got out too. The French Legation by this time was a Vichy set-up; no need to worry about the *Pétainistes*, David Eynsham said acidly to his chief—they were quite happy where they were. But the others had better come with the British—"then Pista can make up one diplomatic train to the frontier for the whole lot of us." The Minister agreed, and the American Legation obligingly radioed a message to the Foreign Office suggesting this arrangement. Since the wireless transmitter in the British Legation had been dismantled, and the Germans had taken over Hungary's entire telephone and telegraph system, as well as the petrol-pumps, this was the only se-

215

cure means of communication with London. The Foreign Office once more concurred—via the Americans—and Sir Hugh went down and put the suggestion to his colleagues.

The Dutch agreed at once; the Belgians hesitated. As the Germans were not actually occupying Hungary, only passing through, it might be better to wait and see, etc. Sir Hugh could not wait and see, and said so; he cut the Belgians out, and asked the Hungarian Government for a train for his own party and the Dutch. He prudently took all these measures in advance, before he had received definite orders to leave; in fact England only formally broke off relations with Hungary on April the 7th. But with the Dutch he had over sixty souls in his care, and must make provision for them. Through the helpful Americans he cabled to Moscow, asking the Ambassador there to arrange to have a diplomatic train sent to the frontier station to meet his party and take it on through Russia, and to organise "forward transport" via the Trans-Siberian Railway to the port of Dairen, bound for Japan and the U.S.A.

But of course everyone knew that the departure of the English was only a matter of time, and now began the heart-breaking business of farewells. The Hungarians—in a desperate situation, menaced alike by Germany and by Russia—had felt, perhaps irrationally, that the presence of the British Legation was some sort of safeguard; and now this was leaving them. They poured up to the Legation and to the houses of the staff, bringing farewell gifts: books, flowers, fruit, huge boxes of Gerbeaud chocolates, as well as touching tiny presents of all sorts—some extremely valuable. Prince Willie came up from Siraly to say good-bye; after calling at the Legation he came along to Rosina's little yellow house. She had been forced to ration visitors to five minutes each, but when he came in she said to Erich— "The Durchlaucht, naturally, remains as long as he desires."

"My dear Rosina, this is so sad. But do tell me—what is this mysterious instruction that you gave to your servant?"

"Only that I didn't want you to be hurried. I make Erich come in and say that I'm wanted on the telephone or something

216

after five minutes, so that I can go on working through the queue."

He smiled.

"You are well organised. But this is most melancholy—and for us it will all turn out very badly, you will see."

"We are so frightfully unhappy about Count Teleki" Rosina said. "Do you know how his wife is?"

"Very brave, as one would expect of her. But it is a fearful loss for this nation."

Mrs Eynsham took the opportunity of thanking the Prince for all his help over the prisoners' parcels—"We owe so *much* to you" she ended.

"It was not so much—and to do it was a pleasure."

It suddenly occurred to Rosina that Prince Tereny might do her one last service, and she told him about the seven freight-wagons of underclothing, now loaded, but still in a siding at the West Station—Colonel Morven, through his sleuths, kept her informed every few hours as to the situation there. "Pista *promised* me it should go" she said rather plaintively, "but it hasn't gone."

"Are you sure of this?"

"It was still there an hour ago" she replied firmly.

"Well, I will do what I can. Things are difficult just now, as I am sure you realise." He changed the subject. "Oria wanted so much to come up and say good-bye to your daughter, but she has influenza."

Rosina made suitable sounds of regret.

The Prince rose.

"I must not keep you. We are *sad*, personally, to lose you— you know that." To her great surprise, instead of kissing her hand he kissed her on the cheek. "Look after your husband" he added, with a sudden brisk emphasis. "I did not think he looked well when I saw him just now."

"Oh, didn't you? No—he isn't well, and all this work and fuss is so bad for him. He hates leaving Hungary."

"I know this. Bon voyage, and au revoir, with God's help."

217

But she never saw Prince Willie again; within six months he had died of a stroke.

When he had gone other leave-takers came in. Among them was a Hungarian diplomat who had returned from Moscow a few months before—when he heard of their proposed route he said: "Take plenty of oranges and lemons; there are none in Russia. And toilet-paper; this is not furnished on Russian trains, nor in the hotels—if you are spending a week or more on the Trans-Siberian you will want your own supplies. And mineral-water—take plenty; it is unobtainable." Mrs Eynsham gratefully took the hint: a net of oranges and lemons, and a stout twin-handled carrier full of toilet-rolls joined the pigskin bag of necessaries which had spent so many months under her bed-table —now at last it would be used, though not wheeled down through the Balkans in old Countess Pongracz's garden-basket. As for the mineral-water, she passed the tip on to Sir Hugh, who ordered several cases.

But Rosina was troubled by what Prince Tereny had said about David. Dr Mendze had examined his ankles after her telephone call, and reported that the swelling was cardiac oedema— "He should come back to the Szanatorium, and remain in bed." This of course was out of the question, and she had asked for drugs to help the condition—"We have a journey ahead of us." The good little doctor sent her up two boxes of pills, a phial of mohphia, and a hypodermic syringe. "The white pills are for the swelling, a diuretic. And if he should get another heart attack, give him first two brown pills, and a small glass of whisky; then an injection of the morphine. Can you give an injection?"

"Oh Lord yes! I give myself an anti-rheumatism one every week."

"Good. I wish you did not leave."

"So do I" said Mrs Eynsham.

The final marching orders for the Legation came on April the 7th; the telegram arrived latish in the morning, and everyone was told at once. Almost the saddest farewell of all took place that afternoon on a forested slope far upstream from Budapest, over-

218

looking the Danube. Lucilla had seen little of Hugo for the past three or four days; she had been too busy, helping to pack the Athens underwear, then encyphering and decyphering floods of telegrams with Horace's overworked Chancery staff—besides making a *triage* of her clothes, telling Bertha which to pack, and herself packing the most precious of her books. But when the news of the Legation's imminent departure was announced she telephoned to him at once, and he came up and drove her out into the country. They left the car in the mouth of a wood-cutters' track, and walked up the hillside till they reached a clearing with a view out over the great river; there the young man spread his coat on a bank of deep moss, as lovers have done for their sweethearts since the golden age of Greece, and they sat down side by side.

"So now it ends?" he asked.

"It ends for the moment—we're supposed to leave the day after tomorrow. What are you going to do?"

"We stay; my Father and I, at least, shall stay as long as we can—we have the employees in our works to think of."

"But if the Germans come in, *can* you?" At that moment Lucilla was acutely aware of the fact that this blonde boy beside her, whom she loved so much, was a Jew.

"If things become too difficult we may send my Mother and Emmi away."

"Where to?"

"Ultimately to America, we hope—but it is not easy to get in there. Probably first to Portugal."

"Portugal? Why on earth?" In 1941 Lucilla had never heard of anyone who went to Portugal.

"Entry there is easy; the climate is delightful; and there are good and very *cheap* hotels. And there is also Fatima."

Lucilla had never heard the name Fatima, except as one of Bluebeard's wives; the Visions and the great pilgrimages were outside her Anglican ken. What struck her, and troubled her, was the idea of any of the Weissbergers having to think of hotels being cheap, after the luxury in which they had always

219

lived, and so generously and hospitably extended to endless guests, rich and poor alike. The tears came into her eyes.

"Oh, I can't bear it! Why should you have to be poor? Why is the world so *mad?*"

He put his arm round her.

"At the moment the world is mad because Adolf Hitler is a paranoiac—and if the Russians, since the Ribbontrop-Molotoff pact was signed his so-called allies, turn on him and beat him it will get madder still! But why do you mind our becoming poor? Do you not wish to be involved with a poor man?"

"Oh don't be idiotic, Hugo! I'm thinking about your Mother —she's not so young now, and she's always been comfortable, with a lady's maid and all that sort of thing. I can't *bear* to think of her in cheap hotels."

He kissed her, but she gave him a little impatient push.

"*I've* got money" she went on, "at least I shall have; Mummy's old Aunt Lucy in Scotland has mints, and she's leaving it all to me. But I shouldn't want to live in the States!" she pronounced with sudden decision.

"Why not?" he asked, surprised.

"Oh, no monarchy, no aristocracy, no tradition—except in the South; just wealth and gadgets! Not having tradition is what matters most, of course; it's like roots to a plant, it gives a sort of continuing *life* to a nation."

He stared at her.

"I had no idea that you thought about things like these."

"That's the misery of it" she said sadly. "We were just beginning to find out what we each did think about all sorts of things, and now we've got to stop. But you'll always let me know what's happening, won't you?"

"Most certainly, my darling. Where do I write to you? To this Aunt who makes you so rich?"

"No—just care of the Foreign Office, London. They're bound to know where we are."

"This is easy." Then, rather embarrassedly, he took a little leather case out of his pocket and snapped it open—from the white velvet an enormous diamond set in sapphires sparkled up in the girl's startled face.

"I wondered if you would agree to a betrothal? You *have* said that you loved me! If so, I should like you to wear my ring."

Lucilla stared for a moment at the beautiful jewel.

"Why sapphires?"

"Your month-stone. I found out from your Mother that your birthday is in September."

Lucilla burst into tears. Oh, he thought of everything—life with him would be perfect. But how uncertain it was that she would ever have life with him—especially if he persisted in staying in Hungary when the Germans came in, as everyone said they were bound to do.

He was distressed by her tears. "Do you not wish to be affianced to me?"

"Yes. But I won't take your lovely, lovely ring—and I don't want you to feel too tied to me, if you should meet someone else." At the back of her mind she was thinking of Hamish— she might be submarined going home from the States, or blitzed when they got to London; she might lose her arms or legs, or go dotty! "Let me look at it again" she said, inconsequently. "Yes, it's sup*erb*. Thank you, darling Hugo."

"But why not wear it?"

"Oh, it's too beautiful—it would get stolen! No." She stood up—the young man rose too. "Give me your hands" she said— surprised, he put his hands in hers.

"I want to be your wife" Lucilla said, slowly. "A year from today let us meet, or else telegraph to one another; if we can't meet then, we try the year after, or the year after that. But for that time I mean to keep myself yours." (This was her more modest version of "Always.") "Thereto I pledge you my troth" she said solemnly, and kissed him on the mouth.

Now the tears were in Hugo's eyes.

"My precious one! I will do as you say. But then, why not the ring?"

"What I said is more than any ring. It comes out of our marriage service. Oh my darling, I do love you so much!"

"I shall love you till I die, I think," the young man said.

That was on April the 7th. On the 8th the hard-pressed Legation staff—trying to combine their private packing, settling of last-minute bills, and paying off their servants with a final rush of work, and receiving the unceasing farewell calls, learned that they had a forty-eight-hours reprieve—the Embassy in Moscow reported to the Americans that the special Russian train could only get to the frontier on the 11th, not on the 9th, as previously arranged. The Ernest Erdöszys came up from Terenczer on the afternoon of the 8th to say good-bye; Ernest had had a little silver matchbox-holder engraved with the words: "Rosina, with Ernest's love. April the 9th, 1941"—he was greatly upset when he found out that the date was wrong. "Perhaps I can get it altered in time."

"No, don't bother, Ernest. The date doesn't matter—what matters is your love! Bless you."

But on the evening of the 9th she learned from Colonel Morven that the Athens underwear, in its seven railway-trucks, was still sitting in a siding at the West-Bahnhof; it had not been despatched. Rosina lost her temper, a thing she did rather easily, and took action. She rang up Pista Horthy at his house.

"Pista? Rosina here. Our stuff hasn't gone from the West-Station, as you promised me it should."

The young man was very apologetic—the mobilisation, etc.

"Yes, I know all that," Rosina said brusquely. "But a promise is a promise. Anyhow, Pista—no, don't interrupt—*listen!* Until that stuff has gone, I don't leave Budapest."

"But your train goes early on the 11th, to the Russian frontier."

"Quite so—but I shan't go on it unless those seven wagons of the prisoners' stuff have crossed the frontier at Hegyeshalom. I know it will be frightfully inconvenient for your Government to have the British Counsellor's wife stay behind when the whole Legation staff has gone, but that's just something you

222

will have to put up with, unless you get that clothing away in time. I shall *know*, Pista, remember—and *I* don't go till *it's* gone." She rang off. And about noon on the 10th Colonel Morven telephoned to her to say that all seven trucks had safely crossed the frontier into German-occupied Austria, and been accepted by the German authorities. Then Mrs Eynsham relaxed a little, and went on with the business of handing over the wool, the names of the knitting-parties, and the undespatched stores to the wife of the American Military Attaché, who had nobly promised to go on sending parcels as long as she could. This lady was another of the "unknowns," like Prince Willie and Mr Smith and Mrs Starnberg, to whom the British prisoners owed more than they realised.

When a diplomatic Mission leaves a country there is usually a certain careful formality about the actual departure—a platform cordoned off, plenty of police in control, a Government representative to make the official leave-taking. But the Hungarians, normally the most courteous of nations, were so rushed and rattled on that April morning in 1941 that nothing of the sort was organised. The train for the Allied diplomats was drawn up at an ordinary platform, unguarded by police; such crowds of the public were milling about on it that the diplomatic parties had difficulty in getting to their carriages—conspicuous among these crowds were German officers in uniform, elbowing people —including the departing diplomatic ladies—out of their way.

"This is outrageous!" David Eynsham said angrily to his chief.

"I know. It will be reported" Sir Hugh said. "Get in and sit down, David—Horace and I will see to everything."

A few of the many friends who had come to the station to say good-bye succeeded in pushing through the *melée* and reaching the train—among them Mr Smith, Mrs Starnberg, and Emmi Weissberger and her Mother; the last three were in tears. So were Erich and Anton, who had brought down the luggage, and now came to report. "Oh, auf Wiedersehen" Anton said, kissing Sir Hugh's hand. "The best, the kindest of masters! Oh!—oh weh! What becomes of us without you?"

223

That was indeed the prevailing note. Rosina, after settling David in a corner seat and checking the hand-luggage—the net of oranges and lemons, and the pigskin bag, at last coming into its own, were all in the rack—got out of the train again, said good-bye to Emmi and her Mother, and kissed Mrs Starnberg.

"You've done so much—I can never thank you. I do hope you'll be all right—I wish you were coming."

"I can't leave Herberth—and he *won't* leave."

"I know. Bless you. Write."

"Rosina, we're off—get in" Horace said brusquely. She did so, and the train pulled out, with waving from the platform and from the windows—then its occupants, feeling curiously dislocated, sat down and presently began to do something rather ordinary, consciously or unconsciously to take their minds off this painful severance from a place and people that most of them had liked so much. Sir Hugh, in his carriage, began to read a copy of *The Times* which had come by the last bag; Colonel Morven lit a pipe, while Gina took out a tiny brocade bag and began to crochet some exquisitely fine lace; Horace Wheatley put on a pair of leather gloves—he hated dirt on his fin-like hands —and began to read a well-bound book. Martha Beckley didn't sit down till she had been along the coaches to see that everyone was all right, particularly the Dutch; she had a bag full of Penguin thrillers, which she handed out right and left, including one for Eleanor Wheatley, who sat unoccupied and gloomy opposite her husband—they shared a carriage with the Morvens, and though he had carefully asked her permission, she disliked the Colonel's pipe.

The Eynshams had a carriage to themselves—they were three, and he was the Counsellor. Lucilla went out and stood in the corridor; Mrs Eynsham, her despatch-case on her knee, began writing letters to prisoners' relations—there were a few late ones that she had failed to answer in the hurry and turmoil of the last few days.

"What on earth are you writing letters for?" David asked ir-

224

ritably. His face was flushed; he was still upset that his beloved Hungarians should somehow have permitted such an ugly muddle at the moment of their departure; those tell-tale corners of his palms were a more vivid pink than ever. "You can't post letters in Russia" he said.

"I know. But as this train will be coming back to Budapest I thought I'd get the steward in the diner, or someone, to post them."

"Fair enough" David said, more equably. But Rosina screwed on the cap of her pen and closed her despatch-case—if David wanted to talk, and she got the impression that he did, her letters could wait.

She was right. When she lit a cigarette he began to speak of Count Teleki's suicide, and the loss that his death meant to Hungary. "He was so able, and had such complete integrity; really their one major standby. Bethlen is getting old, and so is the Regent, poor old boy." Rosina smiled, thinking of the phrase so often on Prince Willie's lips: "I will have a little talk with the Old Boy."

"The Regent has been tremendously good to us" she said.

"Yes. But I'm afraid Teleki Paul's death is the beginning of the end for this darling, decent little country. I wish we could have stayed—I do love it so."

"Dearest, I know you do." She was moved by his distress, but she was also thinking that their departure spelt the end to their efforts to help the prisoners-of-war—a small thing compared with the submerging of a nation, but worth doing. If only they had been able to stay on till the British Red Cross really got going, as it was bound to do in time. Greatly to her surprise, David presently referred to this.

"You weren't here long, Rosie, but you did like them, didn't you?"

"The Hunks? I *loved* them. I even rather liked Anna Dolinski, rabid Nazi that she was, and *before* she saved your life!"

He grinned a little shame-facedly.

"Anna's one of those clever fools, if you follow me. But she can't ever escape for long from her natural good heart—it's always breaking through her perversity."

"She sent me a terrific box of chocolates from Gerbeauds— it must have cost *pounds*" Rosina said. She had had to send a servant out to buy an extra suit-case in which to stow all the sweets and books that people had sent to her—their last-minute bouquets of flowers even now lay wilting in the rack above her head. But she was enjoying this talk with David—they had had so little time to talk of late. And then he gave her his surprise.

"You did a very good job for the P.O.W.s."

"I didn't think you knew much about that."

"Oh yes I did."

"Well now that's over too" Rosina said sadly.

David glanced towards the corridor, where Lucilla stood, pro-filed against the window.

"I'm afraid that child may have taken a bit of a knock over young Weissberger" he said. "I shouldn't have minded her marry-ing him a bit—he's a splendid boy. Do you know how that was left?"

"Not for certain. She didn't tell me, and I never ask. My guess is that she stood him off at the last." Bertha, with a nice servant's deep interest in her employers' affairs, had mentioned to her mistress that the *gnädiges Fräulein* had gone to her room in tears after returning from her last drive with the *Herr Baron*.

"Quite right not to ask" David said, with a husband's insuf-ferable patronage—Rosina, after years of marriage, had become inured to this tedious attitude, and wasn't even much annoyed by it; she mentally said—"Yes yes—how right you are"—aloud she said nothing at all.

"The Min will probably know, or learn, more than either of us" David pursued. "I gather she confides in him. But if you're right, there's another good thing come to an end."

"Oh dear me yes!—what a lot of endings, and how I hate them" his wife replied. "I like things to go on and on."

Lucilla stood in the corridor, alone, watching the Hungarian countryside, so much beloved, flow by. She was at once disappointed and relieved that Hugo hadn't come to the station; she would have wished to see him again, but under his Mother's shrewd eyes it would have been difficult to be sure of giving nothing away; and since they weren't engaged, better not to betray their love. She fretted and puzzled over that—had she done right to refuse to be engaged to him, in the complete uncertainty of the future for them? She couldn't be sure—she had hated seeing his disappointed face as he put that glorious ring, specially made for her, back in his pocket in its little case. She held out her left hand and looked at it speculatively—that tremendous diamond in its circle of sapphires might have been on her finger now. *No!* she told herself; better not, fairer not—she had made it clear that she was his, if marriage ever became possible; till then there was no need of a ring, least of all one so embarrassingly magnificent. As they walked down through the forest she had picked a wood-anemone and brushed it to his lips, and then put in it her note-case—it was there now. That was her pledge of betrothal—humbler and sweeter than the ring, and better recalling their last time together.

A restaurant-car had been attached to the train, in which an excellent luncheon was served; it was followed at 8 p.m. by an equally excellent dinner. Between these two meals the Minister had been giving his mind to their arrival at the frontier, and dealing with the authorities there. He knew that Horace Wheatley, his First Secretary, could speak a little Russian, but not much; it was a relief to him to learn that the attaché who had been seconded from Bucharest was fluent in it.

"That's excellent. Though I daresay the Embassy in Moscow will have sent someone down."

The Embassy had done nothing of the sort; their staff were over-pressed too. After dinner the air grew colder, and the train, climbing up onto the northern spur of the Carpathians, moved more and more slowly; the polite Hungarian *chef de train* explained that there was snow on the track—and indeed the travellers, wiping steam from the windows, could see whitened slopes on either side, and pine-trees whose boughs bent under a heavy white burden. "Goodness, how ghastly!" Eleanor Wheatley said. "Snow as well as all the rest!"

"The snow won't affect you" her husband replied sharply. "You'll only have to step from one train to the other."

He was quite wrong. The Russians used to have very odd ideas about any form of contact with Western countries—this must always be made as difficult as possible. When the diplomatic train from Budapest at last reached the summit frontier at 10 p.m. the train from Moscow was indeed awaiting the travellers, but it had carefully been drawn up 200 yards away—a stretch of snow, fifteen inches deep, separated the two. A Russian Colonel, sent down from Moscow to meet these unwanted foreigners, lengthily explained the reasons for this arrangement to Sir Hugh, through the helpful attaché from Rumania; there was also a prolonged inspection of everyone's passports.

"David, you go along and get into the other train and wait," Sir Hugh said to his Counsellor when this performance was at last completed—it had taken a whole hour. "Horace and I will settle everything—we shan't be long, with Dickie to translate. They say it's along there." He pointed vaguely, and went away into the station buildings with the Russian Colonel; all the men except David went with him, as men do, leaving a train full of women and hand-luggage sitting in the snow in the middle of the night.

"Mummy, I'll go and reconnoitre, shall I?" Lucilla asked.

"Yes do, darling. Gina, will you go too? And get some porters —then we can follow on. No, David!—do sit quiet, as the Min says, till they come back" Rosina said to her husband.

Gina and Lucilla presently returned.

"We've found it, but it's *miles* away; and there are no lights on in it! Have you got a torch, Mummy?"

"It is black-outa" Gina put in.

Rosina had a torch in her bag; she raised what torches there were among the other women—the Dutch Minister's wife had one like a searchlight. "Did you get some porters?" she asked her daughter.

"There don't seem to be any."

"God!" David Eynsham exclaimed angrily—"What a place! We'd better take what we can ourselves."

"Oh don't, David." But he had pulled down her pigskin bag, and insisted on carrying it; with the four bottles of gin, whisky, rum and brandy it was extremely heavy. Gina, Martha, and the typists all took up pieces of luggage and plunged out into the snow.

Two hundred yards of deep snow seems quite a long way in the dark, burdened with luggage. When they climbed up into the Russian train—which mercifully was at least heated—and flashed their torches into the pitch-dark carriages, they were agreeably surprised by their vast size; Russian railways are broad-guage, hence their carriages are much wider than the ordinary European ones.

"There. Now you lie down and rest" Rosina said to her husband; as she spoke she undid the straps of a hold-all and laid two pillows at one end of the long seat, and a rug at the foot. "Undo your trousers—look, there are hooks for our coats." When she had settled him down—"Now I'd better help Martha with all these women and get the rest of the hand-luggage along" she said.

"Why on earth are there no sleepers?" David asked irritably.

"I've no idea—p'raps there are some somewhere further on. But do stay here for now."

"I want some whisky" he said.

"Right you are!" She watched him anxiously as she took a flask from her enormous hand-bag. "Let me take the torch a second, will you? I expect there are glasses somewhere." She was right— in a cubby-hole at the end of the coach, above the usual samovar, was a rack full of tumblers; she took two back, poured him out a drink, and added water from the tap in the wash-place attached to each compartment—the cases of mineral-water were still in the other train.

"Now, are you all right, dearest? If so I'll go and help Martha."
David was sipping his whisky.

"I'm all right" he said.

"Sure?"

"Yes—go along. I'd like that torch, though."

"Of course." She stood it on the floor beside him, where its beam illuminated the green-painted roof of the carriage, casting a faint light over everything. "All right like that?"

"Yes. What a lunacy, not having porters! Try and find Hugh and get him to make these infernal Russkis do the normal decent thing. It's ridiculous that we should have to carry our own luggage, and the lights ought to be on." He was getting angry again.

"I'll do my best. But *please* don't fret, David. Here's the flask, and a spare glass of water, if you want another drink. I won't be long."

She felt her way through the dark corridor, climbed cautiously down the high steps, and stumbled along in the snow towards the distant lights of the station. Besides her concern over David Mrs Eynsham was worried about Martha, who had started influenza two days ago, though she had concealed the fact from the Minister—she had a temperature, and ought not to be running about at night in the cold. Half-way to the station she met Lucilla, Gina and a convoy of typists, all weighed down with miscellaneous baggage; behind them came Martha, also burdened, and driving before her two Russian porters festooned with luggage, urging them on with gestures and loud commands in English.

"Goodness, so there *are* porters" Rosina exclaimed.

"Well there are *two!* Go on, Ivan!—go on, Wronsky!" Martha said, as the men paused when she did; grinning, they obeyed her.

"Is this all?" Mrs Eynsham asked.

"Lord no! But I think two more trips will do it. Anyhow we're making a track in the snow to walk on, that's one thing. Keep *moving*, Ivan!" Martha said to one of the porters who had paused again; the man went on.

"I've left that little buffoon Eleanor in our train" Martha pursued, "and told her not to let anyone in. She says she's not fit to carry luggage."

"I'm sure *you're* not" Rosina said. "Don't come back; go and sit with David, and let me take over. He's in the first coach; you'll see the light, he's got my torch."

"Is he all right?" Martha asked. "He oughtn't to have carried anything, and that leather bag of yours weighs a ton. I'll see to this, Rosina—you go back to him."

"No, *you* keep quiet. Where's the Min?"

"Somewhere in the station, parleying. Do you want him?"

"David wants the lights put on."

"Goodness, I should think so! Ah"—she turned as another little party, also laden with suit-cases, approached them from the direction of the Hungarian train. "Here come the Dutch."

"We go where?" the Minister asked.

"Straight on—our train's just along there. But Your Excellency, it would really be more useful if you left that luggage to us, and went into the station to find Sir Hugh" Martha said. "He has an interpreter, and we simply must have the lights turned on— could you ask him to see about it? It's really hopeless in the dark."

"The train is not lit?"

"As black as the pit's mouth! Do do this, please."

"Then who takes these pieces?" the Minister asked.

"The porters will do it." But in fact when he had turned back towards the station lights Rosina picked up the two suit-cases which he had dumped in the snow—they were enormous, and very heavy—and somehow dragged them along to the foot of the steps into the train. "Make those porters get them up" she said to Martha, who by gestures and loud words did so.

"Now you stay there in the warm" Mrs Eynsham said firmly. "You can look after David; I don't like leaving him alone. Have some whisky—he's got my flask, and there are glasses by the door, here. Gina! Lucilla! Miss Maudsley!—come on, all of you; let's finish this job. What time is it?"

The Dutch Minister's wife, with her huge torch, appeared just then from the next coach; Rosina looked at her watch in the strong beam.

"Good God! It's just on midnight!" She said. "Martha, do look after David."

15

Everything in Russia generally takes much longer than Westerners expect, and is also completely unpredictable. Having left Martha with David, sitting quietly in the warm, Mrs Eynsham addressed herself to getting the transport of the hand-luggage completed with a fairly easy mind. But what masses of it there was! The two Russian porters carried out another couple of trips, along with the Dutch Minister's wife, the typists, and the English staff wives; but when this coolie-party was returning to the Hungarian train for the fourth time they encountered a furious Russian official, who withdrew the porters, boxing their ears with his fists, and shouting angrily at the foreign women.

"I think he says the luggage is not to be moved" said the Dutch Minister's wife, who had been *enposte* in Poland.

"If you know how, tell him to go to hell!" Rosina replied briskly. And in spite of the Russian's angry shouts and theatening gestures they went back into the other train, collected Eleanor Wheatley and the last of the hand-baggage, and for the fifth time humped their loads along that two hundred yards of snow, and lugged them up the high steps into the train for Moscow.

"Well, that's the lot," Mrs Eynsham was just saying in a satisfied tone, when suddenly the lights came on.

"Oh, how splendid! Well done your husband!" she exclaimed to the Dutch Minister's wife. "Now we can sort it all out." And they proceeded to allocate carriages in two coaches to the various members of the party, and to put the appropriate luggage into them. Still no one had come to arrange the sleepers and make up the beds; it was all very un-European, unexpected, and uncomfortable. "Well, we must just put our heads on our hand-bags, and our coats over us" said the Dutch Minister's wife resignedly. "The train is warm; this is one thing."

"When the hell do we start?" David Eynsham asked, rather crossly, when his wife looked in on him and Martha.

"I've no idea."

"We've run out of whisky, too. Where's that mineral water? This train stuff tastes foul."

Mrs Eynsham lifted the pigskin bag down out of the rack and got out a bottle of whisky, took a corkscrew from her handbag, and opened it.

"There you are. I'm afraid the mineral water must be with the heavy luggage; I don't know what goes on about that. Shall I go and see?"

"You'd better have a drink yourself first" David said—but at that moment Horace Wheatley came in.

"Sorry to have left you like this—it's rather a mix-up here. No one understands anything!—that Russian Colonel had never heard of a diplomatic *laissez-passer*, and wants to examine all the luggage. What's happened about the hand stuff?"

"It's all here, in this train" Rosina said.

"Oh splendid! How did you manage that?"

"*Les girls* carried it themselves" David said sharply; his face was beginning to flush angrily again. "I think Morven and Milton at least might have done their bit—*they* can't interpret. Anyhow, where's the mineral water?"

By some mistake, Wheatley explained, the mineral water had been put in the wagon along with the heavy luggage. "But when we get that transferred, it will come into this coach."

"Good Heavens, hasn't it been transferred yet? Have my wife and the typists got to shift the heavy luggage too?" Eynsham asked furiously.

"*No*, David. It will all get done in time; only the Bolos are a bit slow, because they don't know anything about anything. What I came to ask was, is anyone hungry? There's a restaurant in the station where one can get supper of a sort."

234

"David, do you want anything to eat?" his wife asked.

"No! I want to get moving, and go to sleep!"

"Rosina, I brought some sandwiches and a thermos of soup, just in case," Martha muttered in an aside. "That will do for him and me. So do go and eat if you feel like it."

Mrs Eynsham did feel like it. They had finished their last meal at 8.45 p.m., and it was now half-past one; in the interval they had done quite a lot of hard work. She, with Lucilla, the typists, and the rest of the wives once more tracked along through the snow to the station and into the restaurant.

This was a very large room, glaringly lit by unshaded electric bulbs, with bare wooden tables set with coarse crockery. In a corner Sir Hugh and his staff, still deep in argument with the Russian Colonel, sat in a gloomy little group; local Russians occupied some of the tables, on one of which was set a gramophone playing English and French records—a number of shabby men and women were dancing to these in an open space from which the tables had been pushed aside.

"Goodness, fancy their having *Parlez-moi d'Amour* here!" Lucilla observed, sitting down.

"Ah, those are the P.C.O.'s records, and his gramophone" Horace said. "They've never heard one before!—and I'm afraid we shan't get away till they've played through every single disk! He has hundreds, alas! What will you eat? There isn't very much but Bortsch."

Rosina, with memories of Bortsch in the London house of Polish friends—strong and dark as claret, with a heavenly taste of beetroot, and whipped sour cream on top—agreed to Bortsch; but at the frontier station it was rather different, being made principally of turnips and field cabbage, with lumps of dark horse-meat in it; this was high, and smelt terrible. However the soup was hot, and they supped it up, and munched the sour greyish bread served with it, thankfully; but everyone was surprised ultimately to be charged the equivalent of a pound sterling for this meal. The Dutch Minister's wife asked Horace if they could have coffee?

"I shouldn't recommend it—it will be *ersatz* if they have it. Have some tea—you're always fairly safe with tea in Russia, even nowadays, they tell me."

The Russian passion for tea is a curiously persistent thing. Practically every coach on their long-distance trains has its samovar at one end, tended by youths who feed it with charcoal, and brew tea which they serve in tall tumblers, with sugar but without milk; such glasses presently appeared at the travellers' table—fragrant and quite good, even in that sordid place.

"How clever you are, Horace!" Mrs Eynsham said, lighting a cigarette, and sipping gingerly at the scalding liquid. Like all the others she was watching everything in these extraordinary surroundings—the dirty fingernails, necks, and blouses of the girls who served the food and the tea, the clumsy shuffling movements of the ill-clad people who were dancing to the records of the Passport Control Officer's gramophone, the unhappy Sir Hugh, courteously but stiffly continuing his insistence that their heavy luggage must *not* be opened, since they had *laissez-passers;* the table where the Chancery clerks and the Legation porters were smoking.

"Are they all right?" she asked Horace Wheatley.

"I think so—I ordered their food, and gave them roubles to pay for it."

Sir Hugh's party now broke up; the Dutch Minister and the attaché from Bucharest went out with the Russian Colonel and several station officials, and Sir Hugh, with Milton and Colonel Morven, came over to where the women were sitting.

"I *think* we've won" the Minister said to Horace. "They've agreed at last to put our big luggage onto the Moscow train, *unexamined*. But what a performance!"

Horace at once mentioned the mineral water. "Some of that must come into our coaches, Sir."

"Didn't it? Why not?"

"Anton must have made a mix-up this morning—anyhow it's with the heavy stuff."

236

"How do you know that?" the Minister asked rather brusquely. Rosina put her oar in.

"*I* know, because I checked every single piece of hand-luggage from our train into the Russian one. We had to carry most of it ourselves."

"Why?" Sir Hugh asked, still more brusquely—he too was having a very disagreeable night.

"Because there aren't porters, and *all* the men went along with you! What help Geoffrey and Hugo were to your negotiations I can't think" Rosina said tartly, "but they could have been of real use to us. *Five* trips!"

"Now Rosie" Colonel Morven protested—"We had no idea that you were carting luggage."

"This is dreadful" Sir Hugh said. "I am so sorry, Mrs Eynsham." He spoke very formally.

"Oh, I know *you* couldn't do anything" Rosina said. "You had to be arguing." She pulled herself together, ashamed of having lost her temper. "Never mind—it's done now."

"I am inexpressibly sorry" the Minister repeated. He turned to Milton. "Geoffrey, go and find out where the heavy luggage is, and tell Dickie Aston that one case of mineral water must come into our sleepers, *tonight*."

"They aren't sleepers yet" Lucilla put in, in her cool little voice. "The upper bunks haven't been let down, and there are no pillows or blankets or anything."

Sir Hugh frowned; then he got up. He had really had all he could take, a common experience among those who encounter Soviet officialdom for the first time.

"All the same, I think I shall go and sit down," he said.

"I'll take you to the train" Horace said, getting up. "Where is H.E.'s carriage, Rosina?"

"Not in the first coach; in the second one, next to the van Damm's."

The Minister glanced at the tables where his staff and the women-folk were still sitting smoking.

237

"Shall you be all right?" he asked of the Dutch Minister's wife and Rosina.

"I'll finish my tea" Rosina said. "I do likewise" said the Dutch lady.

"I'll stay with them" Colonel Morven said to his chief reassuringly.

"Well don't be too long—we ought to be off as soon as that luggage has been transferred." He looked at his watch. "Merciful Heavens, it's half-past two! Come on, Horace." They went out into the dark and snow.

Presently Horace came back. "The mineral water's been found, and they are making up the sleepers at last" he reported. Rosina had gone over to the table on which the gramophone stood, where the P.C.O. sat gloomily keeping guard over his records.

"How are they doing?" she asked him.

"Oh, a lot to go yet! I'm half inclined to smash them, but they'd murder me if I did, I'm sure!"

"Must we really wait till they've all been played?" Mrs Eynsham asked Horace.

"I'm afraid so—no one has any control over these people." The Passport Control Officer grinned gloomily.

"Go on till 7 a.m., if you ask me" he said.

Rosina, with Horace, returned to the others. "Is David all right?" she asked as they walked through the tables.

"Yes, he seems fine—only he didn't want to be turned out to have his bed made up. He and Martha were laughing like anything when I looked in."

"Then I think I'll have another glass of tea" Mrs Eynsham said. There come times when even the most dutiful of wives feel that they want the pressure taken off, want not to have to *do* anything for a little while—and as the devoted Martha was in charge of David, and he was well enough to laugh, she was glad to sit and relax a little longer, even in that glaring place. The other women followed her example, and sipped slowly at second glasses of tea. And then, the more modern records having been worked through, the gramophone began to blare out "Always."

238

Lucilla sprang up and bent over her Mother.

"I'm going to bed. D'you mind?"

"Of course not, darling. I'll be along soon." Rosina had no idea of the impact of that particular tune on her daughter. "You're next to us, with Martha."

"I know." She said good night politely to the Dutch Ministress, and hurried out. The lumbering Russians liked "Always," and stamped with their feet to beat out the time—the waltz-step was quite beyond their ken.

Suddenly Lucilla came running back. "Mummy, Daddy's ill! Come quick."

Mrs Eynsham threw on her fur coat, grabbed up her bag, and went out with her daughter. "What's happened?" she asked.

"I don't know. Martha came and told me to fetch you—she thinks it may be another coronary" Lucilla panted out, as they hurried along the now deeply-trodden track in the snow—this had frozen, and they slipped and slithered while they ran through the dark.

As they climbed up into the train Rosina heard her husband's voice, raised angrily.

"Then *break* the windows! I tell you I must have air."

"Lucilla, go and open the door at the other end of the coach" her Mother said; she had already noticed that this Russian train had double windows, apparently screwed shut. Lucilla ran off, and Rosina went into the carriage. David was half sitting-up on the long green velvet seat, gasping and waving his arms about. "I want more pillows" he said when he saw her, with almost a child's angrily confident demand. "Have you got some morphia?"

"Yes, David. Just keep quite quiet. You'll have more air in a minute—I'm getting something opened." She took off her fur coat, rolled it up, and slipped it in behind the pillows.

"Have mine too" Martha said, doing likewise.

"That's better" David said, lying back; his wife's presence seemed to calm him a little. "Where's that morphia?" he asked. "God, this hellish pain in my arm!"

"In a moment, David. Here—take these, and chew them"—

she gave him a couple of Dr Mendze's pills from a little bottle in her handbag. He began to chew the pills obediently; like so many sick husbands he had become for the moment, not the head of the household, the master, but his wife's child. Rosina took out a phial of morphine and the little case with her hypodermic syringe and a flask of surgical spirit with which to sterilise it; she set all these on the broad window-sill, and rolled up the sleeves of David's pull-over and shirt—he had taken off his jacket in the hot stationary train. Then, having sterilised the syringe, she filled it with the exact dose of morphia which Dr Mendze had prescribed, and plunged the needle into Eynsham's upper arm.

"You did that rather well—didn't hurt a bit" David said. "Thanks, Rosie." Mrs Eynsham was re-sterilising the syringe; she sprayed the last drops of spirit onto the spot where she had made the injection, and then rolled her husband's sleeves down again. He lay quiet now, with closed eyes; Rosina sat down beside Martha on the opposite seat, and waited. After some minutes David Eynsham opened his eyes again.

"That's lovely" he said. "No pain now. Bless you, Rosie—you're a clever girl!" He closed his eyes once more.

The Eynshams were in one of the old-fashioned double sleepers left over from the Czarist régime, roomy and comfortable to a degree, with two broad seats.

"Did you have some supper?" Rosina asked Martha, in a low voice.

"Oh yes, heaps, and so did David; he took two glasses of soup and three sandwiches, and enjoyed them," Martha replied in the same low tone. "Look, Rosina, now that the train-boys are functioning, I think I'll go and get some pillows—we may want our coats if the heating goes off."

She went out, and returned in a few minutes accompanied by a rather surly youth, suffering badly from acne, who carried pillows, several blankets, and two pairs of sheets. Rosina took two of the pillows and very gently and carefully substituted them for her and Martha's fur coats under David's head; meanwhile the pimply train-boy made up a proper sleeper-bed on the opposite seat. Having done this, he turned to the couch where Eynsham lay, and spoke eagerly in his own tongue—clearly he wanted to make a proper bed there, too.

"*Nyet!*" Martha said—"No" was the only word of Russian she knew. After fluent speech on his side, and repeated "Nyets" on hers, the pimply youth at last went away defeated, with his unwanted sheets.

Lucilla suddenly appeared in the open doorway of the carriage.

"How is Daddy?"

"Quite comfortable. He's had some heart pills, and a morphia injection."

"Oh good. I opened the other door."

Horace also appeared, peering over Lucilla's shoulder, to enquire about David. Martha Beckley took her usual firm grip of the situation.

"Horace, wait outside; Lucilla, you go to bed—with you both blocking the doorway he gets no air at all." Lucilla, looking hurt, went away; Martha followed Horace into the corridor.

"Are both the coach doors open?" she asked him.

"Not the further one. The train-boys don't like them open—they say it wastes the heating."

"Well if they don't like it, they must lump it! Just go along and tell Hugo Morven to open it again, and *keep* it open."

Horace obeyed, and a faint breath of cold air came down the corridor as the Colonel returned. "How is he?" he asked Martha.

"Quite comfortable—but he must have air. When we get moving it will come in from the ventilators, of course. I leave that door to you, Hugo."

"I'll deal with it." He went away.

"Does H.E. know that David's had another turn?" Martha asked Horace.

"I don't think so. Should I tell him?"

"No—what can he do? Let him be; I hope he's asleep."

The First Secretary looked worried.

241

"Martha, do you think David's dying?" he asked. As he spoke the train-boys closed the door at their end of the coach; Horace went along and opened it again, and stood propping it open. "Nyet!" said the train-boys angrily, and tried to push him away; "Nyet to you, you mannerless oafs!" Horace muttered in English; in Russian he said "Diplomatiki" very firmly. "God, how ghastly this is! Well?" he asked Martha.

"I'm afraid so. It's his third go, and that isn't so good. And he's been frightfully angry twice today, so bad for blood-pressure —and he would carry that bag with all the alk in it from our train to this. It weighs a ton!—and he oughtn't ever to carry weights."

"Do you think *she* knows?"

"No one *knows*, yet. You asked me what I thought."

"I know. Oh, poor David!" Wheatley said, with infinite sadness in his voice. "But Martha, if he *does* pass out before we get moving, you must arrange to keep it absolutely dark. There are all sorts of regulations against carrying corpses on trains except in a coffin, in a special van, and with a *Leichen-Begleiter*, a corpse-escort!" Even in his distress he laughed a little at the German phrase.

"Oh yes, I see" Martha said. "H'm." She reflected. "Of course this is the frontier; they might turn him out to stay in Hungary, might they?"

"Exactly."

"But that's impossible! Rosina would insist on staying too, and then we *should* be in the soup! Would it be any good trying to get a doctor, here?"

"Quite hopeless, I should say. He'd probably only be a sort of vet, and it would lead to more complications. Better wait till we're in Russia, and try at Lwow or Tarnopol—they're big towns."

"What happens if we're actually in Russia?—if he should die, I mean?"

"Even there I think we'd better pretend he's only ill. But we shall have longish halts at Lwow and Kiev, and Dickie or I ought

242

to be able to get onto the Embassy and say what's happened—
if it *does* happen—and they will be able to fix something, I suppose. God, what a place for him to get taken ill!"

"Horrible!" Martha said. "And I'm afraid he's really in a bad
way. Horace, I think I must put all this up to Rosina. She won't
lose her head, but she ought to know what is involved."

"All right, you tell her. But oughtn't you to get to bed yourself? What's your temperature?"

"Damn my temperature!" Martha exclaimed. "I shan't die—
one doesn't die of 'flu, at my age. I shall stay with Rosina, at
least till we get moving."

After further argument with the train-boys Wheatley went
off and lay down, fully dressed, in his sleeper; Martha went back
to David's compartment.

"Rosina, come outside for a minute."

Rosina went.

"He seems quite comfortable" she said, as they stood in the
corridor.

"I'm so glad. But listen—" and she repeated to Mrs Eynsham
what Horace had just told her.

"I understand" Rosina said, on a long breath. "All right." Suddenly she choked back a sob. "*Why* does Horace think he's going to die?"

"He doesn't. Only he knows how David's gone on and on working when he wasn't fit for it, and should have stayed in the
Szanatorium and kept quiet—and he has been upset twice today; I expect that's what brought this attack on. Horace only
wanted you to be warned, *in case* anything should happen" she
said carefully. "That makes sense, doesn't it?"

"Oh yes. Thank you for telling me, Martha." Then she too
asked about the possibility of getting a doctor?

"Horace thinks that's hopeless here—there wouldn't be a decent one. I asked him, and he said better wait and try at some
big town in Russia, where we stop."

"I see" Rosina said sadly. "Well now, Martha, you'd better
go to bed. How are you feeling?"

243

"Quite all right. If you didn't mind I'd really rather stay with you—and him."

Mrs Eynsham put her hand across Martha's forehead.

"You've got a blazing temperature!" she said. "One hundred and three, I shouldn't wonder! You go and lie down."

At this juncture two things happened. The train-boys slammed the door of the coach next to the Eynshams' compartment, and Tom, the tall night-porter, approached from the opposite end.

"Excuse me, Madam—I just wanted to ask if there was anything I could do for you? I heard the Counsellor wasn't so well," he said.

"Oh, thank you, Tom. Yes, Mr Eynsham did have a bit of a turn, but he's better now; he's had an injection."

"Miss Beckley should go to bed—she's ill too." Tom said "Miss Beckley, Miss, I got these pills at the station—Sulpha-something. The man said they cure flu." The boxer handed Martha a tube of tablets of Sulfapyridine, then the favourite sulphonamide in use in Central Europe.

"Tom, you're an angel!" Martha exclaimed. She had meant to get some sulphonamide for the journey when her influenza came on, but with all the last-minute rush she had failed to do so—she was unspeakably relieved to have Tom's tube. "Thank you very much indeed. But look—those revolting boys have shut the coach door; it *must* be kept open till we start, for Mr Eynsham to get air. Mr Wheatley told them about it, but now he's gone, they've shut it again."

"Leave it to me, Madam." The tall boxer strode down to the little compartment where the train-boys slept; they had taken to their bunks, but he pulled them both out.

"Open that door!" he said, dragging the two juveniles to it, and pointing. The boys protested—Tom, most improperly and undiplomatically, knocked their heads together. "Now do as you're told!" The boys opened the door and retired, muttering angrily and whimpering, to their compartment. Tom went back to the Eynsham's carriage.

244

"Now, Madam, if you will excuse the suggestion, I should like to stay with you and the Counsellor, while Miss Beckley goes to bed. I shan't be in your way—I can stay in the corridor, and keep an eye on that door at the same time."

"Thank you, Tom—I shall be very glad to have you. Martha, do go to bed."

"Have you taken those pills, Miss?" Tom asked as Martha got up.

"Not yet, Tom. Do you know where that case of mineral water was put, from the heavy luggage?"

"Yes Miss—in the Minister's sleeper."

"Oh how dotty!" Martha exclaimed irritably—she too had taken about all she could that night.

"Don't worry, Miss—I'll fetch a couple of bottles; he won't hear me."

"If he *is* awake, don't say anything to him about Mr Eynsham being unwell" Martha said urgently. "*Remember*, Tom."

"Whatever you say, Miss. I'll be back in a jiffy."

In no time at all the boxer returned with two bottles of mineral water.

"Sleeping like a baby! But these bottles have those caps on, and I can't find my beer-opener. Usually I keep one in me pocket."

"I've got one" Rosina said, delving into her vast handbag; she always carried a beer-opener as well as a corkscrew about with her. Martha swallowed her pills in a glass of *Hunyadi Janos*, and went off to bed. "Call me if you want me" she said. "Bless you, Rosina"—she gave Mrs Eynsham another of her rare kisses as she went out.

"Now Madam, if I might make so free, why don't you lie down yourself?" Tom asked when Martha had gone. "I see your bed's all ready, and I'll keep an eye on the Counsellor, and rouse you if he gets worse."

Rosina's heart sank at the night-watchman's last words. Even Tom expected that David might get worse! But if he did, she must be fit to act, and she was really pretty well worn out. They had breakfasted at 7.15 to be at the station in Budapest by 8, and now—mercy, it was 4.30 a.m.!

"Thank you, Tom. Yes, I think that's a good idea." She went along to the lavatory; on her return she unfastened the belt of her skirt, and then bent over her husband, putting her hand on his wrist. His pulse was beating gently; she spoke to him softly, but he did not answer, nor open his eyes; his hands were warm. She drew the rugs up over him again, and went out into the corridor.

"I'll leave the light on, Tom, so that you can see how he is; it doesn't seem to disturb him—he's sleeping beautifully."

"Won't the light disturb you, Madam? You've had a hard day."

"No, I'm a good sleeper. Everyone has had a hard day—you too, Tom."

"I'm strong, Madam. Don't you worry about me," the night-watchman said. Rosina went back in to the carriage, took a mohair shawl out of her overnight case, and after taking off her shoes wrapped her feet in it and lay down in the clean bed, infinitely thankful to be flat at last, after a day which had lasted for twenty-two hours.

But she did not sleep at first, although she closed her eyes against the harsh overhead light. Her mind went back to their talk after leaving Budapest—all those different endings. Was her life with David going to come to an end too? Her memory went back over all the years of their marriage: the hard parts and the lovely, heavenly parts—oh, she did love him so! With a sharp pang she remembered his words about the blackbird's song, only the other day, and how he had wondered if he would hear it in another spring? In a panic she got up again, and felt his pulse—no, it was quiet, and his breathing seemed easy. She lay down once more, said some brief prayers, and fell asleep instantly.

A few minutes later Lucilla crept along the corridor and peeped in at the door. Tom put a restraining hand on her shoulder.

"Don't you disturb your Mother, Miss. She needs some rest."

246

"How's Daddy?"

"Sleeping beautiful. I'm keeping an eye on him. I've promised to wake Madam if he rouses."

"Well wake me too if anything happens, Tom."

"I will, Miss."

"He looks very peaceful" Lucilla said, a little comforted by the sight of her Father's calm face, sealed in sleep.

"Yes Miss. Is Miss Beckley asleep?"

"Yes. She said those tablets you got her were wonderful; she felt so much better after taking them."

"Glad of that, Miss. Now you go to sleep too." Tom's profession being that of a night-watchman, he liked his charges to be in their beds, and let him *keep* watch. Lucilla went back to her sleeper.

In fact the dying very often do look peaceful—especially when they are under the influence of a powerful drug like morphia. But Tom had been a professional boxer before he became a night-watchman, and had learned to notice any signs of physical change in his opponents' faces. Soon after six he touched Mrs Eynsham on the shoulder.

"Madam, I think he's going."

Being roused from the sleep of great exhaustion feels like having the heart torn out of one's body. Painfully, Mrs Eynsham roused herself, sat up, and stared about her; a pale daylight, whitened by the snow outside, was coming in at the windows. She had not in the least taken in what Tom had said.

"Why are we standing still?" she asked stupidly. "Where are we?"

"Still here, Madam—we haven't moved yet. But Madam, I think the Counsellor is going."

This time his words did penetrate Rosina's poor senses, dulled by sleep; she sprang out of her berth and knelt by her husband. "David!" she said urgently—"David! David!" There was no response. She drew down the rugs and felt his wrist—there was no sign of any pulse at all. She turned and stared up at the night-porter.

247

"Tom! I can't feel his pulse! You try."

Tom tried, also in vain—then he pulled a tiny mirror in a case out of his waistcoat pocket, and held it to Eynsham's mouth—there was no misting; the glass remained perfectly clear.

"Madam, he's gone," the man said, and crossed himself.

"Oh *no!*" she said, in a low wail of protest. "He can't be! He's so *warm*. Help me to lift him up, Tom. David!" She gave his shoulder a little shake.

"Madam, it's no good. I've seen plenty of dead men. Leave him quiet." To her infinite surprise the night-porter knelt down beside her in the carriage, pulled out a rosary, and began to recite the De Profundis—the great sentences flowed over her, even while she still clung to her husband's wrist.

"Out of the depths have I cried to Thee O Lord; Lord, hear my voice . . .

With Thee there is merciful forgiveness . . .

My soul hath hoped in the Lord, from the morning watch . . .

With the Lord there is mercy, and with Him plentiful redemption."

Mrs Eynsham's tears rained down on the rug. Tom, after saying the Gloria, went on—

"Eternal rest give to him, O Lord, and let light perpetual shine upon him." Inexpressibly consoling words!—she repeated them through her tears, and so missed some sentences; when she heard Tom again he was saying what he could remember from the Preface for the Dead. "From Thy faithful, O Lord, life is not taken away, it is but changed . . . there awaiteth them an everlasting home in Heaven. . . ."

With blackbird-song, if they wanted it, Rosina thought with a fresh burst of tears, remembering David in bed that morning, listening to the bird's song from the slopes of the Bastion. He had been right; he would never hear a blackbird sing again in this world. And he had teased her for being "a funny believing old Christian." She raised her tear-stained face to the night-watchman—who after reciting an "Our Father" and a "Hail Mary" had risen from his knees, and was standing at attention

248

in the carriage. Somehow his prayers, so simply and spontane-
ously said, had, she felt, blessed her David's passing.

"Tom, I don't think Mr Eynsham believed much" she said—
really seeking reassurance.

"The Counsellor was a good man, Madam. He always thought
for others—the staff, I mean. And Our Blessed Lord liked people
who do that—not repeating the Name, but doing the Will; He
said so Himself."

"Thank you, Tom—and for praying for him." She got up from
her knees, straightened her disordered berth, and sat on it. "I'd
no idea you were a Catholic" she said.

"Oh yes, Madam. Most Kennedys are Catholics." (Rosina
realised, rather ashamed, that she had never grasped that Tom's
surname was Kennedy.) "But now, Madam, if I might suggest
it, hadn't we better fold the Counsellor's hands?"

Rosina had not thought of this; with Tom's help she folded
David's hands across his breast.

"If you didn't mind, Madam, I'd like him to have my Rosary"
the boxer said, and twined his beads through the folded hands—
then he drew up the rugs again.

"Tom, you realise that no one must know until we start?
Otherwise there'll be a fuss, Mr Wheatley says. We must pretend
he's still just ill"—a sob choked her on the words; while David
had been "just ill" it hadn't been the end.

"I understand, Madam. I promised Miss Lucilla that I'd tell
her if anything happened."

"Wait till we're moving" Mrs Eynsham said, with some difficulty—one sob led to more.

"I'll get you some tea" Tom said— "That's what you need."
He disappeared into the corridor, and Rosina knelt down again
beside her husband and said her own prayers for the repose of
his soul—she tried to remember some of Tom's, they were so
beautiful, and somehow so *potent*—but she could only recall
"Let light perpetual shine upon him," which she repeated fervently.

Tom reappeared with a large thermos of tea and a small glass jar full of sugar, and poured her out a cup in the thermos lid. "Best I can do, Madam. D'you take sugar? You can stir it with my pencil"—he drew this out of the breast pocket of his jacket. "Got it filled in that restaurant place—the best thing there, the tea, if you ask me." Then he produced a short candle, lit it, poured some hot wax onto the window-sill above Eynsham's head, and stood the candle firmly in position. "Always travel with a bit of blessed candle" the boxer said. "You never know."

Somehow the candle comforted Mrs Eynsham too—she felt, as she had felt on All Souls Day at Siraly, how much R.C.s *did* for the dead. While she was stirring the sweetened tea with the night-watchman's pencil, and drinking it gratefully, a noise suddenly arose outside, a tremendous shouting. Tom Kennedy went out into the corridor to see what was happening—it was the Russians, cheering the gramophone onto the train.

"The P.C.O.'s come aboard" he reported. "Now we'll get going." And in a few minutes the train, slowly, grindingly, began to move; Tom went and shut the carriage doors as the cold air blew in.

"Now I'll go and tell Mr Wheatley" he said, "in case there's trouble." Rosina looked at her watch; it was just seven. The last record had been played. Gradually gathering speed, the train glided down into Russia.

LIVERPOOL STUDIES IN SPANISH LITERATURE

LITERATURE

SECOND SERIES